LADY ELIZABETH, MD

ANN BROUGH

Thicket Books

Dedicated to the women who fought for the right
to pursue their own destinies

CHAPTER 1

THE GOSSIP ON THE STREET

T he gossip on the street was all about the new doctor.

As the women cleaned their steps and wiped the grime from their front window panes, the news spread quickly down the narrow street.

"What do you know!" shouted Gladys Plant to her next door neighbour. "There's a new lady doctor at the Blackstone Road surgery.[1] Mrs Fields from the corner shop told me this very morning."

Morgan McKenzie looked up from her step-cleaning, hands covered in red polish.

"You don't say!" she said, "I wouldn't mind signing on with 'er. Anything'd be better than old Doctor Williams—no time for women, nor kids. I'm thinking, if ever I could afford a doctor, I'd give this lady doctor a shot. What's 'er name, then?"

"Don't know. Mrs Fields didn't know either," Gladys replied.

"Anybody know the new lady doctor's name?" shouted Morgan down the street.

Soon there was a huddle of women outside Morgan's house, all of them wondering about the lady doctor.

---

1. Surgery - called a doctor's office in North America

The street of dilapidated terraced houses in the middle of Stoke were mirror images of thousands upon thousands of such streets and houses in the industrial cities of England, Scotland, Wales and Ireland in the 1920s. Their inhabitants represented the vast working class population, who worked too many hours for too little money, and eked out a living to put a roof over their heads and food on the table.

The poverty was crushing, the conditions deplorable, and the misery palpable.

Mrs Alcott, the oldest occupant living on the narrow street, hobbled from the stool outside her house and joined the group of women. She was bent with age, her skin wrinkled and yellowing, the clay pipe she smoked hung in her mouth between the few teeth she had left.

"Put the kettle on, Gladys," she grunted. "We'll all need a cuppa before any more talk."

Gladys Plant led a procession of women through the parlour and into the meagre kitchen, where a blackened kettle simmered over the fire in the black grate. Under the tiny lace-covered window stood a wooden table where cups and saucers were laid out. Mrs Alcott was settled into one of the two chairs beside the table. Once the tea was steeped in the big brown teapot, each of the women added milk and sugar before settling down to continue their discussion of the new lady doctor. Some poured the tea into their saucer and sipped the cooled liquid with relish. Saucering tea was a common practise among the women of the area.

Connie Milner, who lived at the bottom of the steep street bustled into Mrs Plant's crowded kitchen.

"I've 'eard some news," she announced, enjoying the sudden attention of her neighbours. "My Bill just got home from his shift at the pit and e's bin told about a lady doctor starting up on Blackstone Road."

"What do ya think we're all in 'ere talking about?" laughed Morgan.

"I'm supposin' ya all know 'er name then?" Connie jibbed.

Now she really had their attention.

"Doctor Lingford" She said with a relish. "She married Doctor LaPorte from the North Staffs Hospital. Bill's got a mate who worked on redoin' the house. Very posh she is, and a looker."

With this mine of information another brew of tea was served, and the women talked for half the afternoon.

Doctor Lingford was in an alien land. A strange land with no colour. Everything was dark: the buildings, the streets, the clothing the people wore. There were no trees or grass, just rows of dark dingy row houses with red or white steps, and bottle kilns that belched out black smoke, and filled the air with flecks of soot which blocked out the sun. Men, women and children were all thin. Most men were either covered in coal dust from the mines or clay dust from the pottery factories, or "the pots" as they were called. Most girls worked on "the pots" until they married, usually at a young age. They were trained as decorators, and became high-skilled artists, enhancing the fine bone china with hand-painted scenes and flowers. Babies were born at a rapid and regular rate, creating more hardship for the underfunded families.

The new lady doctor was used to the conditions which now surrounded her. Her recent work in Glasgow had introduced her to the desperate struggle for survival among the working poor of city tenements. Yet she had thought moving to North Staffordshire would have offered more of the lifestyle she had enjoyed in her earlier days.

She had been born and raised in the Suffolk countryside, with green fields and trees at every turn. It seemed so long ago. She had never imagined life in her chosen profession would lead her so far away from all that she held most dear.

Why had she agreed to come to such a place as this? Why had she let her husband persuade her?

Opening a medical practice in the The Potteries might prove to be a mistake for the young doctor from a different world.

CHAPTER 2

BORN A LADY

Elizabeth Amelia was the third child born to Lord Arnold and Lady Maud Lingford Her two older brothers, Henry and Percy, were age six and four when she was born. It was of little consequence to either of the boys that a sister had been born into the family. Nanny Wells still took care of them, and they neither saw nor heard from the latest addition to their family. The nursery nanny tended to the baby's needs, and the newborn nursery was far enough from the boys' rooms to cause them no interruption in their daily routine.

The only time the three children were together was after tea, when they were taken downstairs to be presented to their parents for the daily visit. Mama[1] always greeted them with a smile and accepted a kiss on the cheek from each boy. Papa[2] sat in his favourite chair and inspected them from afar, noticing their clothing, cleanliness, deportment, and manners.

Papa always asked the same question.

"Henry, Percy, have you been good boys?"

"Yes Papa," was always the answer.

---

1. Mama pronounced Mamar
2. Papa pronounced Papar

Nanny encouraged the boys to show their parents something they had worked on that day. A painting, or a page of meticulously copied alphabet letters. Sometimes they recited a short poem, or shared a story about their outdoor time. All were offered in a quiet proper manner and without making eye contact with the adults.

Henry and Percy hated it.

Baby Elizabeth usually lay sleeping in the nursemaid's arms for much of the visit. Mama took her for a few minutes after the boys' presentation, and kissed both her cheeks. Papa watched with indifference. Never comfortable with babies, he believed his job as a father, other than as sire, was to keep the estate running to perfection, so that his family could live in the luxury his wealth afforded.

The family had always prided itself on running a profitable estate, providing employment and housing to over two hundred families who lived in cottages scattered throughout the twenty-five thousand acres. Over the decades, a village had evolved from a cluster of cottages in the centre of the estate. At the dawn of the 19th century the village boasted a church, a butchers shop, general store, blacksmiths, school, post office, and even a public house. Generations of tenants had worked on the land owned by the Lingford family, and counted themselves lucky to have a well-respected and successful landlord.

During the second half of the 19th century great estates found it more and more difficult to maintain their properties, and many fell into disrepair. New tax laws, a worldwide recession, and loss of political power among the wealthy had all contributed to the downfall of stately homes in Britain.

Tragedy struck the Lingford family when Arnold's father, Lord Hubert Lingford, died of a heart attack in his early fifties, leaving his son to inherit the estate. Lord Arnold Lingford had worked alongside his father for several years, and knew the estate was floundering. He took immediate steps to secure the future of the ancestral estate, and as the new Lord of the Manor he initiated the first steps to address the financial situation. Some respite was achieved by renting out sections of farmland to outside farmers, with the proviso that labourers would be hired from the estate tenants. It was a temporary solution at best.

As the cost of supporting his growing family increased, the income from the estate was stretched to the limit, and it became obvious to Lord Arnold that the temporary steps he had taken could no longer sustain the upkeep of the manor house and large staff required to run it.

"I will certainly not make a list of dispensable household staff," Lady Maud said. Her husband stood before the grand fireplace in the drawing room and frowned down at his wife. He had made a perfectly reasonable request, had he not?

"Not one single servant would be on that list," continued Lady Maud. "There are more than eighty rooms to be taken care of, not to mention our rapidly increasing family and their needs."

Lady Maud paused to pointedly place a graceful hand on her newly expanding stomach.

"We need extra staff, not less. Another nursery maid will have to be hired, and the boys need a full time tutor now. They should be learning languages, and Mr. Meadows is not qualified past a rudimentary education."

Lord Lingford glared at his wife for several minutes. It was unusual for her to voice her opinion so vehemently. He put it down to her delicate condition, and was reluctant to press the matter further.

"Very well," he muttered, almost to himself. "Then my task becomes ever more difficult. Don't concern yourself, my dear. The house and estate are indeed my responsibility."

With the interview over, Lord Lingford turned on his heel and marched toward the drawing room door, down the wide curved staircase and out of the side door. He did what he always did and headed for the stables.

"Saddle Jewel," he ordered the stable hand.

"Yes, m'Lord," the boy answered, touching his cap before hurrying to prepare the horse.

Lord Arnold pulled on the riding boots he kept in the stable tack room, and calmed himself with the aroma of the stable. The odours of warm manure, straw, and leather mixed together always gave him a sense of peace and tranquility. From a young age he had felt more at home around horses and dogs than he had around people, and it was to this part of his world he clung in times of stress or anxiety. This was, indeed, one such time.

Jewel was Arnold's favourite mount. She was strong and courageous. Larger than the average mare, she never tired of galloping across the vast estate lands. The rider could think more clearly sitting on this horse. He could focus on the immense difficulties he faced, and allow his mind to wander through myriad ideas that could possibly save the world he knew and loved.

His Lordship arrived back at the stables, and leapt from Jewel's saddle sweating and out of breath.

"McCarthy," he yelled as he marched through the swinging doors into the long stable filled with stalls on either side, "McCarthy".

"M'Lord?" said Callum McCarthy, stepping into view from the last stall. "Yes, sir. How can I help you?"

"I need to discuss something with you," panted Lord Arnold. "Let's go to your office, and get somebody to bring me a drink for God's sake. My throat's as dry as a camel's crotch."

Settled with a tall glass of beer, and having caught his breath, his Lordship leaned forward in his chair to ask several questions of his stable manager.

"Do we have enough of a stable to begin a stud farm? How many years would it take for it to become viable? Do you have the expertise to make it happen? How much money will it cost?"

Callum McCarthy's pipe fell from his open mouth as the questions tumbled out of his employer's mouth. He wondered to himself if his Lordship hadn't lost his senses and gone completely mad. How could he even begin to answer such questions on the spur of the moment. It took several minutes of the two men holding each other's eyes before Callum could trust himself to answer.

"Your Lordship, I don't know where you came up with such an idea," he began. "Beggin' your pardon, sir, I believe it must have been the long ride and the wind in your face, that's filled your head with such things."

"Stop that, right now," yelled Arnold. "This is no crazy idea that deserves to be tossed aside. You are the one person in my employ who could get away with addressing me in such a manner, without me having your hide whipped. Take it seriously, man, and answer my questions."

Callum picked up his pipe and relit it, letting the smoke swirl into his face to partially hide his eyes as he continued to contemplate his master's outlandish ideas.

"All right, m'Lord," Callum finally managed to begin. "The stables are more than adequate for the estate's needs at present. There would have to be a major expansion to begin thinking of a breeding program. I do believe I am qualified to supervise such a venture. I have experience with the County Kerry breeding facility in Ireland. As for a time line, that's more difficult to define. I'm thinking three to four years at the very least before a breeding stable could be established. The cost would be astronomical, m'Lord."

Lord Lingford was not deterred by the obstacles Callum McCarthy had outlined. He forged ahead with his dream, selling two large parcels of land to invest in the stable expansion. When Lady Lingford realized her husband would not give up his plan, she reluctantly agreed to advance him a portion of her own inheritance.

Lord Lingford had never been more enthusiastic about anything in his life. After two years of careful planning, he travelled to Ireland with McCarthy to purchase a stallion. It would be the most important decision they would make. The entire breeding program would hinge on the quality of a good stud.

Four of the estate's own suitable mares were joined by eight others from breeders in neighbouring counties.

Callum went back to his roots and asked the advice of his former boss, John Ryan, at the County Kerry stables. John recommended they view at least four stallions, and gave them the details of the stables they should visit in neighbouring counties of Ireland.

It was obvious to them that the third stallion they looked at was an exceptional stud horse. He had the frame, stature and temperament that Callum was looking for. He stood sixteen and a half hands, and upon physical examination was a perfect specimen of equine superiority. He had raced at Curragh in County Kildare for a season and achieved several important wins. During the past eighteen months his performance as a stud had produced six outstanding foals.

Lord Lingford paid a high price for Kilkenny Jack, but he would never regret the cost. The beautiful stallion was indeed the beginning of a dream.

CHAPTER 3

KILKENNY JACK

Henry and Percy Lingford watched in awe as the beautiful stallion was led towards his own stable. Their father had told them, in great detail, about the attributes of the fine horse he had bought in Ireland. A stallion who would be a father of many foals during the future years.

Kilkenny Jack was impressive. He was bigger than any of the horses in the estate stables and his sleek dark brown coat glistened in the evening sunlight as he walked quietly beside Callum McCarthy across the stable yard. The head of the stables glowed with pride as he ran his experienced hand over the steed's muscular neck. He couldn't wait to begin breeding the bevy of mares prepared for this fine horse.

"When will the first foal be born?" Henry asked his father as they walked away from the stables.

"Now that's a good question," Lord Lingford said. Not wanting to go into too much detail, he chose his words carefully. "He will need time to settle in with us. Then he will need time to get to know the mares. McCarthy will supervise the breeding side of things." A clearing of the throat was necessary after divulging such sensitive information to his two young sons. "The mare will carry the baby for almost a year—well eleven months to be exact. So I think you two will have to be very patient."

"Where will she carry the baby, father?" asked Percy, trotting along to keep up with his father's quickened pace.

"Well, like all mothers, the baby will grow inside her," Papa explained, beginning to feel most uncomfortable about the way the conversation was turning.

"Can we watch when it comes out?" Percy persisted.

"We will leave that part of the process to the vet and McCarthy," Papa said. Noticing the downfallen faces of the boys he added, "But you will be able to see the foal very soon after the birth, I promise you that."

Good enough for the two young brothers, they ran into the house and up to the nursery to tell Nanny Wells the good news.

Elizabeth sat in the window seat pouting. She had not been allowed to go with her brothers to watch the famed stallion arrive. Nanny had thought it 'unladylike.' She listened intently to Henry's description of the horse and the conversation with Papa about the foals. She was determined she would be with them when the first foal was viewed. She would talk to Papa herself about that.

Kilkenny Jack proved his worth, and as the mares came into heat and were presented to him, he didn't disappoint, enthusiastically impregnating each one. Three mares were in foal within a few weeks, followed by a continuing number during the course of the first year of the breeding program.

A year seemed an interminable time to be patient. The two young masters of the house counted the days, weeks and months before the first foals would be born. A chart on the wall of the nursery recorded each mare's name, and when her foal was expected. Nanny Wells cut out pictures of baby horses from The Horse and Hound magazine, which the boys stuck to the chart on the day of the expected birth for each horse. Elizabeth was fascinated with the process, and nearly drove Nanny crazy with her questions.

"Why is it taking so long?"

"When will the baby horses be born?"

"What are the mama horses' names?"

"Why is there only one papa horse?"

"Did he marry all the mamas?"

The biggest question was asked of Lord Lingford.

"Will I be able to see the foals when they are born?" Elizabeth asked as she sat on her Papa's lap and looked up at him with her big beautiful eyes and waited for his answer.

Henry and Percy looked at each other knowingly. Papa would say she's too little, they both thought to each other. She was also a girl, and going to see a newly born foal was not appropriate. Mama wouldn't even go to the stables. It was a man's world.

"Darling," began Lord Lingford. "You are too young right now to go tramping around the stables. Maybe when you are a little older. When the foals are up and around, I will take you down to the yard and one of the stable boys will bring a foal out for you to see."

"Stop," Elizabeth said, her lips puckering up and her eyes squeezing shut. "I am already big enough. Papa please. I won't be in the way, I promise. I will stand perfectly still and just look with my eyes. I don't even mind if I just take a peek and then have to leave right away. Papa, please let me."

His Lordship stared at his feisty little daughter. How could a child her age even speak the way she did, he asked himself. He pondered her question, knowing his two sons stood to attention in their place by the oak table, awaiting his response. He chose his words carefully.

"Elizabeth Amelia," he began, using both her names to emphasize his words. "Your brothers will be the first to see the first foal. That I have promised them both. I am prepared, however, to allow you to go to the stables immediately after-wards. It's against my better judgement, but you are so deter-mined to have your way that I will arrange for Nanny Wells to escort you to the stables, where a stable boy will meet you and take you to see the foal."

"Thank you, oh thank you Papa," squealed Elizabeth.

The boys were both downcast as they left the drawing room. Their little sister always had her own way with Papa. Even down to going to the stables, which was their domain. The one thing they shared with their father.

The time dragged on and on, until, on a cold November morning, word was sent to the nursery that the mare, Golden Flame, would have her foal that day. Henry ran to the chart on the wall and circled the baby horse under the mare's name with a red pencil. The boys watched through the window as the vet's horse and buggy arrived. Callum McCarthy was there to greet him, and both men hurried into the stables, where Lord Lingford stood anxiously waiting by Golden Flame's stall.

"How long?" Percy asked.

"Nobody knows," answered Nanny. "Come away from the window now, and let's have some breakfast."

Elizabeth had her nose pressed against the window pane, wishing she was in the stable now to watch what was happening. She didn't understand what was taking so long, only that she was tired of waiting. She would ask Nanny to dress her in her outdoor warm clothes after breakfast so that she would be ready to go when the word came.

Golden Flame had birthed two foals in the past, yet this third one was not an easy birth for her. The foal was bigger than the previous two, because of the size of the sire. The vet worked alongside Callum to reassure the mare and keep her calm. The vet would only intervene if there was cause for concern, and for now it was up to nature to take its course. Lord Lingford paced up and down the stables like an expectant father—indeed he hadn't been this nervous when his children were born. The first foal. It was a prodigious day.

Henry and Percy clattered down the stairs, out of the side hall door, and bolted across the slippery cobblestones to the stables. Their father had sent for them, and they knew what that meant—the first foal had been born. A young stable boy met them in the yard and took them into the stable, holding his finger to his lips to indicate the boys should be quiet as they entered. Lord Lingford stood outside a stall at the end of the long stable, his face flushed and his eyes glittering.

"Boys," he whispered, waving his hand for the boys to come closer."Come and see. The first foal. A beautiful filly."

The tiny foal lay wet and slimy by the side of her mother. She had her head up and Golden Flame licked her foal's nose and mouth as she cleaned away the remnants of the birth.

"She was born just fifteen minutes ago," explained Lord Lingford "She will try to stand up very soon. Watch closely boys. This is what we've all been waiting for."

As predicted the filly struggled to her feet and wobbled on her unsteady legs, encouraged by the mare, who constantly licked her and nudged her gently with her nose.

"Look at that," Henry said, his eyes wide with wonder. "She's up on her feet. It took Elizabeth almost a year to learn to walk. How amazing that a horse can walk so soon."

"It is a miracle," agreed Papa. "Something you will remember all your lives, I'm sure."

Lord Lingford rested a hand on each of his son's shoulders. One of the few times in their young lives that he had shown any physical affection for them. They would remember this day for more than a mare giving birth.

Elizabeth was brought to the stable, as promised, an hour after her brothers. Papa picked her up so that she could get a better view. The filly was now steady on her feet and had her head buried between the mare's back legs drinking hungrily.

"What is the baby doing, Papa?" asked the inquisitive little girl.

"She is having a drink of milk from her mother," said Papa.

"Does she like it?" persisted Elizabeth.

"What do you think?" asked Papa, laughing.

"I think she does," Elizabeth answered, smiling as she watched the first foal enjoying its meal. "She looks like her mama. I wish I could touch her." .

"She's not a pet," said Lord Lingford. "Nobody will touch her for the next few weeks. She needs to be with her mother."

He walked Elizabeth to the stable door, where Jane, the nursery helper, stood waiting for her.

"Run along now," Papa said, patting his daughter on her head.

Elizabeth smiled up at her beloved Papa as she took Jane's hand. He had kept his promise, and she was filled with over-whelming love for him.

CHAPTER 4

TINY GENIUS

Elizabeth knew from an early age that she was different from her siblings. Two more girls were born in rapid succession after her, and she was moved into the 'big' day nursery before her time, to make room for the babies.

With two older brothers dominating the large play area, their younger sister was left to her own devices much of the time. She was content to find a corner away from the boys to look at a book, or build fantastic castles with a set of colourful wooden blocks. However, when Mr. Meadows arrived to take over the education part of the day, Elizabeth insisted on sitting at the work table alongside Henry and Percy, where she listened attentively to the tutor, her eyes unblinking and round with amazement.

Mr. Meadows was baffled by this tiny girl, who learned to read in a matter of a few weeks, and held a pencil correctly to form her letters with perfection. She asked question after question about every subject they studied, leaving the boys to roll their eyes in exasperation. The tutor realized that Elizabeth was a gifted child, who would overtake her older brothers in their studies.

Since Elizabeth had learned to walk, presentation time in the drawing room each afternoon had become an adventure to behold for Henry and Percy. Instead of standing still to be presented to their parents, as instructed by Nanny, their little sister toddled towards her father with her arms outstretched and a smile on her chubby face to melt the coldest heart. Instead of asking Nanny to please remove the child, Lord Lingford actually picked her up and sat her on his lap. Even Mama gasped in disbelief at the sight.

Of course a precedent was set that day, and Elizabeth took her place on father's lap every day afterwards. Added to that, she was allowed to touch his moustache, lift up his lip to look at his teeth, play with his pocket watch, even climb onto her feet, balancing on his lap, to kiss him full on the lips. The boys, who still stood at attention for the entire visit, looked on in amazement at their baby sister's antics.

Elizabeth's first word was "Papa".

Lord Lingford was delighted.

Elizabeth had eyes only for her father. At the end of each daily visit, she condescendingly allowed her mother a brief kiss on the cheek, before joining her brothers to go back to the nursery.

As she grew, she gained more and more confidence. She worked hard at her classes during the day so that she could show her work to Papa after tea.

"Papa," Elizabeth cried as she ran through the drawing room door and headed for her favourite person in the world. "Look at this. I did a whole page of adding sums."

The excited child waved her paper in front of her father's face as she climbed up onto his lap.

"Well, well," Lord Lingford said, his whole face lighting up. "Let me see this. Every one correct. How old are you Elizabeth? You must be at least ten years old to complete such good work."

"I'm only four, Papa," laughed Elizabeth. "Mr. Meadows says he will teach me subtraction tomorrow. I just cannot wait to learn fractions like Henry."

Henry and Percy stood by, envious of the obvious affection their father had for Elizabeth. He had never shown the slightest interest in their achievements, and seemed to only tolerate them at a distance. Mother was absorbed with the new babies during the daily visits, and the two boys were left standing with Nanny by the round oak table, acutely aware that they were on the outskirts of the family group.

The boys had only one place where they were welcomed into their father's life. Every Saturday morning they headed to the stables to have a riding lesson. Lord Lingford insisted on supervising the lessons himself, watching every move they made as they took their instructions from Jeremy Spraig, a very experienced and patient stable hand.

"Sit up straight, Henry," Papa called out. "Back straight, eyes ahead. Loosen your grip on the reins boy. She's a mare not an elephant. Come on, Percy. Dig your heels in. You're in control, not the horse."

Despite the constant stream of criticism from their father, the boys were delighted to just spend time with him and have his attention. Lord Lingford always ended the lessons the same way, with a slap on the back for each of his sons as they dismounted.

"Well done," he said each time, before marching back to the stable.

It was up to the boys to take their horses into the stable, unsaddle and rub them down. Their father insisted that his sons have the "whole experience". They were not to cut corners by having a groom do the dirty work.

Elizabeth begged and begged Nanny to let her go with the boys on Saturday morning.

"No, Elizabeth," Nanny said in her stern voice. "You would be in the way. You will learn to ride side-saddle when you are five next year. His Lordship has enough to do supervising your brothers, he doesn't need you interfering.

"I will learn to ride like the boys," argued Elizabeth. "Not side-saddle. I'm going to go on the hunt with Papa when I'm grown up."

"You will do as your father orders, young miss," Nanny said. "You won't get your own way with everything. I will make a lady of you yet, you mark my words."

Making a lady out of Elizabeth would prove to be a daunting task.

CHAPTER 5
THE TUTOR

The middle child of Lord and Lady Lingford excelled in everything she did. Academically she left Mr. Meadows far behind, and he was relegated to teaching the two younger girls, Lydia and Caroline. Silas Gainsborough was hired to tutor the three oldest children in English, Latin, Arithmetic and Science. Geraldine Faulk came to the house three afternoons each week to instruct Elizabeth in painting, embroidery and piano. Henry and Percy headed outside on those same three afternoons for target practice with both bows and arrows and rifles, with their younger sister gazing at them in envy for being able to be outside doing fun activities while she was trapped in the day nursery with Miss Faulk.

Nanny Wells never tired of reminding Elizabeth how fortunate she was.

No expense was spared when it came to attiring young Miss Lingford in the highest quality clothing and shoes. She was tall and slender, and carried herself with an air of confidence unusual for a girl of her age. Her dark hair curled naturally, and her dark blue eyes were surrounded by long lashes that gave her an exotic charm. Her lips were full and pink, and she had an easy smile that showed a flash of perfectly formed teeth. She already turned heads when she walked through the village, or as she left the church on Sunday mornings.

As predicted, Elizabeth stormed ahead of her brothers in all subjects in the classroom. Inquisitive and curious, she absorbed knowledge like a sea sponge, often challenging her tutor, Silas Gainsborough, with her thirst to know more. Mathematics and science were particular favourites, as the young girl buried herself in biology, chemistry and physics.

The tutor was quite overwhelmed by his young student. The older boys, at sixteen and fourteen, had never shown an interest in the sciences and had begrudgingly ploughed through the bare rudiments. Never knowing what to expect of their sister, she constantly surprised them, bringing objects into the classroom to expand her knowledge: a collection of rocks, herbs, and plants which covered the entire deep windowsill, a large pike from the gamekeeper, and a pig's heart begged from the kitchen, that she cut open to examine the arteries and chambers.

Mr. Gainsborough suggested to Lord Lingford that a specialized tutor for science and mathematics would be a good idea for Miss Elizabeth, unless he should be discouraging such an interest in one so young and of the fairer sex.

"Elizabeth must have every advantage in her studies," declared her father, as he peered over his spectacles at the uncomfortable tutor. "Showing an aptitude for science may be regarded as unconventional for a young girl, but my daughter is unique and, as you have often remarked, extremely intelligent. It would be unthinkable to stand in the way of her interests in this matter."

"Yes, m'Lord," Mr. Gainsborough nodded in agreement. "That is why I broached the subject with you. Shall I advertise for a tutor for Miss Elizabeth?"

"No, no. Leave that to me. I will seek the guidance of a good friend of mine who is in the field. I want only the best."

The best was sought and hired by Lord Lingford. His friend, Professor Bauer, of Oxford University, recommended one of his students for the position. A young man of impeccable credentials, who excelled in his studies of the sciences.

When the term ended at Oxford, Elwyn Thomas joined Mr. Gainsborough to begin his tutoring of ten-year-old Elizabeth.

Elizabeth thrived under the guidance of her new tutor. With his soft Welsh accent Elwyn Thomas led her through the intricacies of chemistry, physics and biology. It was a challenge to keep the studies age-appropriate. Elwyn's young student pushed for more information in every area of study, asking questions that were far beyond her years, and impossible to answer without exposing Elizabeth to mature knowledge her age and gender prohibited.

Painting, embroidery and piano continued to be Elizabeth's nemesis. With constant pleading, she managed to persuade her mother to discontinue the painting and embroidery and continue with only piano, cut down to two afternoons each week. The extra time gained was used to visit the stables to gather information on the mares for the graphs in the nursery. The graphs now covered an entire wall, and information was added each day regarding the progress of each pregnancy.

Kilkenny Jack didn't disappoint. Foals were born with regularity throughout each year, and when the first of them was sold to one of the prestigious racing stables, everybody celebrated.

After consultations with the vet and McCarthy, Percy and Henry had been allowed to be present at a birth. It was the mare's second foal, and was deemed to be an easy birth. The boys were beyond excited when they were called to go to the stables. Even the bitter cold early morning couldn't dampen their enthusiasm as they dressed quickly and ran out of the side door and across the slippery, wet cobblestones.

"Completely disgusting!" Percy announced at breakfast. "I can barely stomach my food after watching."

Piling more toast and sausage onto his plate, Percy sat beside Elizabeth and wrinkled his nose.

"Nothing you should ever see, Beth," he continued. "Henry had to leave the stable."

"No I did not," argued Henry. "It was all over by the time I left."

"All over?" continued his brother. "You never saw the mess that came after the foal. Then the mare began to lick the stuff off the foal. I thought I would be sick. Leave it to the vet and McCarthy, that's what I say."

Elizabeth sat quietly nibbling on her toast, listening intently to all her brothers had to say. She couldn't wait until she was allowed to see a live birth. She knew she would not view it in the same light as the boys. She had studied and studied everything about the process and even seen diagrams, so she knew what to expect. All she had to do was persuade Papa.

Elwyn inspected the huge graph on the nursery wall with interest. The Lingford youngsters had certainly put a great deal of energy and thought into it. The boys' interest had waned over the years, but Elizabeth meticulously entered every detail under each mare's name. Some had foaled two or three times during the past six years, and the information beneath their names stretched almost to the floor.

Elizabeth was busy writing a new entry under Misty River's name, the latest mare to give birth.

"Mr. Thomas," Elizabeth looked up from her writing. "Could you ask my father to allow me to be present at the next birth? He is reluctant to give his permission, but if you explained my interest in biology and my in-depth study of each mare's condition, I think he would listen to you."

"Well, Miss Elizabeth," Elwyn replied, looking down at the ten-year-old. "I have a feeling your father will probably not listen to me in this matter. You are very young and watching the birth of any animal, especially a horse, could be traumatic, even for an adult."

"I wouldn't find it traumatic," scoffed Elizabeth. "I know exactly what to expect, and I would not react as my brothers did.

I have gathered every detail available to me. I've interviewed McCarthy and the vet, who have given me a first-hand knowledge, but it isn't like being there. Please Mr. Thomas, would you give it a try?"

"Very well. I will bring the matter up with his Lordship when the opportunity arises," her tutor agreed.

CHAPTER 6

A NEW FOAL

Two days later Elwyn Thomas spied his opportunity to talk to Lord Lingford. He waited in the stable yard for his Lordship to return from his daily ride, when he would be in the best of moods.

"Well, young Thomas," greeted Lord Lingford as he walked towards the tutor over the wet cobblestones. "How is your student progressing. She giving you any trouble?"

"No, m'Lord," answered Elwyn, touching his cap as he greeted his employer, and falling into step with him as they marched towards the house. "Elizabeth is a model student. Intelligent beyond her years, inquisitive and curious about everything."

"Nothing new there," continued his Lordship."So, spit it out. What has she put you up to this time?"

Elwyn stuttered as he tried to convey his young student's request in an amicable way.

"We have been looking at animal reproduction in an age-appropriate way, of course. Miss Elizabeth is quite obsessed with the stud farm and has kept track of every mare who has foaled in these past six years. The graph covers the entire north nursery wall and is very impressive."

"And?"

"It's like this m'Lord," Elwyn explained. "She would very much like to be present at the birth of a foal, and has commissioned me to ask you for permission."

"She has been asking for many months," Lord Lingford said, stopping before entering the manor house to look into the tutor's face. "My answer is still 'No'."

"May I beg your indulgence, sir?" Elwyn asked. "I completely understand your answer, and would agree entirely if it were not for the insistence of my young student. After working with her, I beg to differ with your decision, and urge you to reconsider. Miss Elizabeth has studied the birthing process carefully, including diagrams and pictures, and has become familiar with the technical and medical issues. I believe she should be given the opportunity, at Mr. McCarthy's discretion to witness a birth. Maybe a mare who has given birth before and will have an easy delivery."

"Oh, Good God!" exclaimed his Lordship, whacking the side of the doorframe with his crop. "There will never be peace until she has had her way in this. Confound her. She wheedles and cajoles all of us until she wins the argument. I will talk to McCarthy and make arrangements. But, Mr. Thomas, I am giving you fair warning that if this all goes badly, I will hold you to blame for speaking on her behalf."

"Thank you m'Lord," mumbled Elwyn.

So it was settled. Elizabeth was to witness the next foaling. She had dashed into her father's study later that day to throw her arms around his neck in thanks, declaring that he was the best Papa in the world, and she would be indebted to him for life.

"Maybe you should thank me afterwards," laughed Papa. "Think of how your brothers' reacted to the whole experience."

"Papa," Elizabeth frowned. "You know me better than that. You know I will absolutely love every minute of it."

Callum McCarthy chose the pregnant mare carefully. Jenny

Lee was a calm, beautiful six-year-old mare who had birthed a foal two years previously with no difficulty. Her second foal was due at the end of May, 1911, and Elizabeth couldn't wait. She visited Jenny Lee daily, stroking her neck and offering her apples, and she was present at the vet's visits, taking notes on all the details of his examination.

It was a warm night in late spring when Callum McCarthy, who had been watching Jenny Lee carefully for a few days, noticed a change in her behaviour. She was restless, sweaty, and skittish. Sure signs that her foal would be born very soon. Probably in the middle of the night. McCarthy sent word to Lord Lingford, who joined his stable master to take a look at the mare.

"What do you think, McCarthy?" asked His Lordship.

"She will foal before too long, Sir," answered the dedicated horse expert.

"Right then. I'll be led by your expertise and send word to the nursery to alert Miss Elizabeth. She may have a bit of a wait, but she won't forgive me or you if she misses it."

Daisy, the young nursery assistant who acted as Elizabeth's chambermaid, shook her young mistress gently as she lay snuggled into her bed.

"Sorry to wake you Miss," Daisy whispered, as Elizabeth's eyes popped open with a start. "Mr. McCarthy sent word for you to go to the stables."

Elizabeth was up in a moment, pulling on her clothes with Daisy's help. She flew downstairs, grabbed her boots in the mud room and was out of the side door and running across the yard in no time. She arrived at the stables out of breath, her eyes shining and her lush dark hair flying behind her.

McCarthy greeted her with a smile, and they walked to the birthing stall together.

"Have patience, Miss Elizabeth," McCarthy said. "All indications are that a foal is on its way, but nature will take its course. I've just sent young Charlie off on his bike to inform the vet."

"Yes, McCarthy," nodded Elizabeth. "Thank you. I am very excited. Can I give Jenny Lee an apple?"

"No, Miss. Not right now. Let her concentrate on what's at hand. She's in some discomfort, but all we should do is watch and wait. She'll take care of the rest.

Mr. Norris, the vet, arrived within the hour and quickly assessed Jenny Lee.

"Well, McCarthy," he said as he stepped out of the stall. "You are spot on with your prediction. She's coming along just fine. "Some leakage, and the vulva's well expanded. We shouldn't have to wait very long."

Elizabeth scribbled in her notebook, eager to record every word the vet uttered. She moved closer to the stall and stood on a crate placed nearby especially so that she could have a better view. As Jenny Lee moved restlessly around the stall, Elizabeth's eyes searched for the signs the vet had spoken about. The mare came closer to her young friend and Elizabeth reached out to stroke her muzzle.

"No apples today, Jenny Lee," Elizabeth said quietly. "You are a fine horse, and you are going to be a fine mother to your foal."

With a low whinny the mare continued her fretful movements, with the liquid beginning to seep more prolifically from under her flicking tail. All of a sudden Jenny Lee was down on her side, panting, her eyes wild and her front legs pawing at the fresh straw around her.

"Help her," Elizabeth cried out to Mr. Norris.

"Everything is going along nicely, Miss," explained the vet. "Jenny Lee doesn't need any help. I will only step in if there is a problem, and right now there is none. Do you know what will happen next?"

Elizabeth collected her thoughts and looked into the stall before answering.

"There will be a lot of liquid to bring the foal into the birth canal. We will see the foal's two front legs first, followed by the nose and head laying on the front legs. After that, the foal will slip out quite easily."

"Well done," Mr. Norris said. "You have done your home-work. You are about to witness the miracle of birth. You will always remember the first one you see, so keep your eyes on Jenny Lee."

The mare panted and pushed, stood up then lay down again, There was the gush of fluid, there were the two front legs, there was the nose enclosed in the sac. Elizabeth held her breath as she watched in wonder. The flimsy sac broke with the next push and the foal slid onto the straw, its nose free to breathe for the first time. Jenny Lee lay very still, resting, but Elizabeth wasn't worried about her now.

"She's resting now," she said. "The umbilical cord is still pumping blood into the foal, so she will wait until it's safe to stand up. Then the cord will break on its own and she will lick her baby."

"If ever I need an assistant, you will be my first choice," laughed Mr. Norris.

Elizabeth beamed, as she watched the new baby's first tenta-tive movements. Two tears escaped from her eyes. What a marvellous experience she had been privileged to witness. As Mr. Norris had said, she would never forget it.

Once the mare was up on her feet and the placenta had been inspected, Mr. Norris shook hands with Callum McCarthy, patted Elizabeth's head and headed back to his bed.

"You should get back to bed too, Miss Elizabeth," Callum said.

"Not yet, McCarthy. I want to stay and watch the foal nurse for the first time, and make sure Jenny Lee is happy. I couldn't sleep yet anyway."

Callum McCarthy shook his head as he smiled at the young girl still standing on the crate. So unlike her brothers, who had literally ran out of the stable after witnessing a birth. She was one in a million, just like her father was always claiming. Callum wondered what kind of life was ahead for her. What would the future hold for a girl of her intelligence and courage? Not the usual path of aristocratic young ladies, Callum thought.

CHAPTER 7

WAR

"You shall name the foal," Lord Lingford said to his daughter the next day. She had spent the better part of an hour giving her father every detail of the early morning birth, and he was quite overcome by her knowledge and awed excitement.

"Black Diamond is his name, Papa," Elizabeth announced proudly, "he will grow up to be the best racehorse at Newmarket. I will follow his career for his whole life".

Percy and Henry appeared at breakfast, scoffing and teasing their younger sister about her visit to the stable during the night. They were soon silenced, when she described her experience in glowing terms, and added that she intended to be at every birth from now on to expand her knowledge.

Later that day in the study, Elwyn Thomas went over his student's meticulous notes and sketches, with ever-increasing admiration. It could have been the work of a graduate student. He realized that he had not been challenging her to the best of her ability, and he knew he must forge ahead at a higher level.

The years melted away, with Elizabeth keeping her promise to be at every birth. Some were difficult and the vet was forced to intervene, particularly if it was a maiden birth. Mr. Norris became so used to having Elizabeth there that he allowed her to assist him on occasion. She climbed into the stall alongside the vet to remove the amniotic sack from the nose of a foal when it didn't split on its own. She helped check placentas and helped disinfect the umbilical stump attached to the baby. She even helped Mr. Norris pull on the forelegs of a foal to help it into the world. She loved every minute of it. It convinced her that her dream to become a vet was the right choice. She would spend her life around horses doing what she loved.

The stud farm was an enormous success, producing high quality foals every year. Word of the stables spread through the counties of southern England and by 1913 there was a healthy waiting list for Lingford horses. The dream had come true.

Elizabeth still begged her father's permission to ride astride, but in this one thing, her Papa remained unmoved and insisted on side-saddle. The two of them met for long rides through the countryside, enjoying each other's company and the wild wind in their faces.

The two younger girls were not fond of horses and preferred to follow their mother's direction, staying indoors to sew and paint. Henry had left the year before for Oxford to read History, and Percy would follow him soon. Both boys still loved to ride when they could, although they had never again had the desire to be present at the birth of a foal.

Elwyn Thomas remained the senior tutor for both Elizabeth and Percy as they prepared for the Oxford entrance exam. Mr. Meadows taught the younger two girls, concentrating on English, French and Geography, rather than mathematics or science for which neither girl had an aptitude.

The whole Lingford estate ran like a well-oiled machine. The manor house was fully staffed and maintained, the agriculture thrived and the cattle production was prolific and prosperous. Lord Lingford was a happy man.

∾

Percy was preparing to join Henry in Oxford. Elizabeth was enjoying a summer break from studying, giving her the opportunity to ride every day. Lady Lingford and her two youngest daughters were busy making preparations for a garden party at the manor house. Lord Lingford had just returned from Ireland, where he and McCarthy had purchased a second stallion, when everything came to an abrupt halt.

On July 28, 1914 Britain declared war on Germany in support of Belgium and France. Rivalry between Germany and Britain and had been growing for years, with Britain's control of the world's oceans and Germany's powerful and aggressive dominance in Europe. Both countries felt threatened by each other.

For Lord Lingford it couldn't have come at a worse time. Just as the breeding program was underway and producing wonderful foals, and with the rest of the estate ticking over nicely, the government appealed for all young men to volunteer to fight for their country. A third of the estate workforce were gone within the first three months of war being declared, leaving every part of the estate, from field workers, to stable hands, to house servants, in dire need of help. No Oxford University for Percy, who joined his brother, Henry, and volunteered to fight the Germans. Both young men were promptly given commissions as officers in cavalry regiments. They were encouraged to choose their own horses from the estate stables, before the army issued a commission for a percentage of the Lingford equine population for military service. Fifty horses were commandeered by the British army, leaving the stables with a handful of young racers, plus ten mares, Kilkenny Jack, and the new stallion, Big Boy, to continue breeding.

It was only due to their location near Newmarket that the Lingford estate was allowed to retain its working stables. Newmarket was one of the few race courses given permission to organize several races each year, for the morale of the country.

As the young men left, the women stepped in where they could to fill the shoes of their sons, husbands or brothers. Even in the stables, Callum McCarthy relented his strict "no women" rules of employment, and four of the young women from the village were hired as stable hands.

England's economy was turned upside down as all funds were channelled into the vast expense of the war effort. Horse racing became a rarity as the racecourses were converted into training camps for the troops, or field hospitals for the injured. Thousands of horses were commandeered into the cavalry, leaving farmers distraught.

Turning the tide of financial ruin for the Lingford estate was a daunting task, and during the war years there were many times when the future looked bleak. Holding onto his dream, Lord Lingford forged ahead, putting his faith in the groundwork McCarthy and his team of dedicated stable hands had accomplished.

Elizabeth's life changed too. Elwyn Thomas joined the army, and studies were set aside until another tutor could be found. Fourteen-year-old Elizabeth filled her days with riding and exercising the horses. Long ago she had won the argument with her Papa about riding side-saddle, and now enjoyed the wonderful freedom of flying across the estate straddling her mount.

She was one of the few people allowed to groom the stallions, who seemed to have a special affinity for the young mistress of the house. Elizabeth longed to ride Kilkenny Jack, but McCarthy forbade it. Kilkenny Jack was too valuable to risk injury from a frivolous and unnecessary ride through the countryside with the young mistress.

The Great War brought despair and hardship to the island nation of Great Britain. It lasted too long and took too many lives. The families who struggled and waited at home began to think it would never end.

CHAPTER 8

LINGFORD IN TURMOIL

E lizabeth's new tutor was an elderly retired professor from Oxford University. Isaac Worthing was very happy with his new situation. He was given a large guest room and ate his meals with the family. He was a lonely widower, having lost his wife of forty years several months ago. His new student confused him from the beginning. Not being used to teaching young ladies in the sciences, it took him several weeks before becoming comfortable enough to continue where Elwyn Thomas had left off.

The Professor was not a favourite with his young student. He was stooped with age, and had a constant annoying cough. He smelled musty, and tended to spray saliva when he spoke. He wasn't interested in horses at all, and shrugged his shoulder with indifference when Elizabeth proudly showed him her research and the graph on the nursery wall. However, he did challenge her in the subjects he taught, and she continued to progress at a rapid rate through first year university courses.

News from the battlefields of France and Belgium were grim indeed. Thousands of men and horses lost their lives as the fight against German dominance seemed never-ending. Injured and wounded soldiers flooded into Britain, as boat after boat carried them across the English Channel to their homeland. Hospitals were overrun in every city and the British Government, underestimated the vast number of injuries. Parliament was at a loss to deal with the ever- growing tide. Help was badly needed, and estate owners, among them Lord Lingford, volunteered to convert their stately mansions into space for convalescing military.

Lady Lingford immediately took charge of the operation, giving instructions that empty bedrooms be made ready.

Once Lingford Manor was registered as a convalescent venue, the military delivered a small mountain of supplies. Military cots were brought in, so that each large bedroom had four beds instead of one. The family bedrooms were in one wing of the house anyway, so the use of guest rooms was not an interference. The lady of the house also converted the billiard room into a makeshift ward, so that soldiers who couldn't manage the stairs had a bed on the main floor.

Along with the cots, boxes of medical equipment, grey flannel pyjamas, socks, and underwear, were delivered. As part of the standard issue for convalescing soldiers they received hospital blue uniforms, and even red and white handkerchiefs and red ties. The towers of boxes were stored in the stable barn until needed.

Lady Lingford gave instructions for the music room to be converted into a small dining room for the family, so that their military guests could use the large formal dining room. Every practical arrangement was made to ensure the comfort of the expected wounded soldiers, even down to digging several more sewer pits to accommodate the extra lavatory waste. In fact the whole house was turned upside down.

Lady Lingford put the word out among the tenants on the estate that more help would be needed to run the house. Kitchen hands, chambermaids, gardeners, and particularly those with experience nursing the sick. Mrs. Formby, the vicar's wife, spearheaded volunteers to attend to the medical needs of the soldiers.

She had some experience of nursing from before her marriage, and called on ladies she knew to join her in the care of the troops.

Eight dishevelled, thin and dirty soldiers were the first to arrive at the manor house on a windy, rainy evening in March of 1916. The house staff were kept busy running up and down the stairs with pails of hot water to fill baths for the tired young men. All eight could manage the stairs with help. They shared the two bathrooms, enjoying the warm water, soap, soft clean towels, shaving equipment, brush and comb at their disposal. They bathed each other's wounds, and bandaged them carefully with the strips of pure white cotton placed on the wash stand. None of them could remember the last time they were clean, or when they had used a commode, or shaved their whiskers.

The chambermaids ran up and down the stairs, fetching and carrying more warm water, emptying commodes, and carrying the stinking, blood-stained uniforms outside to be burnt on the bonfire the stable hands had lit.

Hospital blue uniforms, flannel pyjamas and socks were placed on each bed, some ill fitting, but all clean and smelling of soap. Each soldier looked and felt like a different person as they hobbled downstairs in search of food.

The kitchen was a hive of activity as cooks and maids prepared a hot beef stew for the guests, followed by apple pie. A meal the men had only dreamt about for many months.

Lady Lingford entered the dining room as they were finishing their meal.

"Welcome to Lingford Manor," she said, smiling at the tired young men sitting around the dining table.

"I hope you found everything in order when you arrived. You are our guests and we are all here to make sure your convalescence goes well. My husband, Lord Lingford will see you all tomorrow. There will also be a group of nurses to attend to your wounds."

"Now," Lady Lingford continued. "A small glass of brandy is

in order." She indicated to one of the footmen to follow her instructions, and each soldier was served.

"Thank you, m'Lady," one of the soldiers said.

Her Ladyship nodded in his direction before leaving the dining room. She would make sure her guests would be given the very best of care whilst they were under her roof. She knew from the few letters she had received from Henry and Percy how bad the living conditions were on the battlefield.

The soldiers flipped coins for the opportunity to sleep in a proper bed, the fortunate winners sank down into the luxurious, soft mattresses, with fine linen sheets and pillows full of down, and pulled the thick bedspreads over them. Even the army cots were a luxury, despite the army-issue sheets and coarse grey blankets. It was a far cry from the wet mud of a trench, where a dirty woollen blanket was their only comfort.With full stomachs for the first time in many months, and the brandy warming them from the inside, all eight soldiers sank into a deep sleep, only interrupted by the images in their dreams of the horrors they had witnessed. Some of them cried out in anguish when nightmares overwhelmed them, only to be shaken awake by a comrade, who consoled them with the assurance that it was just a dream.

The following day, as promised, three women arrived with their own bags of medical equipment to assess the needs of the soldiers. Those first soldiers were the lucky ones, with only superficial wounds. No limbs missing, or burns, or eyes blinded. All had various shrapnel wounds that had been treated at a mobile medical unit on the battlefield. None had healed well enough to be sent back into the trenches. They had travelled by horse driven cart to the French coast, and then by hospital ship to the English south coast. Dressings had been changed with some haste before leaving Dover to make the journey to Lingford Manor. As a result the wounds were showing signs of distress, and medical intervention was required.

Mrs. Formby and her two companions set to work immediately, cleaning and dressing each wound with care. With a few weeks of good food, clean clothing, warm and dry lodging, these young men would soon make a full recovery, and be sent to fight again.

Elizabeth peeked through the doorway of the billiard room as the women tended their patients. Mother had strictly forbidden her to go near the soldiers, but she itched to help tend them, even if only to help serve food or freshen water. There was no doubt in her mind that she could change dressings. She never felt faint or queasy, as other young ladies might, when she helped the vet with all manner of procedures in the stables.

"Elizabeth," Mama's voice behind her made the young intruder jump. "Do you not have something more important to do than spying on the soldiers?"

"I'm not spying, Mama," answered Elizabeth. "I'm watching the nurses do their work. Can I not help in some way? I know I could be useful."

Elizabeth put on her most wistful look as she faced her mother, but Mama was not Papa, who would have fallen victim to such pleading.

"A sick room full of young soldiers is no place for a young lady of your position," Mama sighed. "Let the servants and nurses care for them. There is enough help."

With that Mama turned on her heel, glancing over her shoulder to make sure her daughter was following her.

Lady Lingford had no idea what was ahead, and how she would have to eat her words.

CHAPTER 9

MASTER HENRY

The house was unusually still. The servants walked on tiptoe, careful not to disturb the quiet. Nanny, long retired but still living in her room, lit a fire in the nursery and gathered the three young Lingford girls around her. Nanny, who had comforted them many times during their short lives, held out her arms to comfort them again.

The telegram had arrived at dawn, and Hayden, the butler, had hurriedly taken it to his Lordship's bedroom. Hayden had since informed the housekeeper, kitchen and day staff of the contents.

Master Henry had been killed in action.

Lord Arnold and Lady Maud Lingford sat silently in their small sitting room, adjacent to their bedroom. A maid had delivered tea, which sat unpoured and untasted on the table beside them.

Having the title of Lord and Lady, being the owners of a large estate and manor house was of no consequence. They were father and mother of a dead soldier, akin to thousands who sat in the same stupor throughout the country.

The day passed by ever so slowly as Henry's parents and siblings tried to absorb the shock of the news they had received.

Lady Lingford sent for her daughters once she was dressed, and they broke with tradition as they clung together, their tears wetting each other's cheeks. Papa stood still as a ramrod, gazing out of the window onto the rain-soaked land. His thoughts were with his son, dying in a trench in another rain-soaked country across the English Channel. He prayed he had not been alone at the moment of death. He prayed his other son, Percy, was safe somewhere.

Elizabeth had never let her father remain protected by his outer image. From a baby she had broken down the barrier that the rest of the family never crossed. Today was no different. She unravelled herself from her mother and sisters and ran to her father, flinging her arms around him and holding him close. More than his wife had done. More than he would allow anyone but Elizabeth to do. A quiet wrenching sob escaped his throat as he held his daughter. The warmth of her being in his arms spread through his frozen body like radiance from the sun. Here was life. Here was warmth. Here was hope. Here was Elizabeth.

The weeks which followed were a blur for Maud Lingford as she mourned her beloved son. There was a memorial service at the village church with all the estate in attendance. The outpouring of condolences from their neighbours and friends and estate workers were received with genuine gratitude.

The war continued its course, and the wounded returned to England in ever growing numbers.

July, 1916 was hot and stuffy and, even with the windows open, the rooms in the Lingford mansion seemed airless. During the first weeks of the month, news of a great battle, the battle of The Somme, was reported in the newspapers. The poet, Siegfried Sassoon, described the battle as a 'sunlight picture of hell.' On the first day, 19,240 British troops were killed Over the course of the 141-day battle, there were 420,000 casualties among the soldiers from Britain alone.

Elizabeth watched from her bedroom window, as a bedraggled stream of mud-caked men, arrived at Lingford Manor.

Carriages and carts drew up one after the other carrying stretchers laden with the severely injured. Elizabeth leaned her forehead against the window pane. The agony and pain of war spread out beneath her, filling her with despair and sorrow.

Every available space was needed to house the ever growing tide of war-torn bodies, and Lady Lingford gave instructions to clear the morning room and conservatory for extra cots. Every available volunteer was needed to take care of the damaged young men. Mrs. Formby was quite overwhelmed by the onslaught. Not just minor injuries now, but direly wounded men, who needed a doctor's expertise and often surgery to repair the damage they had suffered.

Two elderly doctors from nearby Newmarket took up residence at the manor house to assist the overworked volunteers, followed by Dr.Trantor, an army surgeon, who had been injured himself two years previously, and had now recovered enough to join the team.

Mrs. Formby welcomed any and all girls over sixteen to work alongside the older women. It was Elizabeth's pass into the sickroom. Lady Lingford could no longer deny her, and the young mistress of the house was delighted.

Elizabeth treated every soldier as if he were her brother, Henry, and worked more than her shift required each day, fetching and carrying for the doctors and experienced older ladies, helping to serve meals and fill water glasses, roll bandages, open the daily parcels that arrived with medical supplies. She was not allowed to help with anything personal, like distributing or emptying latrine bottles or bedpans, or sponge baths, as all these tasks were left to the older ladies, or other soldiers who could walk.

Mama insisted that Elizabeth wore her hair tied behind her neck, and had a white cap fixed tightly over her hair. She also wore a plain dress and a starched white apron which showed no hint of a curve in her body. Enough that she was very pretty and every soldier's eyes followed her wherever she went. Mrs.

Formby kept a careful eye on the young mistress as she went about her tasks. She could well imagine what was going on in the young men's heads as they watched her.

Sitting in the evening dusk, bathing the forehead of a delirious young soldier, Elizabeth had a dramatic change of heart. Time seemed to stop and there was a sudden and unexplained silence. The clarity of thought and conviction was so clear it was as if somebody had spoken the words out loud.

"Give up the dream of becoming a vet, Elizabeth. This is what you are meant to do — become a doctor and heal the sick."

Just as suddenly the silence ended and the clutter and sounds of the sickroom returned. The wet cloth on the soldier's hot forehead was as warm as he was, and the young mistress quickly dipped it back into the cold water and replaced it.

The moment she had experienced was etched into her memory and her heart. It was a new dream. One she would not share yet, but would hold close to her until the time was right.

Elizabeth still escaped to the stables whenever she could find time. With so few mares she was still able to be present at almost every birth, and even managed without the vet or McCarthy one dark night in August when Sunwind gave birth to her third foal.

Papa joined his daughter each Saturday morning, when they rode together, although something in Papa's countenance had changed since the death of Henry. To lose a son was something he would bear for a lifetime. A letter from Percy had placated the fear he felt every time he thought about his younger son still in the battlefield.

Lord Lingford was enthusiastic about the racing at Newmarket, one of the few racecourses in England to still be active, although infrequently. The Lingford stable had several young racers to show off, and his Lordship was eager to see them do well. McCarthy trained each of them with an experienced hand, enjoying watching the young horses go through their paces and become strong and fast. It was a distraction from the war and all the bad news, and the men, boys and girls who worked in the stables relished the job they did and the chance to race the horses they cared for.

The soldiers in the manor house were almost equally keen to hear about the horses, and they soon learned that Elizabeth had all the answers to anything to do with the stables.

"Who's racing this Saturday, then?" asked a pale, thin soldier from his bed, as he saw Elizabeth coming into the room with a water jug.

Elizabeth walked over to his bed and filled his glass before answering him.

"How did you know there was a race this Saturday?" she asked.

"We do read the newspapers," he quipped back at her.

"Well, in that case," Elizabeth said. "We have two horses racing. Glen Lacey and Black Diamond."

"Thanks Miss," glowed the young soldier. "I hope one of them wins."

Elizabeth turned as she reached the door.

"Black Diamond is my favourite. He was the first foal whose birth I attended, so he is very special."

The soldier sank back onto his pillow exhausted, but with a smile on his face. Like the hands in the stables, it was something to think about besides the war.

CHAPTER 10

A SON RETURNS

Black Diamond won the race at Newmarket with ease, and McCarthy glowed with pride as he told Miss Elizabeth every detail. Elizabeth hung onto every word, and then ran into the house to tell the soldiers.

The patients housed in the morning room had made their own betting pool, and thrown in what little they had on the horse of their choice. The young soldier who had inside information on Black Diamond didn't share his knowledge, and was thrilled to win the pot of four shillings. Elizabeth laughed at his excitement over such a small amount of money, but also for the joy it brought her to see the young man so happy.

In 1917 the government closed all racing at Newmarket. British resource in the war effort were stretched to their limit. Everyone feared that the war would be lost and they would all come under German rule.

Out in the Atlantic Ocean, ships carrying supplies to the British Isles from America became the target of the German U boats. America had remained neutral since the beginning of the war in 1914, but as Germany attacked more merchant ships, sending them and their crews to the bottom of the ocean, President Wilson, backed by congress, declared war on Germany. The full might of the United States' arms and equipment would be the turning point of the war in Europe. The British people once again began to believe the allies would succeed and overcome their powerful enemy. After waiting for three years for help, the badly depleted British forces would wait for another ten months before troops from the United States began to arrive in Europe, at a rate of ten thousand a day.

The soldiers arriving at the Lingford estate in March of 1918 had optimistic news from France and Belgium. Despite the huge losses of both men and horses, the influx of American soldiers had bolstered the lines of the exhausted British, and the Germans could not hold their positions.

Elizabeth turned eighteen in the spring. She had spent almost two years of the war tending the injured and sick, riding and helping in the stables, and studying when she could. She had held the hands of dying men, supported lame soldiers while they learned to walk again, bathed tired faces and washed grubby hands. She had helped dress wounds and on more than one occasion had helped undress or dress soldiers too sick or tired to help themselves. Through it all she never balked nor blushed with embarrassment.

Some of the soldiers were only at the house for a few days before being transferred to one of the convalescent bases. Others were with them for much longer, as their severe injuries needed surgery and great care afterwards. They could be funny, quiet, tearful, or difficult, but they were all grateful.

It took a small army of servants and volunteers to keep the manor house running during those demanding years. Every person involved worked more hours than they had ever worked during peacetime, and days off were few and far between. The soldiers showered their thanks on the doctors, women, and girls who had shown them such kindness, and many wrote letters to Lord and Lady Lingford expressing their gratitude.

Lord Lingford watched for the mail every day, waiting for some word from Percy. They had received a letter from him in the summer of 1917, telling them he was safe, but had lost his wonderful steed. The six year old mare, Florentine, had been a faithful companion through more than three years of war, and Lord Lingford could feel his son's pain behind the written words. He clung onto the hope that receiving no telegram was cause for optimism, and that his second son must be alive somewhere.

It was the second week of May when a pitiful looking old horse limped its way along the muddy driveway of Lingford Manor. its rider slumped forward, barely staying in the saddle. McCarthy saw him first and ran across the stable yard to grab the steed's reins. He looked into the haunted eyes of the rider, and helped him dismount, feeling his weight as he slid to the ground beside him.

"Master Percy," gasped McCarthy. "Let me help you, sir. Here, give me your arm. Let's get you into the house."

Lord Lingford was sitting in his study when he heard the commotion in the side hallway, and hurried to find out what was happening. McCarthy was helping a dishevelled soldier into the house, and as recognition dawned on Lord Lingford's face, he dropped his pipe on the floor and ran to support his son. Within minutes the whole family surrounded the trio as they made their way into the morning room and lowered Percy onto a couch. The deep gash in his head oozed a sticky residue. His head flopped back onto the soft pillows and his eyes closed. He was home.

"Give him air," his father said quietly. "Ring for water, brandy, anything he wants."

"Darling," Lady Lingford said grasping Percy's cold hand. "You are safe now. You are home with your family. Oh Percy, I've never been so happy to see anybody in my life."

With an unaccustomed show of emotion, she held the back of Percy's hand against her lips.

Percy opened his eyes and gazed at his family. He had often thought during the past four years that he would never see them again. He smiled slowly, and gratefully sipped the water laced with brandy his father held for him. The fortified drink revived him quickly and he raised his head to take a better look at his sisters, who were standing staring at him in wonder.

"Do I look that bad?" he smiled as he caught their eyes.

"No, no, you look fantastic," Elizabeth said, while the other girls nodded their agreement. "It's just so incredible to have you home, Percy. We had almost given up on you."

Percy doubted any of them were as happy as he was at that moment. He had seen, heard and done things in the past four years that would never be erased from his mind. An eternity of days filled with mud, stench, near starvation, suffering, and death, that he would rarely talk about again, but his dreams would be filled with the horrors he had endured long after the war was over.

CHAPTER 11

PERCY RESTORED

The wound in Percy's head had initially rendered him unconscious for several days. When he finally opened his eyes, he had been transferred to a field hospital, and lay amid stretchers of wounded, bleeding soldiers wedged into an overcrowded, unsanitary tent. He wondered, looking back, how any of them had survived. For several days there was no food, no water, no medical attention, and no toilet facilities. The tent became a stifling cesspool of human excrement, vomit, blood and gore. In and out of consciousness, Percy lost all track of time.

Water touched Percy's lips and ran down his chin. He opened his mouth to quench his dry mouth and throat. Finally, some reprieve from the nightmare of carnage he found himself in the midst of. A young, pale-faced man in clothing so dilapidated it was difficult to determine what regiment he served with, held a tin cup to Percy's lips, and supported his head with his other hand.

"All right, mate?" the young man muttered. "Drink it in. Help's on its way."

The tent of horror was slowly cleared over the following week. The men were stripped and bathed. Wounds were bound, and the injured were housed in three newly erected army tents, with space between the cots. Latrines were dug and an old barn converted into a wash house. An army doctor made his way through the list of soldiers, assessing each one's needs.

Percy's head wound was infected and he still had periods of dizziness. He found out from the doctor's adjutant that his regiment had taken a heavy beating the day he had been injured, and the few surviving soldiers had been transferred to another regiment. The doctor issued an order for Percy to be evacuated home. The first step in an arduous journey took him by horse drawn ambulance wagon to a nightmarish few days on an overcrowded hospital train, and finally to another larger field hospital on the shores of the English Channel. A medical ship transported him, along with numerous injured soldiers, to their homeland. Many died during the horrendous trip, and Percy became delirious. Dysentery was their constant companion, causing great distress and suffering. The fetid smell permeated the wagons, trains, tents and boats the sick young men occupied. Percy swore to himself that he would do everything in his power to reach Lingford Manor, even if it meant stealing a horse and riding there alone.

A cavalry stable backed onto the field hospital in Folkstone, where Percy lay waiting to be transferred. He heard the sound and smell of horses, and made his move after dark. Hobbling slowly towards the stable, he sought a steed. The poor animals were a collection of left-over old nags, too unreliable and unhealthy to travel across the Channel into war. With the little strength he had, Percy saddled an elderly mare and pulled himself into the saddle. Slowly he set out for Lingford, praying he would make it home alive.

Percy's recovery was slow. He was weak and tired, physically and mentally. His sisters were his constant companions, urging him to walk a little further each day and eat the good food Mrs. Thompson, the cook, had prepared to tempt him. He wasn't interested in returning to Oxford to continue his education. It seemed pointless to him now. As he grew stronger, Percy longed to be more active, and his father encouraged him to become more involved in the management of the estate. Lord Lingford suggested to his factor, Mr. Darrowby, that Percy might begin his new career by learning the ropes under his expert supervision. The book-keeping and management of the great estate took skill, dedication, and meticulous record-keeping, and would give Percy a panoramic view of how everything worked.

The new venture suited Percy very well, and he quickly became acquainted with the people who worked the land and their various roles. He joined Mr. Darrowby in the weekly meetings with his father and the estate manager, and was soon offering his opinion and advice on issues of concern.

He made a habit of walking through the rooms converted to hospital wards each morning, despite the apprehension he felt as he remembered his own experience. He stopped to shake a hand, or say a few words to the comrades he encountered, knowing their thoughts and feelings mirrored his own. Henry's face often flashed into his mind, taking him by surprise and making him take a second look at an unknown soldier's face lying on a pillow. He knew it wasn't Henry, but he just had to make sure!

CHAPTER 12

A DIFFERENT PATH

E lizabeth continued to tend the injured with renewed vitality and energy. Since the night she had decided to become a doctor, she had dug out her old biology, physics and chemistry books and set herself the task of revising what she had learned with Elwyn Thomas, to prepare for the entrance exam into Oxford University that autumn. Who knew how long the war would last. They had all thought it would be over in a matter of weeks, maybe months. Now it seemed it would go on forever, and Elizabeth was determined she would be in attendance at Oxford at the beginning of the Michaelmas term in September.

Lord Lingford sat quietly at his desk, trying to block out the subdued noises coming from the rest of the house, indicative of the work in progress: the clattering of bedpans, the hurried steps across the stone floor in the entrance foyer, the smashing of a glass, the moans of suffering, the calls for help. The war a constant companion, even among the green fields of England.

Elizabeth knocked and came into the study, dressed in her working uniform, and stood opposite her father, looking down on his tired face and furrowed brow.

"How are you, dear Papa?" she asked. "Do you need anything. Anything at all?"

"I'm well, princess, and not in need. I am all the better for seeing you. The days become a blur after so many years full of the same daily activities and the same hopelessness."

"It's not the same at all," Elizabeth said. "The soldiers are returning with encouraging news. The war will soon be over, just you wait."

"Ever the cheerful optimist, my dear," smiled her father. "You were born to make my life a sunnier place, I swear. What is on your mind that you come disturbing me in the middle of the morning?"

"I want to sit the entrance exams for Oxford, Papa," Elizabeth announced.

She held her breath as she saw the expression on her father's face change, and his frown deepen.

"Elizabeth," said Lord Lingford, "I had not imagined that you would step out of your place in society to follow an academic role. I believe you are misguided in your quest, my dear. Oxford University doesn't allow females the advantage of matriculation. You would do all the work and be given no degree to reward you."

"But things will change, Papa," Elizabeth said. "I am going to be one of the first women to get a degree there."

Lord Lingford cleared his throat and sat with his eyes closed for a moment to gather his thoughts. This daughter of his, always pushing the parameters, never ceased to amaze and challenge him. Born to become a lady, Elizabeth was once again defying the rules and expectation as determined by the social class.

Her exasperated father remembered the earlier times: climbing onto his knee as a toddler, insisting on joining the boys in their studies, demanding she be allowed to go to the stables, the sheer determination to ride astride, and the recent stand against her mother to be allowed to help nurse the soldiers.

Elizabeth knew she should be content to be part of the aristocracy she had been born into. However, women were fighting for the right to vote now. They were challenging the bastions of learning. They were bucking the system, and seeking the same opportunities as men. They were choosing their own partners instead of one chosen for them by their family. It was exciting to be a young woman in such a time.

Elizabeth moved to her father's side and placed a hand on his shoulder. "Papa," she said, "I intend to apply to Lady Margaret Hall. You have to let me try. The Lingford Estate has been the centre of my world, but it is time to venture out on my own, and there is nothing I want to do more than to study and gain knowledge."

Her father took her hand in his and kissed her delicate fingers. He had not expected to have to part with his favourite child quite so soon.

"I plan to read the sciences," she added slowly.

"Darling," her father rose from his chair. "Consider carefully about choosing sciences. These are men's subjects, not women's. You will be out of place, maybe the only young woman, and will find life very difficult among your peers. Why not choose History or English or even French? They would be more fitting for a female student. I doubt Oxford will even allow you to register for such courses."

Elizabeth's smile froze on her face.

"Father," she said, addressing him in a more formal way. "Have you not always encouraged me to pursue the sciences? You even employed Mr. Elwyn Thomas to tutor me, with the express instruction that I was not to be held back in these subjects. I have no interest in History, English, or French. I would eventually like to be a doctor."

"A what?" blustered Lord Lingford. "You are a Lingford, my dear. May I remind you that any career would be frowned upon. You are expected to lead the life of a lady and marry well. I am going against the traditions of family and society by even allowing you to pursue this idea of yours. Don't make this more difficult for yourself."

"I am determined, Papa," she continued. "The first two years of studies at Oxford will probably be limited to English or History anyway, so I will have time to consider what the future will hold for me."

"Very well, Elizabeth," her father sighed. "I know better than to try to dissuade you once your mind is made up. You are as stubborn as ever. I have no doubt that you will do well in your studies, and be ahead of your classmates in every subject. I would be a fool not to give you my blessing."

Lord Lingford drew his daughter close and kissed her forehead.

He wondered how the next phase of her life would evolve. He only knew he would not be by her side, and the thought of it made him despair.

CHAPTER 13

OXFORD

Oxford was a buzz of activity as students gathered to begin the new year of study. Elizabeth peered out from the back seat of the Rolls Royce at the historical spires, the glimpses of grassy courtyards through college gates, the ornate churches and the bustle of the busy streets filled with students. Her trunks were loaded onto the back of the car, and her father's chauffeur, Turner, had driven her the one hundred miles from her home in Suffolk to Oxford.

Lady Margaret Hall, LMH to its residents, was one of the few women's residence facilities in the university town. It was intended for young women of means who wished to advance their studies at a higher level. Each student was provided a private room, and the common areas were spacious and well furnished.

Turner parked the car outside the front entrance and a porter hurried down the steps to carry the bags to Elizabeth's designated room. With no maid to help unpack, Elizabeth busied herself finding room for all her belongings.

"Welcome to LMH," greeted a friendly voice.

Elizabeth looked up from her trunk and saw a red-headed young woman standing in the open doorway.

"Thank you. I'm Elizabeth Lingford. Just arrived."

"I'm Caroline Vincent. I'm in the room next to you. It's my second year here, so I can show you the ropes if you like. We're a jolly crew here at LMH. You'll get to meet everybody at dinner, and you are already invited to cocoa time at nine o'clock tonight in the common room. We're all pretty relaxed, so don't worry what you wear for meals and all that nonsense. If you're anything like me you escaped to leave all that behind."

It was a great start to Elizabeth's college days. Caroline was the perfect, chatty, outgoing person to befriend. Along with two other first year students, Elizabeth was escorted by their second-year friend to meet the other young women living at LMH, many of whose names escaped her memory immediately after introduction. After three days of mealtimes, cocoa groups, walks around the various colleges, tea in the high street, and merriment in the bedroom hallways, they were soon comfortable and at ease in their surroundings.

For Elizabeth it was like the beginning of a vacation. For the first time in her life she chose her own path. When to wake, when to sleep, where to go and who with. Other than mealtimes, which were firmly set, her life seemed strangely her own. She loved the river and enjoyed boating or punting when it wasn't raining. She loved bread and butter and jam sandwiches in the upper library at tea time. She loved knowing everybody by their first names. She attended the literary society's reading of *Wuthering Heights*. She joined the lacrosse club and looked forward to their first practice, along with her new friend, Isabel. The lectures in History and English afforded her a short time of academia, but life at Oxford was so much more than that.

One week into the Michaelmas term six young women at LMH caught some kind of bad cold and were detained in their bedrooms. Meals and drinks were served to them on a tray, carried upstairs by other students. The chambermaids were kept busy emptying chamber pots, when the patients became too weak to use the lavatory. They were constantly cold and fires were lit in every room. Within the month others had succumbed to the same virus, which was reportedly spreading throughout the college community.

The same malady had been reported among the fighting troops, but had been dismissed as a battlefield complaint, smiting the soldiers in their weakened condition.

All lectures were postponed until further notice. The sports clubs cancelled their activities. All other social gatherings were put on hold. The "cold" had been declared an epidemic of the flu and it was spreading at a rapid and deadly rate across the country.

The contagion was so serious that any infected person was isolated from others in an attempt to halt the spread. Masks had to be worn at all times. At LMH professors, students, servants alike were affected, and the women who were not infected became cooks, cleaners, nurses, and aides to the sick. Once more Elizabeth found herself among the workforce, not only tending the sick this time, but working in the kitchen to prepare soup and bake bread, carrying trays up many flights of stairs, filling bowls with warm water and wash cloths to deliver to each patient, and helping them wash their sweating faces and bodies. She fell into bed at the end of the day exhausted.

News from home was full of the same depressing tales. Mama had taken to her bed, and the youngest of Elizabeth's sisters was infected, though not very badly. The horror of the virus in the population of soldiers they were housing was daunting. Two of the downstairs rooms had been temporarily converted into "flu" quarantine quarters. Four of the young men, already weakened by injury had died in the past two weeks.

Elizabeth read the letter from her father with despair. She wondered if she should go home and help, but knew it was the wrong thing to do. She was needed just as much here in Oxford, and all she could do was pray that the epidemic would turn a corner and begin to dissipate.

In the middle of the epidemic, the war in Europe came to an

end. November 11th, 1918 Germany surrendered. The war to end all wars was over, and Britain celebrated a bittersweet victory. So many lives lost. So many men maimed. The economy destroyed. No work, no food, and for many no shelter. The husbands, brothers, sons, sweethearts who returned came home with nothing, to a country with no way to help them, and a raging pandemic of deadly flu cutting through the island country like a furious swath of evil.

The girls who were still healthy at LMH lit a bonfire on the front lawn on the night of November 11th and gathered around the cheerful flames to sing Auld Lang Syne. Abigail Fenwick, one of the hall's board members passed around a bottle of scotch and everybody took a long swig. Abigail had worked alongside them every day since the epidemic began and knew that this was not the way these young women had envisioned their first term of college.

The flu would run its course, infecting sixty seven students and staff at Lady Margaret Hall before it was done with them. The small residence were thankful that most recovered, and they grieved only one death, a young first-year student who had enjoyed only one week of her college experience.

At her father's insistence Elizabeth stayed in Oxford for Christmas. She longed to go home and be with her family, but realized it was safer for her to remain where she was. The Lingford estate was in the throes of repatriating its injured soldiers with their families or transferring them to convalescent homes. The house was in a turmoil as rooms were converted back to their original state, furniture was brought out of storage, cots and medical equipment picked up by army trucks. Mud and dirt from dozens of boots were trodden into the once pristine floors. Doors and walls were scraped and dented. It would take many months to restore order, repair damage, and reinstate the great house to its former condition as the house servants were already strained to breaking point with half the workforce down with the flu.

The young students at LMH decorated the common room with home-made buntings. They chopped down a small fir tree from the banks of the river and carried it back to the house to take pride of place in the hallway. They decorated it with red and silver balls found in a box at the back of the library. They scrounged and begged the local butcher and greengrocer for extra bits of food to tempt the appetites of those convalescing, and provide a feast for Christmas Day, however unauthentic.

Mr. Saunders, whose wife was a benefactor of Lady Margaret Hall, had a large chicken delivered to them on Christmas Eve, and Elizabeth and two of her friends, with a lot of input from the scullery maids, managed to do a pretty good job of cooking it. The outside was a bit burnt, but once the crusty brown layer was chipped away, the flesh was quite palatable, even delicious. A huge pot of potatoes was mashed, and boiled turnips and carrots rounded out a Christmas dinner to be proud of. Lord Lingford had risen to the occasion and despatched Turner to Oxford with a basket of goodies, including Christmas cake, mince pies and shortbread biscuits. It was a feast indeed.

CHAPTER 14

QUARANTINE

The new year brought no relief from the epidemic. It raged on and on, wearing everybody down and dampening all hope of life returning to normal.

For the students at Oxford a whole year of study and activity was destroyed. The residents of Lady Margaret Hall fared somewhat better than most of the other colleges, with their worst experience of sickness hitting them early in the school year. As the young women, and the staff recovered they kept themselves in close proximity to their residence and avoided contact with other students. Lectures resumed, only open to LMH students. They once again ate their meals together, and organized picnics by the river, croquet games, and hikes into the countryside. Elizabeth passed her History and English examinations with honours, and was more than grateful that her year hadn't been a complete disaster.

Papa wrote to give his permission for Elizabeth to spend the summer at home, and she couldn't have been more excited. She longed to see her family, go for long rides with Papa again, wake up in her own room, and gorge herself on the meals cooked by Mrs. Thompson. She yearned for space, for the familiar rooms, for the camaraderie of her lady's maid, Peggy. She wanted the smell of the stables in her nostrils and the sounds of the horses in her ears.

"Mama, Mama," Elizabeth shouted as she ran through the heavy oak doors into the expansive entrance hall. "I'm home."

"Darling, there you are," Lady Lingford hurried towards her eldest daughter with arms outstretched. "We expected you later this afternoon. You must have made very good time from Oxford. Your sisters will be so excited to see you, as will your father and brother. We have missed you dreadfully."

Lydia and Caroline came running down the marble staircase to greet their sister. They looked so much alike they could have been twins, and Elizabeth embraced them both with affection.

"Father is out on the estate, as we were not expecting you until later. He will be sorry he wasn't here when you arrived." Lydia said. "Come into the drawing room, and we'll send for tea and something to eat for you."

"Are you completely well now, Mama?" Elizabeth asked. "What about you, Caroline, did the flu leave you with any ongoing health concerns?"

"We are both well, my dear," answered Mama. "We were among the fortunate, who recovered quite quickly. Sadly many of our staff and workers on the estate were not so lucky and we lost a number of them at the height of the epidemic. The poor soldiers, still in residence here, were the hardest hit. To live through the most outrageous atrocities during the war, only to succumb to the flu makes me question the sanity of it all."

"Enough," Elizabeth interjected, not wanting to be drawn into a long conversation with her mother. "I will have my tea, change my clothes, then I'm off to the stables. I cannot wait another moment to ride."

Percy was striding across the stable yard as Elizabeth burst out of the side door of the house and almost collided with him. He picked her up and swung her around as way of greeting.

"You're back," he said, brushing her cheek with a kiss. "I hope you have all this studying business out of your system. You're home to stay, aren't you?"

"Oh do shut up, Percy," Elizabeth said, as she poked her brother in the arm with her crop. "You do go on and on. It is not a waste of time for me to be studying. I agree this year was pretty much a wash out, but I intend to follow my dream."

"Right," grunted Percy, giving her a deep bow. "Doctor Lingford, at your service. You make me laugh my dear sister. Why not be content to live the life of a lady?"

"Because the life of a lady bores me to distraction. I prefer to be busy, work hard, and devote my life to healing the sick."

Elizabeth spun on her heel and marched away from her brother into the stables. She didn't call a groom, but sought out Black Diamond and led him out of his stall. She knew McCarthy would be unhappy about taking a racing horse for a joy ride, but this was her first time in the saddle for months, and she wouldn't ride any other horse. She saddled the horse herself, talking to him as she did so. As she slid the bit between his teeth, she stroked his muzzle and nuzzled her face into him.

"I have missed you, my beauty," she whispered.

Coming out of the house, and walking towards the stables, McCarthy saw the young mistress heading for the open countryside.

"Damn that young woman," he cursed to himself. "She knows full well not to ride that horse. First day at home and she's already causing trouble."

Black Diamond enjoyed the unexpected joyous ride almost as much as his young rider. Elizabeth was elated as she sped across the fields and under the trees with the wind whistling in her face. This is what dreams were made of, and she could have rode on for ever. All the images of the past months of sickness and restrictions rolled away, and she found perfect contentment on the back of Black Diamond.

Word had already reached Lord Lingford by the time Elizabeth returned, and he was in the stable yard, hands on his hips. waiting for her. She slid from the horse's back and allowed a groom to take him into the stable. Then she turned to face her father.

"Father, I missed you. I could't wait to come home and see everybody."

She kissed him on his cheek and stepped away to take the brunt of the disapproval she knew was coming.

"Welcome home, Elizabeth," her father began. "I see you have wasted no time getting into the saddle. I won't chastise you when you have been away for so long, but you know better than to take a racing horse out like that. I'm surprised. I didn't think you would break protocol and selfishly have your own way. You need to apologize to McCarthy. You know how he feels about the horses we race. I don't like the disrespect for him and the entire stable."

Elizabeth knew better than to argue with her father over this, and she didn't want her homecoming to be tainted by her bad behaviour, so she nodded her head in agreement.

"You are right, of course, Papa," she said. "I will apologize for my lack of judgment."

"Run along then," encouraged her father. "McCarthy is in the stable. You know what to do."

Elizabeth walked slowly into the stable and mumbled her apologies to Callum McCarthy.

"It was the dream of riding Black Diamond that kept me going through the weeks I was away and things in Oxford were so bleak," she added. "It won't happen again."

"Thank you, Miss Elizabeth," Callum said. "We've all missed you around the stables. I hope you'll ride often while you're home. I have a lovely mare named Silver Buttons that I have in mind as a mount for you. She's graceful and brave, just like you, Miss."

Elizabeth smiled at the aging stable master. Like her father, this wise, quiet man had been a constant and positive influence on her life since she was a young girl.

Dinner would be served very soon, and Elizabeth hurried into the house to change. How calm and peaceful it was to be home, among the people she loved. A flicker of doubt entered her mind as she thought about going back to Oxford in August. Life would be less complicated if she stayed at home.

CHAPTER 15

AFTER THE WAR

Summer at Lingford meant lazy days of picnics, lying in a hammock reading a good book, walking through the gardens filled with a profusion of sweet smelling flowers, stretching out on the lawn staring at the night sky, and riding every day, of course. Elizabeth fell into the pre-war pattern readily and easily, yet everything was not the same as it used to be.

The house staff were always polite, but there was a sadness about their demeanour as they went about their duties. Familiar faces were missing. Even Elizabeth's lady's maid, Peggy, had been replaced by a rather dour older woman, who preferred to be addressed by her surname, Sullivan. Peggy had succumbed to the Spanish Flu, along with three of her family members, leaving her grieving mother and two young children to struggle for survival. On hearing the news from the housekeeper, Elizabeth insisted Peggy's mother be found work at the manor house, and she was duly employed as a kitchen maid the following week. Menial work to be sure, but she would earn enough money to keep food on the table and pay the minimal amount of rent on her tiny cottage.

The biggest change was the young men who had been lost

during the war. Older men and even some women had taken on their duties on the estate, and it wasn't uncommon to see them cleaning out the stables, or pitching hay, or herding cattle.

The young men who did return were in high demand as prospective husbands. Having survived the war, they lost no time in living life to its fullest, and rose to the expectations of the young ladies with vigour, scandalizing the older villagers with their open exhibits of affection: a kiss behind the church, holding hands in public, helping a young lady over a style just to take a peek at her ankles, an arm around a waist at a picnic, a risky roll in the hay when more than a kiss and cuddle were exchanged.

Pain, suffering and sorrow slowly slid into memories, and the strong people of Britain found a new path forward without their loved ones by their side. There were new joys and new celebrations. Weddings, babies, and laughter returned. The dead were remembered in stories and tears—they would never be forgotten, but time moved them forward into a future full of hope.

"Are you still bent on returning to Oxford, Elizabeth?" her Papa asked at breakfast on a sunny July morning. "You've had plenty of time to decide. Now you've had a taste of the good life again. I wouldn't be surprised if you changed your mind about all this studying nonsense."

"My mind is unchanged, Papa," answered his daughter with a smile of affection. "I will return to Oxford, and fight for the right to study the sciences."

"Stubborn as ever," commented Percy, his mouth full of bacon. "Seems to me you are doing it just to be contrary."

"Wrong, Percy," retaliated Elizabeth. "That would be stupid, and I am not inclined to be stupid. I believe I am called to be a doctor, and intend to pursue my calling."

"Oh, stop arguing about it," interrupted Lady Lingford. "Elizabeth has always been her own person, and never particularly enjoyed feminine activities as I remember. I cannot even think about some of the indecent encounters you will have in the study of medicine, but it is your choice."

Mama sniffed and rose from the breakfast table to indicate the discourse was over. Elizabeth smiled to herself, and pledged she would never divulge any "indecent" incidents to her mother.

The last thing Elizabeth did before she left for Oxford on August 20th was to visit Black Diamond. She drew the hidden apple from behind her and offered it to the magnificent black stallion, who galloped towards her as she approached the paddock.

"There, my beauty," she said, feeding him the treat and stroking his neck. "I wish I could ride you one more time before I leave."

The horse responded with a quiet neigh as though he understood she was leaving. She had been there the night he was born, which seemed such an age ago, and now he was one of the leading race horses at Newmarket. For the young mistress he would always be her favourite horse, and she knew he could feel the bond of affection she had for him. He gently nibbled at her hair and fingers, before she turned and walked away. He watched her until she disappeared into the house, and tossed his head when she gave one last look back at him.

Lady Margaret Hall was a cacophony of noise as Elizabeth entered the front hallway. Squeals of delight greeted her as her first-year friends gathered around her, hugging her close, and giving her the very best of welcomes. Some familiar faces were missing from the group, having caught the dreaded virus during the summer. Several others told tales of weeks of illness as they battled the flu, and tears flowed at the first cocoa time, when friends shared stories of the people in their families they had lost.

Because of the ongoing flu epidemic, which had killed millions of people worldwide, restrictions were still very much in place in all the Oxford colleges. Gathering with undergraduates from other residences was strictly forbidden, and sports and leisure activities were also curtailed. LMH took precautions to keep their students safe, and offered a variety of activities along with the academic lectures to keep them occupied.

Elizabeth was soon enjoying the camaraderie of her peers as they met for book clubs, croquet competitions, hikes through the countryside, and the intimate nightly cocoa group who sat around the fire in the common room in the dark, sipping their hot drinks and sharing their secrets.

The company of young men was a scarcity. The fear of spreading the flu kept all students in their colleges with their living companions, venturing out only to attend lectures, play a game of cricket, or fish in the river. It was rare to see anybody around Oxford without some kind of a mask covering their nose and mouth.

Going into the second year of the infectious disease seemed an interminably long time for the young students. On top of four years of war, it was unbearable for some, who had fought and returned to continue their education, only to be further impeded in their young lives. Affluent male students treated their comrades to Saturday nights of drinking the best Scotch whiskey money could buy. Many of these hard-drinking party nights went on until the next day and left the participants with a groggy head and upset stomach. Never to be deterred, they were there again the following weekend to do exactly the same thing. Marks and attendance suffered greatly, but despite the deans and professors best efforts, it was impossible to curtail.

The end of the epidemic would solve the problems. Until then, there was some leniency shown towards the struggling student body.

The women's colleges continued to work for the right to attend lectures in the all-male system. For eight hundred years the colleges of Oxford had been a hallowed centre of advanced education for men only. It was seen as a great threat to the ideology of the ancient institution that women now sought to be included. The women were not about to give up. They had already succeeded to some extent in procuring the vote for women, albeit it was a small select group—women over thirty years of age who owned property. For Oxford University the discussions became more and more intense, as many significant public figures and even some professors joined the women in their endeavour.

Elizabeth wrote articles for the newspapers, she created posters and handed out leaflets, she spoke eloquently and intelligently at numerous outdoor meetings, and became well known among the women fighting for their education. Her admission that she wished to study medicine, and be allowed into the science lectures, drew gasps of outrage from the men in the audience.

"Unheard of."

"Out of the question."

"Stick with painting."

"Women have no place in the sciences."

Undeterred, Elizabeth continued to defy the status quo. She was encouraged by other older women who had joined their cause, and she turned a deaf ear to the criticisms of the Oxford elite, who tried to put her down at every turn.

She would study the sciences at Oxford, of that she was certain.

CHAPTER 16

WOMEN NOT WELCOME

For Elizabeth, the second year at Oxford was a whirlwind of laborious meetings, studying, debating, and generally flying in a dozen directions as she dedicated herself to influencing the policy-makers of the university to include female students.

She returned home for Christmas, having missed the previous one due to the epidemic. Although the disease was still prevalent throughout the land, the household at Lingford Manor was confident their precautions had stemmed the contagion. With great delight Elizabeth revelled in being with her family, eating the traditional Christmas fare, and riding with her father despite the bitter weather.

At the end of her second year, she cut her summer vacation short, visiting Lingford Manor for only six weeks, so that she could return to her commitments in Oxford. She joined a group of ten women at Lady Margaret Hall who ramped up their efforts with the Oxford elite for the inclusion of women. By the time the Michaelmas term began no agreement had been reached. The women in Elizabeth's core group were discouraged, and their opposing male counterparts were louder and more obnoxious than ever, declaring women were "an unnecessary distraction" and not conducive to the bastions of learning at Oxford.

On October 7th, the ancient university, announced that a percentage of women would be allowed full access to the colleges. Women would also be entitled to convocation, graduating with a degree upon completion of their studies.

"Whoopee! Rahrahrah!" shouted Deborah and Isabel, as they raced into the common room at LMH. "We did it."

The women's residence erupted into chaos, as the young women, joined by the staff and tutors, hugged each other, before spilling out onto the front lawn. It was a triumph they had only dreamed of, for five decades, since the first young women had dared to infiltrate the world of men, and demand the right to study alongside them. They held hands and formed a circle, then spun around as fast as they could without falling. They yelled and screamed and sang until their throats were raw, and then collapsed onto the grass in fits of laughter.

The male students didn't make life easy. They heckled, teased and were openly rude to any young woman they even suspected of registering for one of "their" lectures. They put up posters and even barricades to show their disapproval. Despite the resistance Elizabeth was among the first women to run the gauntlet walk into Kings College for a physics lecture at the beginning of the spring term. A resounding echo of boos greeted her as she made her way down the steep stairs to find an empty seat. Every eye in the lecture hall was riveted onto her, the only female in the room. She stuck out her chin, formed her mouth into a straight line and looked directly ahead. She would rather have stood up and stuck out her tongue, but would give no man the satisfaction of knowing she was disturbed by their bad behaviour. She would show them what she was made of by her ability to excel in the subject. They would learn to eat their words.

"Elizabeth Lingford?" Dr. Jamieson, Professor of Physics questioned, gazing around the packed lecture room. "Make yourself known."

Elizabeth stood.

"Ah, Miss Lingford," continued the Professor. "I am unequivocally aware that you are the only female student. You may want to reconsider your decision to take a physics course when you realize the standard expected. My advice would be for you to swallow your pride or whatever else has motivated you to join us, and leave before the lecture begins. It would be a grave mistake for you to struggle through the lectures and course material with so obvious a disadvantage."

Every eye was concentrated on the female in question, awaiting her response.

Elizabeth held the Professor's eyes, and remained erect, feeling the warmth of a blush filling her face.

"I appreciate the advice, sir, but have no intention of leaving. I believe I am entitled to be here."

Her voice was clear and loud enough for the entire lecture hall full of men to hear. She sat down in her seat and stared ahead, trying to calm her heart from banging in her chest.

"Very well!" Professor Jamieson said curtly. "You have been advised of my misgivings. Your downfall will be upon your head, not mine, Miss Lingford."

Elizabeth had only joined the high-level physics class to prove a point, to herself and others, that a female student was as capable as her male peers of excelling in the subject. She did also relish the thought of learning and studying a subject she had enjoyed as a sixteen year-old, under the guidance of Elwyn Thomas. It would be challenging to delve into the world of atoms, mass and density once more, and she looked forward to giving her agile brain something tough to work on.

The male students continued to discriminate against her. They called her rude names, and threw paper missiles at her during lectures. Not one kind word was exchanged. Despite her resolve, Elizabeth almost ran out of the lecture hall a few times.

The course material was harder than she had ever imagined, and she had to go back to her earlier years of study to build on what she already knew before she could move forward. She passed the first two papers by a hair, but gained confidence, worked harder, and raised her mark significantly by mid-term, which caused Professor Jamieson great irritation.

"Good for you, Beth," Isabel said, giving her friend a massive hug. "You passed. You passed with a solid B grade. That is so amazing. We're all super proud of you, old bean."

The other girls in the cocoa group clinked their cups in salute to the first of them to venture into the "man's world".

"Maybe those snobby undergrads in the men's colleges will be more congenial now they see we can hold our own with the best of them," Isabel continued. "It's also going to encourage more women to be courageous and read whatever subjects they choose."

By the time Elizabeth's third year at Oxford was complete, she had a Bachelor of Arts degree in her hand. She headed home at the end of June for six weeks of pure joy, her heart light, and her head spinning with thoughts of her future.

CHAPTER 17

DESPAIR

The summer months flew by in a flurry of excitement. Percy was married to Phoebe Mortensen, whose father, Lord Mortensen, owned a large estate near Bury St. Edmunds. The wedding was a splendid and extravagant affair, hosted by the Mortensen family, with the Lingford household travelling the short distance to enjoy the celebrations.

The young couple settled into a splendid new accommodation built on Lingford land, so that Percy could continue his work overseeing the daily business of his father's estate.

The two youngest Lingford girls, Lydia and Caroline, were accomplished and beautiful. Their company was much sought after by the gentry of the county, and there were invitations to picnics, balls and dinner parties enough to keep them occupied throughout the year. Lady Maud delighted in her two younger daughters, who were always dressed in the very best gowns, groomed and pampered by their personal maids, and devoted in their pursuit of painting, embroidery, and music. They were, in fact, everything to admire in young women of their standing in society.

Elizabeth threw a wrench into the established expectations. She wore mostly trousers during the day, as she was either going riding or returning from riding. Her hair was tied into a bun at the nape of her neck, she never used creams and lotions on her face, and her hands were roughened with short nails from being outdoors much of the time. Lady Maud frowned her disapproval whenever she saw her eldest daughter striding into the house looking like one of the stable hands.

Lord Lingford couldn't have been happier with Elizabeth. She was more like him than any of his other children, even Percy. She was still his favourite person to spend time with, particularly to ride with, and he missed her desperately when she was away in Oxford. Summer was the time to drench himself with her company.

The rain had finally stopped and it was a particularly warm, fresh Tuesday morning. Just the day for one of their extra-long rides. Father and daughter headed to the stables after breakfast to begin their day together. Anticipating their arrival, Callum McCarthy had given instructions to have their two favourite mounts, Silver Buttons and Sweet Charlotte, ready to go.

It was a perfect day. The rain from the days before clung to the leaves on the trees, sprinkling the riders as they rode under the branches. The ground was soft and pliable beneath the horses hooves', and the wonderful smell of the sun-warmed earth filled the air.

Lord Lingford rode ahead of his daughter through a particularly narrow pathway of the woodland, being careful to keep his head down and his arms close to his body. Elizabeth followed close behind, admiring her father's exceptional riding skills.

Suddenly, he slid from the saddle, his right foot caught in the stirrup, and he was dragged along by the powerful horse. Time slowed down and the world went quiet. The ground seemed to rush up towards her; the trees appeared taller and denser. Her eyes blurred and lost their focus, and she couldn't breathe.

Elizabeth snapped out of her stupor, as she gasped for air. She still couldn't hear any sounds, but realizing the danger, raced to catch the fleeing horse. Grabbing the dangling reins, she slowed the frightened animal to a stop before jumping down from her own mount to run to her father's aid.

Lord Arnold Lingford lay face up on the muddy ground.

"Papa, Papa," Elizabeth cried.

Her thoughts were all mixed up. She couldn't think properly. She knew she should be doing something, but what?

"Check for a pulse," she said to herself. "Check if he's breathing."

She checked his wrist, then his neck, then put her head against his chest, willing herself to hear or feel the steady rhythm of life. There was none.

She held her hand against his mouth. Watched his chest. Put her cheek close to his open mouth, thinking her cheek more sensitive than her hand. In desperation she shook his shoulders fiercely, willing him to breath.

"Papa, wake up," Elizabeth shouted. "Wake up. Please wake up, dearest Papa."

She knelt beside him, staring at his peaceful face. She stroked his forehead. She held his hands. She kissed his cheek. She didn't cry.

As her legs began to cramp beneath her, she moved to lay beside her father, her head on his strong shoulder. They would stay here, the two of them, in the woods, where it was quiet and where they could be together.

The horses grazed nearby, content with the chance to eat, and happy for the rest.

As the hours ticked by Elizabeth didn't feel the damp seeping into her body. She could hear a bird somewhere singing its evening song. It sounded beautiful to her.

Silver Buttons and Sweet Charlotte, sensing this was no ordinary rest stop, moved over to nuzzle Elizabeth with their soft noses, making her stir and look at them in wonder. Horses, here in the woods? Then she remembered, and cuddled closer to her father. She had to let him know how much she loved him.

Callum McCarthy was anxious. The master and young

mistress had been gone for far too long. He knew they often stopped off to visit estate workers, or have a bite to eat in the village pub, but even so they had never been this late. He glanced at his pocket watch for the twentieth time before calling out to Jack, one of the stable hands, to saddle two horses.

Callum knew his master's favourite routes for riding with Miss Elizabeth, and the two riders wasted no time heading across country towards the woods.

The two horses hidden in the trees were the first to hear the approaching hooves, and both whinnied their greeting. As Callum and Jack moved closer to the riderless horses, they reigned in quickly, and slid from their horses to run to the silent, still couple on the ground.

"Oh, my God," whispered Callum.

Elizabeth had fallen into a deep, dreamless sleep, and lay as still as her father beneath the shade of the trees. At first glance it looked to Callum that they were both dead, and his knees buckled under him at the sight of it.

"Lord Lingford, Miss Elizabeth," he shouted, praying he would get a response.

Elizabeth woke with a start. Somebody had called her name.

Callum almost cried with relief when he saw her eyes open. He put a hand under her arm and tried to help her up, but she pulled against him.

"Leave me be McCarthy," she whispered. "I have to stay with my father. He needs me."

Callum could tell by the look of him, that his master had long since died, and his heart ached for the loss of him, and for his daughter who couldn't face the truth of it.

"Let us help him, Miss Elizabeth," Callum said gently. "Jack and me. We can help him onto his horse and take him home."

"My father is dead," Elizabeth said slowly. "I cannot leave his side. I have to let him know how much I love him. I don't want him to be alone. I will stay here with him. You can go back to the house now."

"Well now, Miss," continued Callum in his most persuasive manner. "I think you both would be more comfortable at home. The Master wouldn't want you laying out here in the woods with him. He would want you to go home and be with the Mistress and your sisters and brother at such a time. Come on now, Miss. Let me and Jack help you onto your horse."

With great difficulty Elizabeth allowed herself to be led to her horse. She had become sore and stiff from laying on the forest floor for so long, and she needed help to move and mount her horse. She sat like a statue in the saddle watching McCarthy and Jack lift her father. They lay him across the saddle with his head and arms dangling on one side and his legs on the other. Then the sad procession made its way slowly out of the woods and headed towards Lingford Manor.

CHAPTER 18

BACK IN THE SADDLE

A watery sunlight filtered through the open window as dawn broke on a new day. The bedroom was cool and still, echoing the atmosphere of the house and the occupants. Elizabeth stretched her aching limbs gingerly, wondering at first waking why she was so sore. Like an explosion in her head the memories of the day before filled her mind, and she wished she hadn't woken to face reality.

Her beloved father was gone!

She drew the blankets over her head, trying to block out the daylight and the memories, and return to darkness. All she could see were the trees above her head as she lay on the ground beside the man she loved more than any other human in the world. How could she face the moments ahead: the days, weeks, months and years ahead, without her father? It was unfathomable to comprehend a world without him.

Lord Arnold Lingford's death affected the entire estate and beyond. He had been loyal and courteous to all, and was admired by his peers, his tenants, and his servants. The stable hands, who were his closest acquaintances, were inconsolable, particularly as they had seen him ride off on his favourite horse the day before, with his daughter beside him, and not a care in the world. The men and boys took turns brushing down the two horses brought home from the scene of the tragedy, somehow attempting to assure themselves and the animals that all would be well. Callum McCarthy paced the stable yard from early light wondering at the injustice of losing not only his employer, but his friend.

The family gathered in quiet groups throughout the day. Not talking very much to each other, but all drowning in their own sorrow. Lady Maud kept to her bed that first day without her husband, only allowing her daughters a brief visiting time to share each other's tears.

In the days that followed, the Lingford estate was at a stand-still. Only the necessities of life were attended to. The household staff, although in mourning themselves, made a concerted effort to take care of the grieving family. Quietly and respectfully they cooked and served food, continued to maintain the upkeep of the large house, and welcome the stream of guests who came to call and offer their sympathy. Dozens of pots of tea were brewed and consumed, along with a variety of delectable confectionaries baked each morning by the devoted kitchen staff.

Throughout it all Elizabeth was in a daze. The heavy weight of sadness overwhelmed her. She couldn't stay in the house, and she couldn't go to the stables, so she walked. Mile after mile across the fields, giving no thought to the route she was taking, and filling her thoughts with memories of Papa. Without knowing it, she was healing.

Although the sun shone brightly out of a perfect blue sky, the day of the funeral seemed dark to Elizabeth. She moved through the day with her senses only partially aware of what was happening around her. People everywhere mumbled their sympathies to her.

Saint Mary's Church in Bury St. Edmunds was filled with mourners. Through her veil of diminished senses, Elizabeth felt her heart skip a beat as she followed her mother and brother out of the secluded side chapel into the chancel. The sound of the majestic organ filled her head and chased away the dullness of sorrow. She thought she may be in heaven as she marvelled at the grandeur of the old church. Papa would have hated all the pomp and ceremony of the funeral, she thought. It was, however, the expectation for a man of his public stature.

It had been a week since the funeral, and the young mistress had avoided the stables. McCarthy was worried that she may never ride again, and took a great liberty in approaching her.

"Good morning, Miss," McCarthy called to Elizabeth as he saw her hurrying across the stable yard to walk the fields. He caught her up with some effort, and strode beside her.

"Well?" questioned Elizabeth, keeping her eyes on the fields ahead.

"Miss Elizabeth," began the stable master. "Forgive the intrusion on your time. I watch you set out every day, and always hope you will turn towards the stables. I cannot imagine how you feel, but I think I know you well enough to realize that, like your father, you would find comfort in the horses."

Elizabeth squeezed her eyes shut for just a moment to quell the tears that threatened. She turned to face her old friend, who looked how she felt, tired and old.

"You should not have approached me," she said. "I would rather be alone."

"Please, Miss," the stable master continued. "Give it some thought. I wouldn't presume to give you advise if I hadn't known you since you were a youngster. You need to ride again. You need to face your memories of that tragic day, so that you can move on. His Lordship would want you to remember all the wonderful rides you had together, and not dwell on that final ride."

Elizabeth began to walk away, striding through the soggy field, tears spilling down her cheeks. Callum McCarthy stood with his head bowed, thinking his words had fallen on deaf ears, but the young mistress turned and faced him once more. She retraced her steps, keeping her eyes fixed on the man who had stood beside her in the stables during the births of so many foals, who had never shown her anything but the utmost kindness, who had cared for Black Diamond and the other horses with excellence and never-ending patience and affection.

"You have been a dear friend," Elizabeth said. "Your advice, although unsought, is sound. You were closer to my father than anybody outside the family, and I appreciate your loyalty and support."

Elizabeth bit her bottom lip as she wrestled with herself. It would be hard to follow Callum's advice. The memories the stables evoked were too painful.

"Come with me, Miss," McCarthy said quietly. "Let's go back together and just check out Black Diamond. He has missed you."

With a knot in her stomach Elizabeth walked beside the stable master towards the house. The stables awaited her, like a vast cavern of memories, which Elizabeth had done her best to avoid since her father's death. She hesitated and McCarthy touched her arm gently to reassure her and urge her forward.

Hay, leather, manure, and the wonderful smell of the horses filled her nostrils. Her senses slowly came alive as Elizabeth drew in the odours of the stables, odours that brought back the feeling of peace and tranquility. She was surprised that the dreaded recollection of her last ride didn't surface.

Black Diamond's neck muscles rippled with excitement as he saw her coming towards him. He snorted and tossed his head, anxious for his favourite human to reach him. Elizabeth reached up and put both arms around his powerful neck, nuzzling her face into him and feeling joy seep into her soul.

"He's been waiting for you, Miss," exclaimed McCarthy. "He never reacts like that to anybody else."

Words couldn't express how Elizabeth felt as she stood stroking and patting Black Diamond. Callum McCarthy had been right. This was where she would find the inspiration to carry on without her beloved father, enfolding herself in the atmosphere he had loved, and where she felt such comfort.

Silver Buttons was saddled and ready to go later that day, and Elizabeth, accompanied by Jack, set off with trepidation for her ride. All the things she loved about riding repelled her misgivings, her senses returning, as she felt the wind in her face, the reins in her hands, and the exhilaration in her spirit.

CHAPTER 19

A VOICE FROM THE PAST

L ord Lingford's estate and title were inherited by his only living son, Percy, as was the law. Lady Lingford and their three daughters were each given generous bequests in the will. Percy and his wife decided to stay in their own beautiful home so that his mother and sisters could remain in the manor house until such time that other decisions might have to be made.

Elizabeth's inheritance made it possible for her to continue her education.

Enrolled in all the science classes she needed for the study of medicine, Elizabeth settled into her fourth year at Lady Margaret Hall. It was her second home, and she greeted her returning peers like sisters. She took up occupancy of a large room on the first floor, leaving the third floor smaller rooms to the first and second year students.

Without the restrictions of a pandemic, Oxford returned to its former social community. Men and women could meet for tea in the high street, attend dances and concerts together. Boats were on the river once again, full of students, laughing, chattering, and flirting.

There were still few women in the science courses scattered

between the various colleges of Oxford. Physics, Chemistry, Biology and Anatomy were still the domain of men. Only the bravest and most determined young women dared enter the hallowed halls of the science buildings. Elizabeth found, to her surprise, that the discriminatory remarks levelled at her the year before were considerably reduced. A few rude, even crude remarks, she could put up with, when the majority of the male students left her alone. She made a pact with the other women students that they would never sit together in the lecture halls, but scatter themselves between the male students.

The vast majority of criticism still came from scientists and doctors alike, who added the weight of their authority to the discussion regarding the education of women. "Overtaxing" of the brain during study, for example, was frequently pin-pointed as a cause of infertility, flat-chestedness, spinal curvature, extreme sensibility of nerves, irritability of temper, attacks of disease, dullness of the brain, weakness, and degeneracy. Females, it was suggested, should be instructed in cookery, needlework, knitting, and religion, thereby learning how to be a good mother and wife.

[1]The young women in medical studies needed a strong stomach, a sense of humour, and a resilience of spirit to endure the graphic and sometimes terrifying specimens floating around in bottles of formaldehyde. Dissection and examination of body parts, stinking with the obnoxious liquid, was not for the faint of heart.

As a matter of delicacy, Professor Aston had removed the two life-sized charts of the male human body, leaving their twin charts of women's bodies in full view. The imminent Doctor Aston did not hide his distaste of the young women students who had infiltrated his sanctuary. He rarely acknowledged their presence, and skirted around all issues regarding male genitalia, much to Elizabeth's amusement. She hid her smile, put down

---

1. All true statements

her head and studied hard, proving by the high marks she achieved that she could hold her own against her fellow students.

The wind whipped around Elizabeth's legs as she made her way to Queen's College library on a Saturday morning in late October. The library was bustling with students quietly scanning the massive collection of books, or reading at a study carrel. She couldn't find what she needed, and decided to move to the Physics rooms to get her nose into the research she needed for her next paper.

A voice from behind the stack of great tomes made Elizabeth stop in her tracks. A quiet voice, speaking in a whisper, but with a lilting accent so familiar to her that she held her breath waiting for the next small vocalization. Could it be? She hardly dared peek around the end of the aisle of books to confirm her supposition. Plucking up courage, her curiosity getting the better of her, she took the plunge and walked nonchalantly into the adjoining aisle.

"Elwyn Thomas," Elizabeth gasped before she had time to think.

Her former tutor looked up from the book he held and blinked at Elizabeth in surprise. He excused himself from his companion and moved towards her.

"Miss Elizabeth," he murmured grasping her hand and looking into her eyes. "What are you doing here?"

"Shhhhhh," came a sound from behind the books.

Elwyn motioned to the door, and taking Elizabeth's elbow they quickly and silently exited the library.

Former tutor and student walked out into the courtyard in front of the library, and headed towards one of the seats around its perimeter. They stole glances at each other, noting the changes they had both gone through since their last meeting a seeming lifetime ago.

"Miss Elizabeth," Elwyn said, sitting beside her and looking into her eyes. "I don't believe it. After all this time. How is your family? Are you a student? What are you studying?"

The questions spilled out of his mouth unheeded.

"Let me catch my breath," gasped Elizabeth. "I have questions of my own. The last time I saw you, you were heading off to war, leaving me to struggle on without you."

The years between them had seemed such a wide chasm back then. She had been an innocent fourteen year old, and he a mature twenty-two. Now at twenty-two and thirty respectively, the gap seemed far less.

Elwyn walked with a slight limp, and had a scar running down the side of his face beside his right ear. There were noticeable silver hairs at him temples, and his eyes held a burden from somewhere dark and sad. His smile and voice were as Elizabeth remembered them, and she warmed to the comfort it gave her to be in his presence again.

"Do I still call you Mr. Thomas or sir?" she asked, laughing. "Please don't keep calling me 'Miss Elizabeth.' Just Elizabeth… or Beth is better."

"Then you must call me Elwyn," he replied. "I am no longer your tutor, but a friend from long ago. So much has happened since I saw you last, but I often recall the years at Lingford Manor and how much I enjoyed being with you. You were an amazing student Mmm.. Oops! Beth. Such a mind for one so young. Tell me what has happened over the years."

"I have a better idea," Elizabeth said, rising to her feet. "Because I have to meet somebody shortly at my residence, could we arrange to meet again? Maybe for a meal?"

"Of course," he agreed immediately. "Let's do that. The Eagle and Child is one of my favourite places to eat. Are you free tonight? If you tell me where you're staying I could collect you around seven o'clock."

"I can rearrange my plans and join you instead," Elizabeth said. "My residence is Lady Margaret Hall. Do you know where it is?"

"Of course. Who doesn't? See you later then," Elwyn started to walk away, then turned and called, "Beth. Thank you. I can't wait to hear all about your life."

Elizabeth smiled and waved, aware that her heart was beating loudly in her ears, and that her face was flushed. What a wonderful surprise to have found an old friend, or was it more than that?

CHAPTER 20

ELWYN THOMAS

So much to say. So many memories to share. They made their way along the narrow walkway, through the park beside the river, neither of them talking, but comfortable and easy with each other's company. The Eagle and Child tavern offered them a small table in a quiet corner, and they finally sat facing each other ready to talk.

Elizabeth shared her experience of the war years; her work attending the soldiers living at Lingford Manor, birthing foals, her revelation to become a doctor, her brother's death in battle, her long journey to gain women's rights at the university. She paused, not able to relate her most painful memory.

"You have been busy," Elwyn smiled. "My years seem to have been eaten up with the war. Four years of unspeakable misery, best left without words. I returned home to Wales after the war to... well, recuperate, shall we say. A time of healing. I accepted a junior position at Manchester University last year, but it didn't work out. I'm afraid I idled my time away after that, private tutoring, teaching for a term at a boys school, and helping my family on the sheep farm."

The food and beer they had ordered arrived, and gave them both time to pause their stories and enjoy the fare.

Elwyn never took his eyes off Elizabeth's face. She had matured into a stunningly beautiful young woman. He remembered the gawky girl of fourteen with an intellect far beyond her years, and a determination and strong will he had rarely encountered since. He felt shabby and old beside her, aware of his worn jacket, and his untidy beard. His life had been taken from him at twenty-two years of age by a war he hadn't wanted to fight. The four years since seemed a blur. Apart from one very short and disastrous fling with a married woman, he had not even been out for dinner with a woman until now.

Elizabeth was just as fascinated with her former tutor. She didn't notice the shabby jacket or the greying hair, but focused on the same green eyes she remembered, full of kindness and understanding. The same deep Welsh-accented voice. The smile that showed the row of even white teeth between the bearded lips.

"What of your family?" Elwyn finally said, pushing his empty plate aside and swigging the froth-topped ale. "Is your father still riding every day?"

Elizabeth looked down at the table, unable to meet Elwyn's eyes.

"Papa died, Elwyn. I was with him on a ride and he died. I tried to help him, but I couldn't."

Elwyn reached for her hand, imagining what a terrible ordeal it had been for her.

"Beth, I am so very sorry," he murmured. "I know how much you loved him, and how much he adored you. I have never seen such a bond between father and daughter."

"I know," Elizabeth said. "I am so grateful for the wonderful memories I have of him, and our great times together. I'll never ride a horse without thinking of him. I am so happy to be able to talk to you about him. Somebody who knew him and liked him."

Walking back through the park, Elwyn told Elizabeth that he had come to Oxford to work with Professor Jefferson in the

Physics Department at Kings College. As a junior faculty member, his salary was small, but he was continuing his education at the same time, and was confident he would gain a full professorship upon completion of his doctorate.

They laughed together at Elizabeth's stories about the male students' behaviour when she joined a physics class.

"You taught me well," Elizabeth said. "I dug out all my old study material and had to work very hard to pass that class."

"You are amazing," laughed Elwyn. "Your determination to have your own way has never failed you, has it?"

"Never," laughed Elizabeth. "Speaking of having my own way, do you want to do this again sometime?"

"How could I refuse, knowing you always get your own way," Elwyn quipped. "Would you like to wrap up warm and go for a punt on the river on Saturday? I'm quite the expert these days."

"Brilliant! I accept," Elizabeth answered.

"Beth?" Elwyn asked "I must ask if you have a young man, or anything?"

An answer didn't come immediately, giving Elwyn some concern that he had overstepped his evaluation of her availability.

Elizabeth burst out laughing when he stopped walking.

"You are funny," she said. "There is no young man in my life Mr. Thomas."

Relief spread across Elwyn's face as he continued to walk, and when they arrived at Lady Margaret Hall and Elizabeth kissed his cheek before running up the steps, he was elated beyond words.

He reminded himself that the kiss on his cheek had been given by Lady Elizabeth Lingford, his former student. That he was a humble and very poor junior professor more than eight years her senior. As he walked to his rooms, he chastised himself, on the folly of his amorous feelings for Elizabeth. He could still feel the effects of her closeness, the soft brush of her lips, her smile, her lovely eyes, her laughter and her passion. His student had faded into the past and been replaced by a vibrant and beautiful young woman who had swept him off his feet.

Elizabeth ran up the stairs to her room, her head spinning and her heart thumping. Her old tutor seemed but a memory, and the Elwyn Thomas of this time and place a totally different person. She didn't recall him being so handsome, but then she had rarely considered him as anything other than her tutor. She threw herself across her bed and ran her tongue over her lips, tasting the saltiness of his cheek, and she couldn't wait to taste more of him.

CHAPTER 21

DAYS FULL OF LOVE

S uddenly life was all about Elwyn. The trip on the river, when he had held her hand to help her in and out of the punt. The walk along the river bank the next day, where he had taken her elbow to help her over a particularly muddy patch. The walk back to LMH in the dark after a choral concert at St. Peter's was worth another kiss on the cheek from Elizabeth, and a return kiss on the cheek from Elwyn.

A picnic on the cold damp grass beside the river meant they had to sit close together for warmth. Elwyn had spread a woollen blanket around their shoulders. With their upper arms and even thighs touching, the first real kiss was not far away. It was Elizabeth who turned her face towards his first, and because she was completely irresistible to him Elwyn touched her lips with his, very gently. It was over in less than a second. However, the effect on every part of their bodies remained, forcing them to turn to each other for more.

Elizabeth had never had such a kiss. It took her breath away and made her mouth fill with sweet liquid, that wet her lips and flowed onto Elwyn's lips. He was enraptured with her, and parted his lips to drink in her sweetness, pushing the tip of his tongue between her open lips to taste more of her.

The physical reaction to each other startled them both, as they gasped for air and clung onto each other, desperately wanting so much more than kisses.

Whistles from a passing punt full of students sent the couple scurrying apart, laughing as they scrambled to their feet, faces glowing and knees weak.

Elizabeth changed out of her damp clothes in her room at LMH, her body warmed by the recollection of the shared kisses, and intimate embrace on the banks of the river.

Snow skimmed across the courtyard like lines of fine sugar the next morning as students, wrapped against the cold, hurried to their classes. Elizabeth headed to Magdalen College for her biology class, clutching a woollen scarf around her head against the biting wind. It was a long walk on such a day, and she was relieved to reach the old college buildings and shelter from the elements within their strong stone walls. The lecture hall was at least warmer than outdoors, although the students kept their coats on and rubbed their hands to keep the cold from taking over their ability to write notes legibly.

The work was difficult to say the least. A Master's degree from Oxford was not easily or casually attained. Elizabeth had to apply herself diligently to her studies if she had any hope of passing final exams. Determined to do well, Elizabeth put aside romantic thoughts of Elwyn as she devoted her time and energy to catching up on her neglected and overdue papers. Difficult though it was, she welcomed her old tutor's help with physics and biology, meeting him in the library or common room at Lady Margarets Hall, where close contact was unacceptable.

Elwyn found it difficult to sit in close proximity to Elizabeth, without touching her. His eyes sought hers and relayed to her what he was feeling. His body reacted to his desire, even in the confines of the women's college, and he struggled to gain control of his emotions. Even so, he worked with his love, going over her notes and helping her research her papers.

As a reward, she earned high marks in her studies, and they were able to take a break as Christmas approached.

"I wish we could stay together in Oxford for Christmas," Elizabeth whispered as she snuggled into Elwyn beneath the stone arch of the courtyard gate.

"I too would much prefer to be with you than go to Wales to be with my family," Elwyn replied.

They had been to a Christmas carol service at Christ Church Cathedral, and then on to a roast beef supper at Magdalen College. Now, here they were on their way back to LMH the night before they were to leave to join their families.

"Beth," Elwyn said, holding her close. "Would you come back to my rooms with me tonight?"

The air hung in silence around them, glistening with frost and halos of frozen breath. They remained like the stone surrounding them, statues frozen in time, waiting for an answer.

Elizabeth stirred in his arms and looked into his eyes. The frost in his beard made him look older than he was, but she only focused on his eyes.

"Is it too awful of me to say 'yes'?" she asked. "Knowing what 'yes' would mean?"

"For me it's the opposite of awful," Elwyn answered. "I can't imagine anything I want more. We are leaving in the morning, but will take the memory of tonight with us. That would mean everything to me."

They linked arms and walked back the way they had come, through the now quiet streets, their footsteps crunching on the frosty ground.

Elwyn's rooms were plain and drab, but he lit a fire and warmed some cocoa and soon the glow of the fire and warmth of the drink thawed their cold bodies.

Elwyn sat on the floor at Elizabeth's feet and took each of her feet in turn, warming her frozen toes with the palms of his hands. He ached for her, but wanted to give her time to relax and be comfortable being totally alone with him for the first time. No prying eyes, or students passing by to whistle and hoot. Only the crackle of the fire, and the illumination of its glow.

"This is so perfect," whispered Elizabeth, closing her eyes and sipping her chocolate. "I want to hold this moment forever. Seal it in my memory for the rest of my life."

"We will make many more memories together, Beth," Elwyn said. "This is just the beginning."

Elizabeth slid onto the rug beside him, taking his hands in hers and kissing the palms. Her face glowed in the firelight, and Elwyn thought he had never seen a more beautiful sight. He kissed her gently, pulling her close. It took his breath away. He calmed himself as he held her, knowing his body was responding far too quickly, and he desperately wanted the first time making love to Elizabeth to be another perfect memory, and not a frantic burst of passion, over in seconds.

It was unknown territory for Elizabeth. She knew the biological facts well enough. Around a stud farm, she had years of experience watching the whole operation between sire and mare.

Her heart thumped wildly in her chest as she clung to Elwyn. She would never admit she was apprehensive, even scared. He was older, and more experienced in these things. He had told her about an affair with a married woman years ago. By comparison, she had only shared a few brief kisses with a student when he had walked her back to LMH after a concert.

Layers of winter clothing were cumbersome and difficult to remove with ease. They held each other's eyes as shirts, trousers, skirts and woollen jumpers fell to the floor at their feet, leaving them standing facing each other in their undergarments. As they moved to embrace, Elizabeth felt the evidence of passion from the man she was with, pressing into her through her silk knickers.

The rug in front of the fire seemed the warmest spot in the room, and the couple sank again to lie beside each other. Elwyn gently helped Elizabeth out of the last of her garments, and removed his own underpants. He lay on his side gazing into her eyes fighting for control once more.

"You are so beautiful," he murmured, kissing the tip of her ear, her neck, her breasts, as he slid his hand between her legs, in search of the very core of her.

Elizabeth gasped as the sensation gripped her like nothing she had known. His fingers searched her and stroked her, until she cried out in ecstasy. She wanted to look down to see Elwyn before he entered her, but she clung onto him instead and allowed him to open her legs wider and gently push himself inside. He moved slowly, careful not to hurt her or scare her. She bit into his shoulder as the vibrations he had begun with his fingers increased a thousandfold, and she shuddered and threw back her head as she felt him explode into her.

They lay together without talking for a long time. Elwyn still above her, and still inside her. When he finally lifted himself away from her and moved to her side, she turned to face him and kissed his mouth, trying to reveal how much she loved him in that moment. He reached for his underpants and tucked them between her legs to soak up the fluids draining out of her. An act of such caring she almost wanted to cry.

It was a night to build memories. Making love for the first time, then the second and third time, until the whole night had slipped by and the pale light of dawn came creeping through the frost-covered window. Elwyn piled more wood on the fire and brewed tea. He made toast with lashings of butter, and they sat in awe of each other as they shared their breakfast.

CHAPTER 22

PROFESSOR

It seemed like a dream to Elizabeth. She travelled home thinking only of the night she had spent with Elwyn. She hadn't wanted to leave him that morning, but he had helped her dress and walked her to her college very early so that she could finish her packing and be ready when the car arrived to pick her up. She was already counting the days until she could see him again.

Lingford Manor without Papa! How dreary it seemed. Mama lived through her two daughters, and derived great pleasure in watching Lydia and Caroline take the county by storm with their beauty; invited to every social occasion, every dinner party, every ball, every racing event at Newmarket. Percy ran the estate as his father and grandfather had done before him. He managed the business of the estate admirably. Although Percy's love for horses was unlike his father's, he worked closely with Callum McCarthy to increase and develop the breeding stable.

Invited to Christmas festivities along with the family, Elizabeth donned her finery and smiled her way through the various functions, though she would have preferred a cup of cocoa in front of a roaring fire, dressed in nothing at all, enclosed in a soft blanket with her professor.

The blanket in front of the fire became the favourite spot for Elizabeth and Elwyn during the long harsh winter months. The spires of Oxford, the river, the tea shop in the high street, beer at the Eagle and Child Pub, were the backdrops where their love flourished.

They studied into the early hours, taking little time for relaxation, even at the weekends. Both had their sights set on the high expectations their chosen careers demanded.

Snippets of time, snatched after an exam or a celebration of a good grade on a paper, were precious and the couple treated themselves to a meal at the pub, or rented a boat on the river, accompanied by a bottle of wine.

Despite the long hours of study and classes, Elizabeth also found time to drink cocoa with her friends, attend book-club meetings, and play an occasional game of field hockey. She remained at LMH, but often stayed the night with Elwyn, cuddling into his warm arms and resting her head on his beautiful soft curly chest hair. She loved the smell of him, the taste of him, and the touch of him. She was idyllically happy.

Spring term was drawing to a close. Elizabeth had done well and looked forward to beginning her second year of sciences when she returned to Oxford after the summer break. Elwyn was quiet and nervous as he awaited the results of his PhD dissertation, and the decision from the college regarding his professorship.

"Pack an overnight bag, darling," yelled Elwyn as he burst into his rooms, where Elizabeth was curled up on the sofa with her head in an anatomy text book. "Celebration time! We are going up to the city, dinner at the Ritz, the whole works."

"What?" Elizabeth cried, jumping to her feet and catching his excitement. "Are you mad? What are we celebrating?"

"Please," Elwyn answered, holding his hand out in front of her like a stop sign. "Address me as Doctor Thomas, professor of Physics."

"Oh my Lord, Elwyn," Elizabeth gasped. "You did it, my darling Welshman."

She was in his arms in a flash, kissing his bearded face, laughing at his elation.

"So much to do now," Elwyn Whispered between kisses. "Move out of these old rooms. Get a splendid place instead. I have the whole summer to create a new life. I begin in August as Professor of Physics at Kings. I am flying so high."

He spun Elizabeth around, landing her on the sofa. He was so intoxicated with his finally achieved success and the joy of sharing it with the beautiful woman he loved, he hardly knew how to bear it. Buttons rapidly were undone, clothes discarded around them, until they lay skin against skin, still laughing and showering each other in kisses.

CHAPTER 23

LIVING IN SIN

E lizabeth headed to Lingford Manor to spend most of
the summer with her family. Elwyn joined Elizabeth
for her sister, Lydia's, wedding in July. The stately
home was full to capacity with guests and Elwyn was quite at a
loss what to make of it all. He had seldom seen such decadent
living, even in the years he had lived there as tutor to Elizabeth.
Every mealtime was an extravaganza of delectable dishes,
paraded into the formal dining room by elegant footmen. The
culmination each day was dinner, when everybody, dressed in
their finery, ate and drank through several courses of chef's
expansive cuisine.

Percy walked Lydia down the aisle, in place of their father.
The entire family and half the county attended the service in
Saint Mary's Church, with its pealing bells, cavernous sanctuary,
spectacular domed ceiling, and long aisle. It took several
minutes for the wedding party to slowly walk from the narthex
to the altar. For Elizabeth it brought back memories of the last
time she was in the same church for Papa's funeral, and she
flicked away a tear. Now it was the location of a wonderfully
happy ceremony. A new memory to replace the other etched in
her mind.

As the guests departed and the manor house returned to a more normal routine, Elizabeth confided in her mother that she would be sharing accommodation with Elwyn upon her return to Oxford. The news was not received with joy.

"Have you no regard for the family name, Elizabeth?" Lady Lingford challenged her daughter, her eyes glinting with unfamiliar anger. "Living with a man who is not your husband is not the behaviour expected, or indeed demanded, by the position this family holds in society. Your father would be ashamed of you, as am I."

"Rest assured, Mama," Elizabeth replied. "Nobody outside the family will even know, and the friends we have in Oxford won't care. I will be travelling to London, studying at University College Hospital intermittently during this next year as part of my training. I am determined to become a doctor, despite every obstacle placed in my way. Marriage is not in my immediate future."

Lady Lingford dabbed her eyes with her delicate lace handkerchief, knowing it was futile to argue with her stubborn daughter.

"Be content with knowing the county gentry approve of your younger daughters," Elizabeth continued. "Lydia, married to Lord Middleton, and Carolyn courted by young Jacob Shaftsbury. You should be quite content, Mama. Not to mention Percy, who runs the estate and stables even better than Papa, and has produced an heir already."

Lady Lingford forced a smile at the mention of her grandson, Henry, named after his dear uncle. She acknowledged with a slight nod that she did indeed have much to be thankful for.

Elizabeth brushed her mother's cheek with a kiss before hurrying to change into her riding clothes. The call of the horses, still so strong from childhood, urged her to leave the world of upper-class snobbery behind, and ride with the wind.

Elwyn didn't enjoy riding, but encouraged Elizabeth in her passion. She rode every day, sometimes accompanied by her brother, Percy, who delighted in showing her the improvements he had made on the estate. It was obvious from what she saw and heard that the new Lord Lingford was a successful manager of the lands under his supervision.

Life began anew when Elizabeth and Elwyn returned to Oxford. A fine apartment overlooking the river was their new home, furnished simply and tastefully. Luxurious compared with Elwyn's old rooms or Elizabeth's room at Lady Margaret Hall, with shared bathrooms, and little privacy.

Elizabeth watched the River Isis from the balcony of the flat, flowing majestically towards the capital city, where it would become the River Thames. She sipped her tea and thought about the year ahead of her. Her time would be split between Oxford and London. She was enrolled in University College Hospital, one of the few hospitals allowing a limited number of women to study medicine. Many of the teaching hospitals in London, who had admitted women students during the war years, no longer saw the necessity to educate the fairer sex as doctors. It seemed it would always be an uphill battle for women like Elizabeth. She wondered, not for the first time, at the enormity of her presumptuous ambition.

CHAPTER 24

LONDON

London! The capital city! How different it was from Oxford's quiet, studious way of life. Streets full of people, all seemingly in a hurry, pushed their way through the crowded pavements. Automobiles mixed with horse-drawn vehicles made for chaos in the busy streets, especially with hand drawn carts still weaving in and out of the traffic. The city was noisy, dirty, and vibrant. Divided into defined areas, Londoners knew what to expect in each borough. It was a city of vast differences between rich and poor. The rich lived in luxury in large houses with servants to provide for their every need. The poor lived in the worst slums imaginable, sometimes two or three families sharing two rooms, with shared running water and toilet facilities.

Elizabeth, being among the fortunate elite class, lodged with Lady Margaret Hennessy, in Russell Square. An old friend of Elizabeth's mother, she had lost her husband in the flu epidemic. Childless, she had struggled to find her place in society, or even contentment in her own home.

Lady Margaret was elated to welcome Elizabeth into her home and, for the first time in three years, she felt alive. The household staff were more than delighted that their mistress was finally showing an interest in daily life, and they worked hard to prepare the large bedroom overlooking the square. Chef was given a list of Miss Elizabeth's favourite foods and Sally, the chambermaid, was allocated as lady's maid on the days the young medical student stayed at the house.

University College Hospital was a bustle of activity at every time of the day. The same prejudices held here as at Oxford, with the women students being shielded from any unnecessary contact with male patients. The establishment went to great lengths to keep parts of the male anatomy covered during autopsy or surgical observation. Elizabeth would not be granted access to wards until the following year. Nevertheless, the knowledge was invaluable, the amount of reading and studying immeasurable, the exams more and more demanding, and the amount of sleep negligible.

Each day, from her first day of classes, she encountered people in the streets around the hospital who looked different and sounded different. Many looked almost transparent they were so pale and thin. They shuffled along in a tide of sadness, faces bearing no expression, bodies bent and worn. In all her years at Lingford Manor, living among country folk on the estate, Elizabeth had never seen evidence of such despair.

The lecture halls, as in Oxford, were filled with male students. The same smirks, jokes, nasty comments, and insulting behaviour were present at all classes, usually egged on by the professor. Women in the medical profession were an unpopular and unwanted faction.

The months flew by, with Christmas in Wales among the beauty of the hills. The Thomas family welcomed their son's girl-friend into their midst, showering her with affection and declaring she was the loveliest girl they had ever seen. A cosy double bed was ready for them on the second floor of the old stone house, with a fire blazing in the grate and views of the snow-covered hills from the tiny dormer windows. There was no question of them sleeping separately, although they were extra careful in the quiet of the night that their love-making was muffled if not silent. Snuggling in the soft bed, listening to the wind howl and roar outside, Elizabeth had never been happier.

~

The great hall at University College in London was filled to capacity. It was warm and airless and Elizabeth could feel a trickle of sweat running down the middle of her back. She sat with the rows of graduating medical students—one of the few women among so many men. She smiled as she thought about the guests sitting behind her, waiting to see their graduate be presented; Elwyn, her mother, two sisters and brother among them.

Had it really been six years of study? The last two years had all been at the London Hospital, where Elizabeth had continued to be a guest of Lady Hennessy's. Three years of gruelling work, learning from experience as well as classes about the astonishing and incredible creation called the human body. She had never become accustomed to the fragile condition of many of the poor of London. The cost of a doctor was beyond their means, and the hospital was a last resort for people who were deathly sick with one foot already in the grave. For many it was a place to die, although still more chose to stay at home and not even try to prevent the inevitable. Yet occasionally patients recovered against all odds. A glimmer of hope that shone throughout the hospital, and urged the students to keep going.

Elizabeth was reminded again and again about the young soldier during the war whose hand she had held while he died. She held many more hands during the two years on the wards, and cried many tears for the poor whose lives were cut short for lack of good food, warm clothes, safe lodging, and love. All the things she had grown up taking for granted.

"Beth," Elwyn cried, hugging her close after the ceremony.

"Stop," smiled Elizabeth, remembering Elwyn's announcement years before. "Please address me as Dr. Elizabeth Lingford."

Laughing she threw herself back into Elwyn's arms and kissed him, much to her mother's disgust.

"Well," Lady Lingford said, greeting her daughter with a brief kiss on her cheek. "I am amazed you have graduated. A doctor! I question who will ever want a woman as a doctor, but there you are."

"Well done, Beth," Percy said, giving his sister a hug. "Papa would be so proud, as am I."

Lydia and Carolyn joined in with the congratulations, before they left to join Lady Hennessy at her home in Russell Square for a celebratory luncheon. Their host welcomed them with her usual grace, declaring that Elizabeth was the best student in London, and like a daughter to her. She dabbed at her wet eyes as she gathered Elizabeth into her corpulent arms.

"My dearest Beth," Elwyn whispered, when they were alone in the room Elizabeth had slept in for three years. "Now for a complete rest. Instead of going to Lingford Manor right away this summer, you and I are going to Italy for a whole month. First to Venice and then to Sorrento. We will eat spaghetti and drink red wine and sit in the sun. What do you think?"

"You are my darling man," Elizabeth said. "What do I think? I think it is the very best idea. Italy with you for a whole month. How could I not be thrilled just by the thought of it."

A new phase of life was just beginning for them, and they embraced the excitement that it offered. Professor and doctor together.

CHAPTER 25

VENICE

The sun beat down on the narrow canals of Venice, producing a pungent aroma; not unpleasant but reminiscent of an earlier less hygienic age. The city pulsated with life. Visitors crowded St. Mark's Square and queued for gondolas. Every unique trattoria was filled with hungry tourists enjoying the sumptuous Italian cuisine.

The doctor and the professor strolled the cobblestone alleys, crossed myriad bridges, delighted in listening to a string quartet outside the Doge's Palace, while sipping red wine, and made love in the twilight in their beautiful antique room in the Hotel Monaco.

If Venice had been deemed "wonderful," the second part of their Italian holiday in Sorrento was even more so. A magical town, with magnificent views of the ocean and a calm and serene lifestyle. Oxford and London seemed so far away, and they treasured the sunny days they were together in Italy.

"Marry me, Beth," Elwyn said, as they gazed into each other's eyes across the small table in the corner of a tiny trattoria perched on the cliffs of Sorrento. "I have loved you for so long. I adore you, and want to spend every day waking up with you beside me. Say you'll marry me, my love,"

"We have both waited, my professor," smiled Elizabeth. "Let's get married while we are here. Let's not wait. I don't want a big white wedding. I just want to be your wife."

It didn't seem to matter to the elderly priest in the small church on the outskirts of the town that they were not Catholic. He spoke enough English to get through the vows, his cheerful, rotund face glowing as he gave his blessing. His loyal deacon acted as witness, along with a young woman from their hotel, who they had befriended. It was done. They were married.

The newly-weds travelled to Lingford Manor when they returned to England.

Lady Lingford's eyebrows arched in surprise, or maybe anger, as she heard the news from her daughter.

"Married?" she exclaimed. "You were married in Italy?" Without a member of your family present?"

"Mama," answered Elizabeth, moving towards her mother to touch her arm, which was instantly withdrawn. "Elwyn and I have lived together for so long. The marriage was only an official conclusion to a union we made long ago. Please don't be angry with me. Be happy for me. It was what we both wanted."

"Typical of you, Elizabeth," Lady Lingford spat out between clenched teeth. "Not a thought for your family. Did it never cross your mind that your mother might want to be at your wedding, along with your sisters and brother. Do we mean nothing to you?"

"We didn't want a big fancy wedding, Mama," explained Elizabeth. "I've lived away from home for so long—not like my sisters who have been at home with you. It was the right decision for Elwyn and me. We couldn't be happier. We didn't mean to go behind your back, or make you feel unwanted, that is why we came directly here, to Lingford, as soon as we arrived in England."

"I believe you deliberately choose to conduct your life to annoy me, Elizabeth," sniffed her mother, now letting tears of frustration flow. "You were always your father's child, right from the time you were a toddler, barely giving me a second glance. Well, now you are married to a Welshman who used to be your tutor, what will people think?"

"A Welshman who is wonderfully clever; a university professor who is admired wherever he goes, who is kind and generous. People can think what they like. He is everything a woman could ever want in a husband and partner." Elizabeth walked towards the drawing room door before proclaiming as her exiting remark, "And he's absolutely great at making love."

Lady Lingford thought she may faint. She rummaged through her velvet bag to find her smelling salts, sniffing them in delicately to bring herself back to normal.

Elizabeth's sisters were more enthusiastic at the news of the wedding, although saddened that there had been no big ceremony to take part in. Percy was equally happy for his sister, and swung her around before planting a kiss on her cheek.

"We must have an after-wedding party, don't you think?" he questioned Lydia and Carolyn. "Mother will come around, especially if we fill the house with the local gentry. She will have to put on her good face for them all. Let's do it this weekend before you go back to Oxford, Elizabeth. We can rustle something up in very short order. What fun!"

Before Elizabeth and Elwyn could object the party organization was under way. Lydia and Carolyn wrote invitations all the next day and had them couriered to the various important families in close proximity. It would be the party of the summer, and Lady Lingford would be somewhat compensated for missing the social aspect of her eldest daughter's wedding.

Extra staff was employed to clean the manor house from top to bottom, prepare food, make up extra bedrooms, and run the hundreds of errands needed to pull off such a gathering.

"Let us enjoy this, Beth," smiled Elwyn on Saturday morning, as they lay in bed thinking about the day ahead. "You will be the centre of attention, as you should be, and your family will love being able to celebrate our marriage with you."

Elizabeth buried her face into her husband's chest, smelling the familiar mixture of sandalwood and sweat that she adored. She slid her hand over his stomach and down the outside of his thigh, then up the inside of his thigh to find more soft curly hair.

"Begin the day this way then," she murmured, enclosing him with her hand.

Elwyn needed no encouraging, and turned her over so that he could kiss her mouth.

"My pleasure, Mrs Thomas," he sighed.

Maggie, Elizabeth's personal maid, had been told not to enter the bedroom until she was called for, but today was a special day and there was so much to do. Surely the young mistress would want to be up and bathed and dressed early.

Maggie opened the door quietly and peeked into the room.

"Oh my Lord!" she gasped before she could stop herself.

She quickly closed the door again and ran along the hallway and down to the basement to sit and wait for the bell to jingle on the bell board. Her face was red as a beet and tears stung her eyes as she sat staring at the bell board, dreading now the summons to help her mistress. She couldn't get the picture of what she'd seen out of her head. At seventeen years of age, it was shockingly graphic. She was an innocent country girl and knew nothing of what went on in the bedroom of married people.

Eventually the bell did jingle and Maggie made her way back to the bedroom, still red in the face and not daring to make eye contact with Elizabeth.

"Maggie, don't worry about it," her mistress said with a smile. "No harm done. We were just starting the day with some loving. Now let's get on. I need your help to look my very best, and you do such wonders with my hair."

The day seemed to go by slowly waiting for guests to begin arriving. Overnight guests arrived in the middle of the afternoon to have their luggage taken to bedrooms and give them time to rest and dress properly for dinner. As the dinner hour approached, a cavalcade of impressive latest-model cars lined the driveway, driven by proud chauffeurs who had spent the day buffing and polishing their vehicles into impeccable glory. The gentry alit from each car as it drew to a stop at the entrance to the manor, to be greeted by footmen who directed them into the manor house, discreetly gathering hats from the gentlemen to be labelled and stored during their stay.

Elwyn looked out from the bedroom window at the parade below and sighed. He was not part of this culture or this class. It bothered him that he was drawn into all the fuss, and he would have preferred to be sitting quietly by the river eating a picnic with his sweetheart. He was dressed in uncomfortable, restrictive clothing. His valet had helped him dress, and even sprinkled some kind of perfumed cologne on his hair before running a comb through it and making him look every inch a Lingford. But for Elizabeth he would not have succumbed to any of it. He took a deep breath and watched as his wife came into the bedroom from her dressing room, looking like a royal princess. Her dress was the palest lavender and floated around her as she moved. She wore pearl earrings and necklace to match, and her hair, which normally flew around her face, was pinned into an upswept style scattered with tiny pearls.

"Elwyn," she laughed. "You are staring! Do you approve of your made-over wife?"

"How could I not stare at you? Look at you!" Elwyn said, walking towards her to take her in his arms.

"Don't," Elizabeth said, her eyes twinkling with merriment. "You will crumple me and it's taken an age to get me looking like this. I feel stiff and awkward, especially after wearing very little in the way of undergarments in Italy for so long. I'd forgotten what a corset felt like. Ah well, we must act the part. At least for today."

Then glancing at Elwyn, she stopped to admire him.

"You look pretty dapper yourself, Professor," she murmured,

brushing his cheek with a kiss. "What on earth is that smell? Did you let Hawkins perfume your hair?"

"Please Beth, have mercy," Elwyn laughed. "I had no option. He just took complete control of me. Is it really bad?"

Elizabeth took his arm, assuring him that it was quite appropriate. They made their way downstairs to join the party.

CHAPTER 26

ALONE

Had the wedding party really only been six months ago? Everybody dressed up in their finery; laughing, eating, drinking, dancing. Champagne flowing and the Manor House glittering. Mother at her best in the centre of everything, telling everybody how proud she was of her doctor daughter and her wonderful new son-in-law. Elwyn, resplendent in evening dress, winning the hearts of the gentry, dancing with her until her feet ached. Falling into bed at two in the morning, still laughing as they scratched and rubbed their skin where the tight clothing had left welts and creases.

Elizabeth gazed at the boxes piled around her in the Oxford flat and tried to remember what they contained. How would she know? She hadn't packed them. Mother had sent servants from Lingford Manor to do all the work. She was only there to gather together her books and personal items she cared to keep. The rest would be put in storage for now.

A car was waiting to take her home to Lingford Manor, but she couldn't tear herself away from the room she stood in—not yet.

Two days after the wedding party, they had left for Oxford. A bright sunny day. Newly married with their lives in front of them. The girl on the bike had come from nowhere. She shot out in front of them from a path coming out of a field. Elwyn braked and swerved to miss her, sending the car careering across the narrow road, through the hedge and into an oak tree. It took all of ten seconds.

Elizabeth woke to bright lights and white walls. Was she in heaven? Her mouth was dry and her head ached. When she tried to move her head, shooting pains jarred her senses and she closed her eyes tightly against the pain. A soft touch on her hand, and a quiet voice whispering her name, made her carefully open her eyes again.

"Elwyn?" she tried to say.

"Lie still, Miss," a voice near her ear spoke. "Don't move. I'll get the doctor."

Panic rose in Elizabeth's throat as she remembered the bike in front of the car.

"Elwyn," she screamed. "Elwyn."

He hadn't survived the accident they told her. She was lucky to be alive.

Lucky! Lucky!

She wanted to die too. Why was she alive, when Elwyn was gone?

"Please, God," she pleaded. "Take me too. Don't leave me here without him. Don't leave me here alone. Life without my love will be unbearable. There is no life without Elwyn."

Days slipped into weeks of despair and anguish. Her body was broken, and recovery was slow and painful, but the loss of her dear husband was more than she could bear. She wouldn't eat, couldn't sleep, and spent the days in grief and sorrow. The family visited often, trying to encourage her to try, if not for her own sake, for theirs. Percy even brought her old friend, Callum McCarthy, to see her, hoping the talk of the stables and horses would spark something in Elizabeth.

The old man sat beside his young broken mistress, not knowing what to say. He sat for a long time in silence, before deciding he would talk to her like he always had over the years.

"Remember the day your father died, Miss Elizabeth?" he began quietly. "That was an accident too. Should never have happened. None of us expected it, least of all yourself. Do you remember lying beside him in the woods, not wanting to leave him? You loved him so much, and still do I suspect. You didn't want to ride again, you were so heart-broken. You did though. You got back up onto a horse. You're a brave, courageous woman, and you can get past this tragedy as well. You won't forget, and you won't stop loving your Elwyn, but you will live your life with purpose, just like you've always said you would."

Callum's eyes filled with tears as he spoke to Elizabeth, who lay in the bed not acknowledging she could even hear him.

"Come on now, Miss," he continued slowly. "Get back in the saddle."

Elizabeth closed her eyes. Throughout her life this kind man had advised her and taught her. Only he knew how much she had loved her father. Only he knew how much she loved the horses.

She opened her eyes and reached for his hand.

"McCarthy," she whispered hoarsely. "Get my saddle ready."

The old stable master squeezed the tiny, frail hand in his. Enough had been said.

Elizabeth had been transferred to a convalescent home from the hospital. When she was fully recovered she insisted that her first trip would be to Wales to visit Elwyn's grave. Joseph Graham, a chauffeur from Lingford Manor, drove her. She was exhausted by the journey, and happy to reach the Thomas house before dark, where a warm meal and comfortable bed awaited her. Overwhelming grief flooded Elizabeth as she lay in the bed she had shared with Elwyn. His mother accompanied her to the grave the next morning, where both women knelt in the earth weeping for their loss.

Elizabeth knew she would never recover completely, but she would get back in the saddle. It would be waiting for her when she journeyed to Lingford the following day.

CHAPTER 27

LETTER FROM A FRIEND

Riding every day, even through the snow and wind, strengthened Elizabeth's body and mind. Callum accompanied her, as her father had done many times, and she was glad of his company. They hardly spoke, but to have her trusted old friend beside her gave her immense comfort.

Lady Lingford was sensitive enough to leave her daughter alone to do as she chose. Other than make sure there was good food provided for her, she watched and waited for her eldest daughter to heal. The loss of Lord Lingford had caused similar distress for her ladyship; a distress that she still felt keenly at times. Elizabeth would find her way, as she had done, but in her own time.

Family distractions also helped ease the pain of losing Elwyn. Percy and Phoebe had produced another child, a girl named Rose. Another baby arrived shortly after Rose, when Lydia gave birth to a bouncing baby boy, called Stephen. The three grandchildren were frequent visitors, and kept Elizabeth, her mother and sister, Carolyn, busy. There was nothing quite like cuddling a baby to break through the most despondent mood.

The stables were busier than ever with mares foaling regularly, which thrilled Elizabeth even more than the human babies. She was again a part of each birth when possible, delighting in the whole process, and never tiring of seeing the newborn foal struggling to stand on wobbly legs.

In this environment Elizabeth slowly recovered her sense of purpose. By the beginning of summer she was thinking ahead about where her life might lead now she was on her own.

Doctor Derringer had his practice close to Lingford, and took care of the needs of the estate workers as well as the family. Elizabeth went to see him privately to seek his advise.

"I'm ready to move on, Doctor Derringer," she began. "How feasible is it for me to join your practice, just for a few hours each week to begin with?"

"Well, Elizabeth, you jump right to the point don't you," the doctor smiled. "Let me be perfectly frank with you, my dear. It would not be a good place for you. The estate workers would not feel comfortable having you as their doctor. Maybe some of the women, but certainly not the men. My advice would be to seek a practice away from Lingford, if you can. You have too many close ties here."

Elizabeth thanked him for being so frank, and agreed that his advice was sound. She had to move away and be courageous enough to begin her life as a doctor in some other place. But where?

It took a few days to find the box containing her personal papers, books, and other miscellaneous items, which had been stored in the attic of the manor house. She went through the mass of information looking for the names, and hopefully addresses, of her former classmates at University College Hospital in London. She carefully set aside the pertinent information on several women who she considered friendly enough to approach, and began composing letters asking about their work after finishing their degrees. It was a stab in the dark. She had no idea if any of the letters would reach their destination. Her peers could have moved anywhere in the past year. She needed to find a starting point to plan her future, and finding out where other women doctors had found work was imperative.

The mail was delivered promptly twice each day, and Elizabeth watched and waited for replies to her letters to arrive. It was a long wait, nothing for more than a month. Then one morning there it was. A reply from Jennifer McPhee, the tall thin Scottish girl with the uncontrollable mass of black curly hair. Elizabeth tore it open and ran into the drawing room to read it. Jennifer explained that her friend's letter had been redirected by her former landlord, and had been delayed in reaching her.

The woes of finding a practice that would employ a woman doctor were outlined in detail in her letter. No work in or near London at all. The door was closed at every avenue Jennifer had tried. Even the hospital where they had trained decided not to employ women, and the newly qualified doctor had earned money to pay her rent and buy food by offering her services as a midwife to ladies who could afford to pay a few pounds for the benefit of a qualified physician. After months of struggling to make ends meet, Jennifer had accepted an invitation from an old friend of her father's in Glasgow to work at The Glasgow Royal Maternity Hospital. She accepted the position and was the only physician employed there. The hospital, Jennifer explained, was funded by donation and bequests, and her salary was far beneath the remuneration of male doctors working in other hospitals. Even so, she assured Elizabeth that she was dedicated to her job, and intended to continue working at the hospital for the foreseeable future. She encouraged Elizabeth to think about moving to Scotland, where the opportunities for employment as a woman doctor were far greater than in England.

Scotland! Elizabeth knew nothing about Scotland. She had heard that the Glasgow teaching hospitals were more inclined to accept women students, and knew of several young women who had taken the plunge and journeyed north to finish their education. She talked to Percy about it after dinner that night.

"Do you think it wise to move so far away, Beth?" her brother asked. "You have been through so much, and I wonder if you are strong enough yet to make such a decision. You don't know anybody in Glasgow, do you? Well, mother has a cousin or something who lives up there, but not somebody any of us are close to. I would feel easier about you pursuing your dream if you were closer to home."

"That's the point, Percy," Elizabeth said. "I have only this one letter to go on, but know it to be true from my own experience of the discrimination that exists. If I can work as a doctor in Scotland it's worth taking the chance. Elwyn always believed I could do anything I set my mind on. He was always so confident in my ability to achieve my goals. I am determined to succeed. My father and my husband believed in me. I can't let them down. I have to keep going."

Percy smiled at his beautiful sister. She had come a long way since the accident. He had to add his own belief in her, because she was so courageous, so determined, so Elizabeth.

"Come here, stubborn woman," he said holding out his arms to embrace her. "You go off to Scotland and show them your stuff. I join with Father and Elwyn in cheering you on. You are a formidable woman, and you will succeed in your dream of working as a doctor no matter the obstacles placed in your way. You have overcome so many already. What will be a few more to you, sweet Elizabeth?"

One other reply came a few days later from Margaret Phillips, who had married and given up the idea of becoming a doctor to settle in the London suburbs with her politician husband. She wished her friend good luck finding a position anywhere.

Elizabeth set her sights on Scotland. It seemed the only option.

CHAPTER 28

LAST RIDE

E lizabeth bit into her toast and looked at her mother sitting across the table from her.

"Mama, Percy says you have a cousin in Scotland," she said.

"I do," replied Lady Lingford. "She lives in a rather beautiful house in Dumbarton. I visited her a number of years ago. Climate didn't suit me—very damp! Don't you remember her coming down when your father died? She only stayed a few days."

"No, Mama, I don't remember her," Elizabeth said. "I have corresponded with a friend working as a doctor in Glasgow. There are opportunities for women to work there in the medical profession, and I am hoping to find a position. Do you think I could stay with your cousin? I believe Dumbarton is quite a short drive from Glasgow."

"I don't believe you will ever give up your dream,"sniffed Lady Lingford. "I will write and ask my cousin about staying with her. She would probably enjoy the company of a young woman at this time in her life. They never had children, and her husband spends his days shooting and drinking whiskey."

Cousin Jocelyn was duly contacted, and was delighted at the

prospect of Elizabeth coming to stay. Arrangements were made for a car to take Elizabeth to London to catch the train to Glasgow, where cousin Jocelyn's chauffeur would meet her.

The day before taking her leave of Lingford Manor, Elizabeth walked to the stables to meet McCarthy for their daily ride. She inhaled the pungent, familiar smell of the horses, hay and leather that greeted her, imprinting it on her memory. Her favourite mare whinnied as she stroked her neck, whispering her intent to come back to visit often.

"Shall I saddle her up, M'Lady?" questioned Michael, a young groom who looked after Lucky Lady with utmost care. "Mr McCarthy is saddling Mister Jarvis."

"Yes please, Michael," Elizabeth replied. "Thank you. You take such good care of her. This is my last day of riding before I leave for Scotland tomorrow. I hope to be back for a visit, so I leave Lucky Lady in your excellent hands. Be sure to ride her regularly for me."

"Yes Madam. It will be my pleasure. She's a grand horse."

It was such a perfect day. The blue sky above, the green meadows full of wild flowers spread like a carpet before them, and the companionship of contented old friends galloping in the wind.

"Well, Miss Elizabeth, I must say you make me proud." McCarthy said as they slowed to a trot on their way back to the stables. "I've watched you overcome some big hurdles in your life, but none as devastating as the last one. Now you're off to Scotland and a new life. May I wish you every success. I hope everything works out for you. You deserve it."

McCarthy set his eyes on the grand old house ahead ,and clenched his teeth to quell the emotion he felt for the young woman he had known since childhood.

"McCarthy, thank you," Elizabeth said, touched by her old friend's words. "When you told me to "get back in the saddle", after Elwyn died, I never imagined I could do it. But your words spurred me on that day, and made me want to try. Life will never be the same for me, I know, but I won't stop trying and I have you to thank for that."

They rode on in silence, content with each other's company. The old stable master would miss riding with her more than he dared say, and wondered if this would be their last ride together.

The whole family gathered that night for dinner to say their goodbyes to Elizabeth. It was a bitter sweet parting in some ways. They all worried that Elizabeth was still not fully recovered from losing Elwyn, and would find life very difficult living so far away from her family. Percy made her promise that she would return to Lingford if things didn't work out the way she planned, and Carolyn announced that she would go to Dumbarton in a few weeks time to see how her sister was coping.

Elizabeth shook her head and smiled graciously. They all meant well, and she understood their concerns, but she was determined to make a success of her venture. She wanted to practice medicine and spend her life doing what she had studied so hard to do. If moving to Scotland was the way to accomplish her dreams, then she was ready to take on the challenge.

Lady Lingford and Carolyn were at the door the next morning to see her off. Mama dabbed her eyes and allowed her daughter to give her a brief hug before stepping into the car on her way to London.

Waving goodbye, Elizabeth sat back and relaxed into the plush leather seat in the back of the Daimler. She was happy to be on her way. Away from her mother's constant prying and questions. Away from painful memories. It was time to be on her own and in control of her life again.

CHAPTER 29

GORDON HOUSE

As arranged, Cousin Jocelyn's car met Elizabeth at Glasgow Train Station. The chauffeur waited on the arrival platform holding a sign high in the air which read, "Doctor Elizabeth Lingford." The driver touched his cap as he greeted his passenger and took care of her luggage. Elizabeth settled into the back seat of the car, while her chauffeur stowed her bags into the boot and jumped into the driver's seat to begin their journey to Dumbarton.

The streets of Glasgow were dirty and drab, without colour of any kind. Even the people were dressed mostly in grey or black. The tenement buildings lined the narrow streets and shut out the sky, a pall of greyness hanging over the old city. Elizabeth shivered despite the warm temperature.

As they left the outskirts of Glasgow the greyness and poverty were transformed into rolling green hills, trees, and distant glimpses of a fast flowing river. A prolific array of wild flowers covered the roadside, and birds and butterflies shared the hedgerows surrounding fields full of crops or cows.

The car turned into a tree-lined driveway where Cousin Jocelyn's great house came into view across a shimmering lake. Gordon House was an impressive sight with the sunlight dancing on the limestone facade. Lingford Manor was small by comparison. Elizabeth gazed at the regal stately home, and wondered that her mother had failed to mention the size and grandeur of her relative's residence.

"My dear Elizabeth," gushed Cousin Jocelyn as she came down the steps at the entrance to the house. "You have no idea how delighted I am that you are here to visit. Come inside. You must be tired after your long journey from London."

Jocelyn gave instructions for Elizabeth's bags to be taken upstairs to the east-wing bedroom, and rang a bell to order refreshments. The interior of the house was as impressive as the exterior, with its cavernous entrance hall, elegant curved staircase and beautiful decor. Elizabeth followed her host into a light-filled conservatory full of plants and flowers and comfortable, cushioned armchairs.

"Please make yourself at home, my dear," Jocelyn said. "It's so lovely in here in the late afternoon."

A young maid carried in a tray and placed it on the low table in front of her mistress.

"Would you like lemonade, or maybe tea?" asked Jocelyn. "And help yourself to sandwiches and cakes—whatever you like. I want you to treat our home as if it were yours for as long as you like. You'll meet my husband, Kenneth, at dinner. He is a man of few words, so you mustn't worry if he doesn't respond to you all the time. He enjoys the outdoors; shooting, riding, and things like that, so we don't see much of him, except for dinner."

Jocelyn fussed with the refreshments, making sure her young guest had everything she wanted, and Elizabeth was quite relieved when she was finally shown to her room by the housekeeper, Mrs Campbell, to rest before dinner.

Plush carpets covered the bedroom floor. A four-poster bed piled with luxurious satin pillows and cushions was lost in the spacious room. Every detail spoke of a desire to please the guest, with silver handled combs, brushes, and all kinds of lotions laid out on the dressing table. A beautifully engraved wash basin and jug sat on an ornate oak side table, with piles of fresh towels and face cloths beside it. Elizabeth's luggage had been unpacked for her and her clothing housed in the chests of drawers and large wardrobe. Two wide windows looked out onto a rose garden with a fountain cascading water over white rocks. Through a discrete door at the back of the bedroom was a water closet containing a bathtub and flush toilet—something they didn't have at Lingford Manor.

As there were only three of them, dinner was served in a small dining room off the drawing room. Warned that Sir Kenneth Cunningham was not the talkative type, Elizabeth decided to completely ignore the caution and start the conversation.

"I hear you enjoy the outdoors, sir," she began.

"Hmm," Sir Kenneth offered, continuing to eat his meal with enthusiasm.

"I too love to ride," Elizabeth continued. "My favourite horse is a five-year-old mare named Lucky Lady. I've spent my life around the stables, even helping with the birth of foals since I was a young girl. My brother has one of the most successful stud stables in England, with a waiting list for the foals."

Sir Kenneth looked over his spectacles at the young woman sitting opposite him. Nobody spoke to him in that way. He was used to eating his dinner in silence. His wife rarely talked to him, except to inform him of some social commitment. Elizabeth met his stare directly, and managed a small smile.

"Well, well," he muttered, putting down his knife and fork to consider this strange turn of events. "You ride do you? Have a favourite horse? Even foaled a few? Unusual is that!"

Jocelyn fidgeted in her seat and looked anxiously from her husband to Elizabeth.

"Did you enjoy the venison, Elizabeth?" she asked, trying to divert the conversation away from her husband.

"Never mind that," cut in Kenneth. "We are talking horses here, damn it. Do you shoot as well?"

"No," answered Elizabeth. "But I would appreciate being able to ride while I'm staying with you. Do you think I could be accommodated? Indeed, I would rather enjoy riding with you if you are open to the idea."

Sir Kenneth gulped his red wine and wiped his moustache on his napkin.

"We have a number of excellent steeds here at Gordon House. Probably find one to suit you. The stable master's name is Robertson. Good man. I ride promptly at 8.30 each morning."

"Would you allow me to accompany you, Sir Kenneth?" asked Elizabeth. "You could show me around the estate. I would be most grateful."

By now Cousin Jocelyn almost needed resuscitating. She had rarely heard her husband speak so many words to anybody in their thirty years of marriage. She stared at their young guest not knowing what to make of her.

Servants cleared the main course dishes and ushered in the lemon soufflé dessert, giving all three diners a chance to pause, each with their own thoughts.

Sir Kenneth ate his dessert, frowning at his wife and avoiding the bright eyes of their guest. The silence was uncomfortable, all of them waiting for the answer to Elizabeth's question.

"Meet me at the back entrance hallway at a quarter past eight tomorrow. Be punctual. I will not wait."

With that, he cleaned his moustache again, drank the rest of his wine and left the room.

"My dear," choked Jocelyn, looking down at her untouched lemon desert. "Did you not hear me tell you that he didn't like to talk? Now you are actually going to ride with him. He never rides with anybody. Always alone, unless he's with the hunt. I would not believe any of it if I had not sat here and witnessed it with my own eyes."

"Don't worry about it, Cousin Jocelyn," laughed Elizabeth. "He was very kind to agree to ride with me. I know how to deal with men who don't communicate well. I had plenty of practice with my own father, and I have a feeling Sir Kenneth and I will become great friends."

Jocelyn fanned her face with her napkin and looked like she might cry. Her husband going riding with somebody, and that somebody a young woman whom he barely knew.

CHAPTER 30

SIR KENNETH

R iding attire was brought to Elizabeth's room by Jenny Kilbride, the young maid assigned to take care of her. Boots, Jenny explained, would be available at the stables.

The house was a bustle of activity the following morning when Elizabeth hurried down the stairs to meet Sir Kenneth, and she was grateful for the help of several servants who directed her to the back entrance door.

They walked together silently across the cobbled courtyard towards the stables. The familiar smell of the horses greeted them as they pushed open the heavy wooden doors into the large stall-lined building. Elizabeth inhaled deeply, filling her lungs with the scents which had brought so much comfort and peace to her over the years.

"Good day, madam," a tall grey-haired man greeted her. "Please follow me and we'll have you fixed up with boots right away."

Properly attired, Elizabeth joined her host.

"Robertson, bring Doctor Lingford's mount out into the yard," Sir Kenneth instructed.

Elizabeth was impressed with the chestnut stallion as he was led toward her.

"What's his name?" she asked Robertson.

"Red Clover, but he answers to just 'Red'," the stable master said.

She stroked the horses' head, and held her hand in front of his nose while she spoke softly and gently to him. She stood still, allowing the horse to take a good look at her. Lastly, she allowed the stable boy to cup her boot and assist her into the saddle.

"Ready?" said Sir Kenneth between clenched teeth.

The terrain was rugged and very different from the green fields and meadows of the Lingford Estate. Elizabeth was grateful for the company of Sir Kenneth, who trotted ahead of her over the rougher patches of heather and rock. The wind whipped around them, stinging their cheeks, and sending dust into their eyes and nostrils. The deep gorge below, full of frothing water, filled Elizabeth with delight. The strenuous ride was just what she needed after her travelling day.

Sir Kenneth nodded his approval of her riding skills as he slowed his horse to a walk before entering the stable yard.

"Well done," he muttered. "Not easy trails."

"Thank you for letting me ride with you, Sir Kenneth," Elizabeth replied. "It was most enjoyable. Different from the country-side where I'm from, but I enjoyed every minute and hope you will let me ride with you again."

"Hmm," Sir Kenneth offered. "I ride at the same time daily. Enough said!"

Elizabeth smiled to herself as she dismounted and handed the reins to the stable boy. Not exactly an invitation, but not a dismissal either. She would ride with him whenever she was able, or until he got tired of her and told her she wasn't welcome.

Cousin Jocelyn was all of a dither about the morning ride when Elizabeth joined her in the breakfast room.

"I don't believe I even know Sir Kenneth any more," she

babbled. "Letting you ride with him. Whatever has come over the man? You, who are a young lady. Well, I would not have believed it possible. He has very little patience for women at the best of times. You must have bewitched him, Elizabeth."

"Not at all, Cousin," laughed Elizabeth. "I was grateful for his company this morning. It could have been a treacherous ride on my own. I shall ride with him again very soon. In fact, whenever I am able."

Jocelyn rang for more tea and fresh toasted oatcakes.

"I think we are all in for a very interesting visit with you, Elizabeth," she quipped.

No more than ten words were exchanged between the two riders over the following three days. Elizabeth studied her companion, trying to read his stoney face with its furrowed brow and pinched lips. There was no indication that she was unwelcome, nor was there any sign Sir Kenneth enjoyed her company. He guided her on a different trail every day, showing her the stunning, rugged beauty of the Firth of Clyde where the great river emptied into the Atlantic Ocean. Elizabeth was in awe of the landscape around her, and as she glanced at Sir Kenneth she glimpsed a man full of pride and love for his country.

How lovely it was to rest. To be away from the family, and all the things that reminded her of her loss. Elwyn was always with her, sitting quietly reading a book, or riding in the mornings, and especially when she was alone in her bedroom at night. Then the tears would come and she longed for his strong arms around her, and felt her heart would tear into shreds with grief.

Enough rest, thought Elizabeth. Time to move on and make a trip into Glasgow to meet with her old friend Jennifer McPhee. She asked Sir Kenneth about transportation and he offered to give her a ride into the city, where he had an appointment the following afternoon. He agreed to drop her off at the Royal Glasgow Maternity Hospital where Jennifer worked. His appointment would take two hours, and Elizabeth would be picked up after that.

At two o'clock the chauffeur-driven Rolls Royce Phantom dropped Elizabeth outside the hospital before taking Sir Kenneth to his appointment. As usual, the journey had been silent, but it seemed a more congenial silence after the days of riding together.

The hospital had the familiar smell of carbolic. Elizabeth asked at the enquiry desk for Doctor McPhee and was directed to the second floor and given instructions to follow the rabbit-warren of corridors that led to "Maternity Unit Four," where her friend was working.

Jennifer was seated at a large desk flipping through a pile of papers before her. She looked up as the door opened, and then jumped to her feet to greet Elizabeth.

"You came," Jennifer smiled. "Good for you, old bean. You couldn't have timed it better. Come down to the tea room with me and we can have a proper chat."

The two old friends linked arms as they walked down the corridor and into the scantily furnished tea room, which consisted of a few tables and odd chairs, a sink, a small gas ring to heat the ancient kettle that sat whistling gently on the dim flames. China mugs hung on hooks above the sink and a milk bottle sat in a bucket of cold water on one of the tables, along with two cans marked "sugar" and "tea".

Settled with a cup of tea each, Jennifer continued with her conversation.

"One of our most ardent admirers and supporters bequeathed quite a generous amount of money to our maternity hospital when she died a few months ago. The board has met several times since hearing about the endowment, and decided only this past week that we can go ahead and hire another doctor. I am so overworked, and fortunately they all recognized the fact. If you're interested, Elizabeth, you would fit the position perfectly. The work is so rewarding in many ways, and you are so desperately needed. And wouldn't it be such fun to work together? What do you say?"

"Give me a minute, Jen," gasped Elizabeth, laughing at her friend's enthusiasm. "I'm a little taken aback at having this opportunity drop into my lap like this. To work alongside you would be amazing, especially here where the need is so great."

Elizabeth sipped her tea and tried to clear her head. Jennifer allowed her friend the time to consider the offer, and sat quietly across the table from her trying not to appear too impatient.

"If you need time to think about it, please don't feel rushed into a decision," Jennifer finally broke the silence. "I barely gave you time to catch your breath, sorry."

"No, don't be sorry," Elizabeth said. "So many thoughts are flying through my mind, I need to take a walk outdoors to think clearly. Normally, at home, I would head for the stables and go for a ride, but a brisk walk would help, don't you think?"

Jennifer nodded her agreement, and Elizabeth gathered her coat and gloves and walked out into the cloudy evening.

What was she afraid of? Wasn't this the opportunity she had hoped for? To work as a doctor? All the difficult years of education and training, the rejection for her profession from family, and society, loss of her dear Elwyn and the long recovery time after the accident. Now, the future was before her. A new life. The Glasgow Maternity Hospital was the first step, the chance to practice professionally, to gain experience and confidence.

It had only been thirty minutes since Elizabeth had left, and she made Jennifer jump as she burst into the tea room, out of breath from hurrying to find her friend.

"Yes, the answer is yes, I accept the position to work with you, my dear friend."

CHAPTER 31

THE ROYAL GLASGOW

During the trip back to Gordon House, Elizabeth contemplated her new position with the Royal Glasgow Maternity Hospital. It had taken less than two hours to map out a plan for the immediate future. Jennifer had invited her friend to stay at her sparse flat, where there was a spare bedroom. Not the luxury Elizabeth was used to, but basically somewhere to sleep, close to the hospital. The Board had asked for her to begin as soon as possible, and three days from now would be her first day.

At dinner that evening, Elizabeth broke the news to Cousin Jocelyn and Sir Kenneth that she would be living in Glasgow and working at the maternity hospital.

"Good Lord, my dear girl, have you thought this through?" Jocelyn exclaimed. "I believe the Royal Glasgow is a charity hospital, depending on bequests or donors. Not the kind of position your mother would approve of, I think."

"It is exactly what I want to do," Elizabeth answered. "In fact, I cannot wait to begin, knowing that my years of training will be put to good use, and working alongside my friend. My dream of being a doctor is finally going to be fulfilled."

Elizabeth tucked into the venison stew with relish, and met Sir Kenneth's curious gaze across the table.

"A doctor for women then!" he mumbled. "Quite right, quite right."

"You must come to Gordon House whenever you can, Elizabeth," Jocelyn continued. "Whenever you are not working. I know Sir Kenneth will miss you riding with him."

"Indeed," Sir Kenneth added.

"You are both so kind. I will take you up on the invitation whenever possible. Riding with Sir Kenneth has been such a pleasure. I look forward to many more adventures exploring this beautiful land."

A letter was written and sent to Lingford Manor by the first mail the next day, so that the family were aware of Elizabeth's plans.

Sir Kenneth insisted on accompanying her to Glasgow the day before she was to take up her position. The car waited outside each shop while Elizabeth bought the things she needed for the empty room at Jennifer's flat. Bed linens, pillows, blankets, towels, wash basin, lamp, small table, warm rug, and a collection of essential items to make her tiny space more comfortable. She spotted a framed picture of horses galloping across the wild highlands and added it to the pile in the boot of the big car.

Andrew Campbell, the chauffeur, helped move all the purchases into the second floor flat, where he looked around with distaste at the meagre surroundings. His small lodgings over the garages seemed palatial by comparison.

On Jennifer's advice, Elizabeth dressed in her tweed skirt and jacket with a discreet pale blue silk blouse underneath. She swept her hair into a neat french bun, and used the dark hair clips she had purchased to secure it in place. She completed the outfit with lyle stockings and sensible brogue shoes. With her doctor's bag firmly in hand and filled to the brim with her collection of instruments gathered over the years, Doctor Elizabeth Lingford crossed the street to the hospital to begin her work.

The hospital was fortunate to have a renowned obstetrician on call, a doctor who had pioneered the first caesarean section surgeries, and who shared his knowledge and experience throughout the maternity medical community of Glasgow.

Jennifer and Elizabeth, as the two resident physicians, dealt with every aspect of care for the women they served. University College Hospital in London had been a revelation for Elizabeth, where she experienced her first encounter with poverty and deprivation. It prepared her somewhat for the horrors of Rotten Row, the nickname for The Royal Glasgow Maternity Hospital.

Rows of narrow beds lined each ward, with barely a foot between each bed. Volunteer orderlies worked tirelessly changing dirty sheets, replacing sodden pillows, emptying chamber pots, and providing the patients with food and water when it was available. Two wards were isolation units, housing pregnant tuberculosis patients, women so undernourished and emaciated that they often could not maintain their pregnancies. Babies born in these wards were either stillborn or died shortly after birth, bearing the deficiencies of their poor, sickly mothers.

Venereal disease was rampant in the city, with young street-walkers earning a meagre living serving the dockers and sailors around the dockland. Dirty Dick's Pub[1] was the meeting place for such liaisons—the girls would write the cost on the bottom of their shoes in chalk, to be shown to the prospective clients when they crossed their legs. A different price for a variety of options. Syphilis was not curable, but treatments with bismuth, arsenic, and mercury gave some relief, despite the side effects they produced. Working among these unfortunate girls and women was particularly distasteful, as the disease symptoms often included pus filled pustules and a stinking, sickening discharge.

---

1. Dirty Dick's Pub was the actual name of a pub in Glasgow where prostitutes plied their trade.

Women came to the hospital in desperation, when their medical conditions were far beyond the help of neighbours and relatives. Women who had tried to abort their babies with all manner of sharp implements, wives who had been beaten by husbands, who laid the blame for a new pregnancy at their feet, girls in their early teenage years who had been judged and disowned and thrown out to fend for themselves, and a host of starving, weak souls, heavily pregnant and begging for help.

Into this sad, and seemingly helpless assemblage, Elizabeth was thrust.

"The ward supervisors send the women in labour to section six," Jennifer explained, as she spread sheets of notes in front of Elizabeth. "This is where we work most of the time. Many of our patients have given birth at home, so don't require a fuss, or very much supervision. History notes accompany every patient, so you'll soon pick up on the cases that need special attention. We keep the VD patients separate, because of infection. Also the TB patients are kept in a separate side ward."

"My head is already spinning," Elizabeth said, scanning through the papers before her.

"Don't worry," Jennifer said, calmly. "We will work together for the first few days until you are used to the system. This work is not for the faint of heart, my friend. When we are not in the delivery section, we will try to see other patients on the wards who need our attention. We do what we can, but there will be many women who don't survive. We have to focus on the ones we can help."

Taking off her jacket and donning a large white apron, Elizabeth prepared to shadow her friend.

CHAPTER 32

BEARING THE UNBEARABLE

Tired to the bone, Elizabeth dragged herself back to the flat at seven o'clock that first night, leaving Jennifer to write the day's notes for section six.

Shadowing Jennifer had only worked out for about two hours before the birthing section exploded with patients and the two doctors had their hands full to deal with the onslaught. Elizabeth was grateful for the experienced volunteer midwives on section six who handled the normal deliveries with ease and expertise.

The day began with a difficult breech presentation needing the expertise of both doctors, followed by a TB patient who was having trouble breathing during the last stages of labour. It was terribly trying, occupying both doctors for hours, but both babies were delivered successfully and, a kind volunteer brewed tea for the new mothers, midwives, and doctors.

Quickly back to work, a young teenager screamed her way through each contraction, and upon examination, Jennifer talked with Elizabeth, who agreed they should send word to one of the consultants. The labour could not progress any further. The girl's pelvis was just too small. A runner was sent to the home of Doctor Sebastian Hope, who was on call that day. An eminent obstetrician and surgeon, he arrived within the hour and quickly determined he would perform a caesarean section. Surgical intervention was the only way to save both lives. The patient's pelvis was too small to allow natural labour to continue. He required Jennifer's assistance, which left Elizabeth to cover the other patients.

Elizabeth lost track of the number of patients she saw from then on. She scribbled quick notes on the bottom of the patients' forms, and hoped that they would be legible at the end of the day. A woman was carried into the hospital by two strapping dockers who were directed to take her directly to section six.

"This is 'er fourth," one of the men told Elizabeth."No problems with the others, but this one's different. Lots o'blood. Lots o'pain. Dunno what's 'appenin'."

"Let's take a look," Elizabeth said, instructing the men to lay their charge on a narrow bed in a side ward. "Why don't the two of you step outside while we help her. What's her name? Is she your wife?"

"Maddy's 'er name. She is mine. This, 'ere's 'er brother."

There was indeed a lot of blood. Maddy panted and screamed, sweat running down her face along with tears. There was no chance for the baby, but Elizabeth could save the mother if she acted quickly. She reached inside the distressed mother and eased a bloody, battered placenta away and into a bucket A baby girl came quick enough afterwards, and Elizabeth place her gently onto a table, where a volunteer wrapped the tiny lifeless body in a soft cloth. Maddy was exhausted and in a terrible mess, but alive. Margaret, one of the older women volunteers came to help take off her blood-sodden clothes and sponge her stained body, then helped her into a cotton nightgown and placed a large soft wad of cloth between her legs.

"There you are, Missus," Margaret soothed. "That feels better, don't it?"

"I couldn't save your baby, Maddy," Elizabeth said. "There were some complications and the baby didn't survive. You should recover well after rest. I'll tell your men folk they can come in now, shall I?"

Maddy nodded, even managing a small sad smile.

"Doctor Lingford," shouted a voice from the corridor outside. "You're needed."

What was that smell? The small room off the main ward reeked, and Elizabeth realized she was in the venereal disease part of the delivery section. The volunteer in the room quickly offered her a mask, and Elizabeth gratefully accepted. There was an aroma of lavender in the mask that took the edge off the putrid air in the room. The woman was in obvious distress, and no wonder. Upon examination Elizabeth observed dozens of sores which covered the patient's perineum and surrounding genital area. The pain must have been excruciating as the birth approached, stretching the infected skin and splitting the sores.

"You poor girl," Elizabeth whispered, caring nothing now for the smell, but only for the young woman laying on the bed before her.

"Fetch warm water and as many clean cloths as you can find," she instructed the volunteer. Contractions were coming every couple of minutes sending the expectant mother into screams of anguish.

"Hold the warm cloth onto her sores," instructed Elizabeth when the volunteer returned. "Be gentle, she is in great pain."

Elizabeth hoped the warm clean cloths would help ease the pain, and also clean the area ready for the emerging new life. Despite every effort, the tiny under-developed baby didn't survive, and the mother would not live long, as the disease was too advanced.

Elizabeth dragged herself slowly to the tea room and sank into the nearest chair, joined, minutes later, by Jennifer and Doctor Hope.

"This is Elizabeth Lingford, Doctor Hope," she said, smiling at her friend.

"How happy we are to have another doctor on staff."

"Welcome, Doctor Lingford," greeted the eminent doctor.

"Thank you," said Elizabeth. "How was the outcome?"

"Very good," said Jennifer. "In fact, a miracle. Tiny mother and tiny baby both healthy and doing well, thanks to Doctor Hope."

Good news after a day of tragedy was just what Elizabeth needed. She felt drained after the hours she had spent trying to save lives, and the day was not over yet.

The two doctors sped around for the rest of the afternoon and into the early evening, tending to the women who needed them most. They dressed the wounds of the beaten and broken, treated the syphilis patients with mercury and bismuth, listened to the wheezing lungs of the worst of the tuberculosis cases, and popped back and forth to section six to check on the birthing units. Six more babies were born, with midwives in attendance and no complications.

It hadn't all been bad. Mrs. McGregor's group of church ladies had delivered enough of their home-made potato and leek soup to feed the entire hospital. The frail, thin women rolled their eyes and smiled at the first taste, and gobbled up every last drop, the warmth filling their tired bodies. With buns and jam for tea, it was a stellar day for the patients of The Royal Glasgow Hospital.

"Sorry it's been such a hair-raising day, Elizabeth," Jennifer said, as they sat sipping tea and eating a stale bun left over from tea time. "The shadowing idea was a bit of a joke."

They both laughed.

CHAPTER 33

DON'T COUNT THE DEATHS

"D
o not count the deaths," Doctor Hope counselled the two young women doctors. "Count the women and babies who are alive because of you."

Jennifer and Elizabeth sat side by side in the section six tea room at the end of another exhausting day. Strands of hair fell around their faces, having long escaped carefully pinned buns. Once white aprons were now stained with blood, urine and worse. Shiny leather shoes were scuffed and dirty, the feet inside them aching and sore.

"I come bearing good news," continued Doctor Hope. "The Glasgow health and social welfare department has agreed to increase the number of health care workers in the city. Fourteen instead of six. We are hopeful they will reach more women at risk. We are pushing for clinics in the most needy communities to offer advice and practical help on all women's health issues, including prenatal and postnatal care."

It was good news indeed. It would mean early detection of problems, and referrals from the health workers. It would have a positive effect on the tragic emergencies the doctors dealt with on a daily basis when women arrived at the hospital too late for intervention. More health workers in the community would be the difference between life and death for many mothers and their babies.

The first weekend Elizabeth had off was more than a month after she began her work in Glasgow. She travelled to Gordon House by bus early on Saturday morning for two days of rest, good food, and a luxurious bed.

"My dear Elizabeth," greeted Cousin Jocelyn bustling across the room to envelope her young guest in a warm hug. "You have surprised us. Come and sit. I'll send for tea and food. You are so thin, my dear.

The hot tea and buttery crumpets tasted like nothing Elizabeth had eaten for many weeks. She gobbled them down, letting the butter run down her chin and closing her eyes with the joy of eating something so delicious. Cousin Jocelyn stared at her in amazement, but didn't interrupt until her guest had finished three of the crumpets and finally sat back in her seat, dabbing at her chin and mouth, and smiling at her host.

"Dearest," Jocelyn continued. "Tell me all about the hospital and how you have settled into life in Glasgow. Sir Kenneth and I have missed you. I hope you can stay with us for a good visit."

"Just for the weekend, I'm afraid," explained Elizabeth. "I have to travel back to Glasgow tomorrow. I am so grateful to you, Cousin Jocelyn, for your hospitality. Two days here with you will feel like heaven on earth."

"We will fill the next two days with good food, relaxation and conversation," Jocelyn said. "You look completely tired out. I promised your mother I would take care of you, and here you are looking so pale and thin. You are obviously working more hours than is healthy for a young lady. Now, off you go to your room to rest. We must make sure these next two days are a time of recovery for you."

Oh, to fall onto a soft bed with down pillows, to drift off to asleep at eleven o'clock in the morning, to awaken to only the sound of birds twittering outside the open window, to wash away the grime of the big city with the warm water in the adjoining bathroom. Even after only a few hours, Elizabeth felt refreshed and at peace.

A wonderful creamy chicken soup was served at lunch, with freshly baked crusty bread, slices of ham, four different cheeses and a variety of fruit. Elizabeth wondered if it was rude to eat so much as she gorged herself on the feast before her, so different from the usual dry bun and strong tea eaten in haste between seeing patients.

The quiet flower-filled garden was the perfect place to explore that afternoon. Elizabeth lay in the garden swing gazing up at the trees above her and drinking in the clear fresh air. She fell asleep again, unable to satiate her need for sleep.

Sir Kenneth's delight was obvious when he greeted her at dinner.

"Elizabeth," he said, taking her hand and escorting her to her seat at the table. "My dear. You have been missed. I hope you are up for a ride in the morning."

"Yes indeed, Sir Kenneth," Elizabeth answered. "I wouldn't miss it. How I have longed to join you. There is nothing quite like riding a horse to bring the world into focus, and raise one's spirits."

Sir Kenneth beamed his approval and raised his glass of claret in a toast to his young riding companion. Cousin Jocelyn was once again bewildered by her husband's behaviour, having had little conversation with him since Elizabeth had left for Glasgow. Their guest had certainly bewitched the non-communicative, withdrawn Sir Kenneth.

As the time drew near for Elizabeth to return to Glasgow, she wondered about the choice she had made. The past two days had been filled with good things, and she wasn't looking forward to plunging back into the chaos awaiting her. There was so much need and so few hands to do the work. She would work alongside Jennifer, and trust she was making a difference in the lives of the women she cared for.

Sir Kenneth accompanied her as Andrew Campbell once again drove her into the city.

"Goodbye, my dear," Sir Kenneth said as the car drew up to the tiny flat facing the hospital. "Please come and stay again very soon. Nothing gives me more pleasure than riding with you at the beginning of the day."

Elizabeth leaned over and kissed him on the cheek.

"I promise I will visit soon," she said.

Sir Kenneth touched the cheek she had kissed as the car pulled away from the curb. He couldn't remember the last time anybody had kissed him, and unexpected tears stung his eyes.

CHAPTER 34

WINTER IN GLASGOW

A never-ending stream of women sought refuge and treatment at the Royal Glasgow, and the two young women doctors continued to work long hours throughout the autumn.

As winter descended like an icy blanket, and the winds whipped around the old stone buildings in the centre of Glasgow, it seemed the patients arriving at the hospital were even more frail and worn. The cold penetrated into their bones and the lack of food and good shelter exacerbated the ailments tenfold. The diseases caused by poverty continued to spread through the worst neighbourhoods.

Women recovered or died. Babies were born alive or dead. The winter months were merciless. The cold penetrated every crevice and crack in the old hospital, leaving the patients shivering between blankets that were too thin, and adding to the misery they already endured. Little could be done to enhance the patient's hospital stay, except to provide medical intervention and care in the most dire of circumstances.

Mrs. McGregor's volunteer group were kept busy providing warm soup on a daily basis; often only potato soup, but occasionally donations of ham or vegetables upgraded the basic dish into a substantial meal. A local bakery joined the donor's group and provided day old bread each day, giving the hospital a reliable source of food for their needy women. Other church groups around the city occasionally dropped off contributions like currant loaves, Dundee cakes or tea biscuits, bringing smiles to some of the drawn faces on the wards. Despite their best efforts there was never enough food to nourish all the women.

Elizabeth made the trip to Gordon House when she could, savouring the few days of normality and gaining strength, both physically and mentally, to go back into the fray and work among the women of Glasgow.

Her sister, Carolyn, joined her for Christmas at Gordon House. Doctor Hope had arranged a schedule of volunteer midwives to cover for Elizabeth and Jennifer for three days, so that they could each spend time with their families. He remained on call at his house in the city, which was the best Christmas present he could have given to his young colleagues. It meant they would not worry about being away from their patients.

Cousin Jocelyn enjoyed hosting Christmas with two young guests to spoil and pamper. The house was dressed from top to bottom with cascades of festive decorations. A tall Christmas tree stood in the hall, covered in blue and silver balls, tinsel and candles. The house was filled with guests on Christmas Eve as the Cunninghams celebrated with their traditional feast, followed by an evening of carols. Carolyn had brought a dress for her sister to wear, cognizant that Elizabeth would not have an appropriate evening gown. Despite being away from Lingford, the two young sisters enjoyed the festivities immensely, particularly the Christmas Day outdoor pig roast. They sat on hay bales, bundled in warm blankets, drinking hot rum punch while they watched the male staff man the fire and keep the meat cooking. When the pig was cooked, the entire household staff joined the family for the feast.

Carolyn journeyed home with the knowledge that her sister was thriving and appeared in better spirits than when she had left Lingford four months before. She would have good news to report to the rest of the family at Lingford Manor.

After saying goodbye to her sister, Elizabeth joined Sir Kenneth in the car to drive back to Glasgow. Their legs were covered in thick warm blankets. As usual, no conversation took place for most of the journey, until they were driving through the outskirts of the city.

"Sir Kenneth," Elizabeth began, "I wonder if you would consider donating to the hospital I work for? The women suffer greatly with the cold, and the blankets are old and threadbare. I believe our patients would benefit greatly from warmth, and it would aid in their recovery."

"What are you saying, Elizabeth?" gasped Sir Kenneth. "Why have you not come to me before now? Threadbare blankets! Unacceptable! Write down the amount you need, and leave it to me. Cold is a killer."

The kindly man continued to mutter "Unacceptable! Unacceptable!" under his breath. during the rest of the journey. It took only a matter of days before two hundred thick woollen blankets were delivered, and the women cried with the comfort they gave. Elizabeth was forever grateful for her friend's generosity. She learned a valuable lesson— to ask for help earlier.

"Do you remember when you first came to work with me?" Jennifer asked, as she sat beside her friend on the settee in their tiny flat. "I didn't think you would survive."

"Me neither," laughed Elizabeth. "It seems like years ago, yet it's only been four months. We've seen some changes for the better. More food, more volunteers, another consultant on board, the health workers in the community, and of course the blankets."

"The numbers on the TB wards are down," continued Jennifer. "I'm confident that the health workers will eventually have some success in preventing the rapid spread of venereal disease, despite the appetites of the sailors and dockers."

Spring burst into Scotland with blossoms covering the fruit

trees in the parks and surrounding countryside. Doctor Hope, always on the edge of creative medical innovations, travelled to Manchester to attend a week of lectures. Presenters were renowned obstetricians and gynaecologists who shared their research and practical application to the hundreds of doctors and students in attendance. One presenting doctor in particular made an impression on Doctor Hope. An eminent surgeon, Doctor Julius LaPorte, gave a spell-binding lecture on his work at The North Staffordshire Royal Infirmary, performing caesarean section surgery. The surgery was revolutionary in Dr. Hope's eyes, as he compared it to the surgery he performed at several maternity hospitals in Glasgow. After the lecture Dr. Hope made a bee-line for Dr. LaPorte, who was being besieged by other doctors.

"Why don't we arrange to meet elsewhere!" shouted the surgeon as he was trapped into the corner of the lecture hall. "Give me an hour. I'll rustle up a meeting place in the meantime, and meet you in the lobby of The Britannia Hotel."

The crowd lessened their grip, allowing Dr LaPorte to escape. One hour later Dr. Hope, along with a few dozen others, were waiting in the lobby of the hotel.

As promised the surgeon ushered his crowd of admirers into a meeting room on the main floor, where chairs were already waiting.

"On behalf of us all, thank you, Dr. LaPorte, for doing this," said a young man from the front row. "I think we all have questions, and we really appreciate your time."

"Let's get on then," answered Julius LaPorte. "I would be happy to answer if I can."

The following two hours were filled with layer upon layer of questions and answers. Dr. Hope's head spun with all the incredible things he was learning. In addition to the verbal information, Dr. LaPorte made use of the blackboard and chalk on one of the walls, and drew diagrams with details of surgery, instruments used, anesthetics, and aftercare. The room buzzed with excitement as the men chatted about all they had learned in a few short hours. They would be returning to their own hospitals with an arsenal of new and creative ideas to improve maternity care.

Dr. Hope approached his new hero with some trepidation. The man had already been more than kind by inviting them all to two further hours of teaching.

"I wanted to thank you personally," Dr Hope said, shaking the hand of the surgeon. "Rarely do I have the opportunity to hear such a lecture, and this past two hours was a dream come true for me. I cannot thank you enough, and I cannot wait to get back to Glasgow to share the knowledge you have imparted."

Dr. LaPorte smiled and nodded.

"You are most welcome, Dr ?" he said, his head tilted to the side as he asked for a name.

"Dr. Hope, sir. I am a consultant at several Glasgow hospitals, but most of my work centers around The Glasgow Royal Maternity Hospital, which is a charity hospital for the poor. As you may imagine, the hospital has a very meagre budget, especially when it comes to surgical needs. What I have learned from you in just a few hours will make a difference. I wanted you to know that."

"Thank you, Dr. Hope. I think you are aptly named, sir."

CHAPTER 35

EXPERT ADVICE

W ith his head full of all he had learned, Doctor Hope told Elizabeth and Jennifer all about his meeting with Julius Laporte. Full of praise for the surgeon, he outlined some of the improvements they could implement in their own surgical unit.

"I hope you don't mind," Doctor Hope said as he hurried into the hospital two weeks later. "I've invited Doctor Laporte to visit us today. He is attending an alumni event at the University, and I wanted him to see the work we are doing here. He plans to arrive at about ten o'clock this morning. I thought that would be a good time. Rounds out of the way, so to speak!"

Nodding in agreement, Elizabeth and Jennifer looked at each other and frowned. It was always stressful to have visiting doctors descend on them in the middle of a busy morning. This doctor in particular was beyond intimidating. They both hoped there would be no last minute disasters to contend with. Mrs Gillingham was in labour, but it was her third baby, and they expected no complications—the midwives would attend to her. Marion McDonald however was another story. She was from the TB ward and needed close supervision as her labour progressed. Her pelvis was small, and she was so undernourished and frail, it would not be an easy delivery. Maybe it would progress slowly and give the doctors time to meet their visitor before having to attend.

As the clock in the front hallway struck ten, Dr. Laporte and two of his junior colleagues pushed open the door and greeted the waiting entourage with warm smiles and strong handshakes.

"Thank you for coming to visit us," Doctor Hope said. "We may not be up to the standards you are accustomed to, but we serve the poor women of Glasgow to the very best of our abilities. I think you will be surprised and pleased with the quality of care they receive, and the high standard of our nursing staff and volunteers—led, of course, by these two amazing young doctors, Doctor Jennifer McPhee and Doctor Elizabeth Lingford."

"Doctor Hope speaks very highly of you both," Julius Laporte said. "I'm looking forward to taking a look at your work here."

"It's a team effort, Doctor LaPorte," answered Elizabeth. "Our midwives and volunteers contribute as much, if not more, than the two of us. We serve a diverse and needy community."

The small group of doctors strolled through the wards, evoking curious stares from the rows of women lining the walls. Julius LaPorte stopped to speak to a number of the patients, who were mostly struck dumb by the handsome gentleman. A few of the more brazen of them in the VD ward answered him with an obscene comment, which he heard with a smile and moved on.

"Thank you," Doctor LaPorte said, shaking Doctor Hope's hand at the end of the tour. "It has been an eye-opening experience to say the least. You are indeed doing marvellous work here. I commend you all for the high standard you have set under immensely difficult circumstances."

"I am in Glasgow for one more day," the eminent doctor continued. "Would you do me the honour of joining me for dinner tonight at the Central Hotel?"

His eyes looked from Doctor Hope to Elizabeth and Jennifer, including all three of them in his invitation.

"I think I can answer for us all," Doctor Hope beamed. "We would be delighted."

"Let's say eight o'clock then," Doctor Laporte confirmed.

With midwives covering the evening shift, Elizabeth and Jennifer dressed for dinner and Doctor Hope picked them up outside the flat to drive them to the Central Hotel.

Dinner anywhere was a rarity for the two young doctors. Dinner at the Central Hotel as guests of a handsome and renowned doctor was unheard of.

Elizabeth sat opposite their host, uncomfortably aware of his eyes on hers during the meal. She learned he was a widower, having lost his wife ten years ago. Jennifer jumped in to tell him Elizabeth was widowed also, very tragically losing her husband in an accident. The grey eyes, full of sympathy, caught Elizabeth off guard and she bit her bottom lip and looked down quickly, not wanting him to see the grief written on her face.

"We share a common grief then," Doctor LaPorte said gently. "But let's not dwell on the past tonight. Let's look into the future stretched before us. Tell me about plans for the maternity hospital."

The conversation switched to medical talk, and they all participated in what their hopes and dreams might be for the future. Where improvements could be made. How more mothers and babies could be saved. How to fund more trained staff, more quality food, more equipment in wards and birthing rooms, an improved caesarean section surgery.

Doctor LaPorte expressed his desire to work more closely with the hospital. He offered to travel to Glasgow on a regular basis, to instruct and teach the surgery he performed to save a mother and baby in crises.

"My dear sir," Doctor Hope said, his face lighting up with excitement. "How can we ever thank, or repay you? Your intervention in the area of caesarean births would be life-changing for so many of our poor unfortunate women. I do my best with the little knowledge I have, but my skills are primitive, and under your guidance could be so much better."

"Agreed," chimed in Jennifer. "We lose many of our very young girls who cannot deliver their babies on their own."

Elizabeth smiled her agreement.

Doctor LaPorte travelled to Glasgow for three full days each month, bringing with him new surgical instruments donated from the hospital in North Staffordshire. Three young men who were studying at the university were soon part of his group of students, attending the surgical instruction the doctor conducted at the maternity hospital. They witnessed the superior surgical procedures the gifted doctor had refined, and in turn offered their help with caesarean operations when the eminent surgeon was not in town.

News spread quickly among the women of Glasgow that an assisted surgical birth when there was no other option was nothing to fear. The success of live births and mothers who recovered quickly from such intervention was proclaimed a miracle among them all.

Elizabeth assisted many such births, and rejoiced when she laid a healthy baby into the arms of a grateful mother. With the extra help of the three students, both young women doctors were able to reduce their long hours of work. They had Doctor LaPorte to thank.

CHAPTER 36

STEEL GREY EYES

Try as she might, Elizabeth couldn't stop thinking about Julius Laporte's steel grey eyes. He had been visiting and operating at the hospital for more than a year, and had affected every aspect of the small surgical unit. Sometimes his visits were untimely with no caesarean section procedures slated. It was on these visits that he busied himself reorganizing the surgery, consulting with Doctor Hope on upgrading equipment, as well as helping diagnose and treat some of the women brought into the hospital in dire need.

His visits always included dinner at his hotel for the three Glasgow doctors, and they formed a close relationship as they socialized and got to know each other better. On one such visit, Jennifer was away visiting family in England and Doctor Hope had a meeting of the city medical board. Elizabeth tried to make her excuses, but Doctor LaPorte wouldn't hear of her backing out of dinner with him.

"Elizabeth, how nice," her host greeted her as she joined him in the dining room of the Central Hotel. "Just the two of us".

"Yes, just the two of us," repeated Elizabeth, trying not to make contact with those eyes.

"I can recommend the halibut," Doctor Laporte chatted on.

"Freshly caught this morning I hear. They do a wonderful lemon sauce as a dressing. But I should let you browse through the menu and choose for yourself."

"Oh, the fish sounds excellent," Elizabeth replied. "Always my first choice, rather than a red meat."

She couldn't avoid looking at him forever. Raising her eyes to meet his, her heart flipped, and she hoped he wouldn't detect her reaction. He met her eyes and smiled, white even teeth showing below his greying moustache. He was many years her senior, and she couldn't imagine why she found his eyes so endearing. She felt she was betraying Elwyn somehow by being so attracted to this other man.

Doctor LaPorte ordered their food, and turned his attention back to Elizabeth.

"Now, tell me more about your home and family. You said you were from Suffolk. I am not familiar with that part of England."

"Yes, I was born in Suffolk, Doctor Laporte," Elizabeth answered.

"Stop!" her companion said quietly. "Julius, please. We have known each other far too long for you to keep calling me 'Doctor'."

Another skip of heart beats caught Elizabeth off guard. She quickly regathered her thoughts and continued. She told him about the estate and her father's influence on her life. She told him about the horses and how much they had meant to her growing up and how she had clung to them for refuge and rescue when life became intolerable.

He listened to it all as they ate their halibut and drank white wine. He was enchanted by her, and never wanted her to stop telling him her story, as he watched her full lush lips between bites of her food and her continuing saga.

He had completely devoted his life to his work since losing his wife so many years ago. What else was he to do? He had decided long ago that he would never meet anybody else. He didn't want to. He didn't need to. Now his senses were stood on their head with this beautiful young doctor sitting across from him. He had watched her work on the days he spent in the maternity hospital, admiring her from afar, not only for her beauty but for how she cared for each woman in her care. A genuine empathy emanated from Doctor Lingford, whether she was treating a young teenage prostitute or a middle-aged, poverty-stricken woman, who had been "caught" on her change of life with an unwanted pregnancy. Her manner never changed. She was never judgmental or condescending, but treated each patient as her equal.

Dessert was served, with Elizabeth choosing a chocolate soufflé, and Julius his favourite raspberry torte.

With her story half finished, Elizabeth looked over at her host, who smiled his encouragement for her to continue. She hesitated, knowing it would take some courage to call him by his first name.

"Well, Julius," she finally got it out. "I only skimmed through quickly, but I don't want to go into any detail about Elwyn, my husband. Only to say he was my everything, and losing him in a tragic accident has taken its toll. Coming to Glasgow was the best decision I could have made, and I am grateful every day for the people who have helped me recover and move on with my life."

"My dear," Julius said, taking her hand in his. "I am familiar with this journey you have been on. I buried myself in my work after losing Phylis. Until now my life has been occupied with only hospitals, patients and the next surgery."

Elizabeth left her hand in his, and met his eyes, drinking in the affection she read in them. They sat silently holding their gaze until the waiter came to clear the table.

Laughing, Julius ordered coffee and chocolate.

"Now you know my secret," he smiled. "Elizabeth, you have turned me inside out. I think about you every minute, and the time drags by endlessly when I am not with you. I suppose, because this has come as such a shock to me, and after years of living alone, I feel brave enough to share my feelings with you. I loved Phylis. Now, impossibly to me, I think I love you more. I am hoping you are not thinking me an old fool at this moment."

"No, not a fool, Julius," Elizabeth assured him. "I really do not know what to say. I would be lying if I told you I felt nothing for you. Your eyes have haunted me since the day we first met. You are everything I admire most in a man, and I feel wonderful when you are near. I would like to know you better though. This is the first time we have been alone together, and I am overpowered by your candour. Can we spend some time together? Just the two of us?"

"You are unbelievable," Julius said. "You are not dismissing me with no hope, and I am content with that. Yes, yes, we must be together. Can you get away for a weekend perhaps? Could it be soon?"

Elizabeth laughed, and Julius joined in.

"What?"

"You. You are in such a hurry. I will talk to Jennifer about covering for me. Would next weekend be too far away to satisfy you?"

"Elizabeth," Doctor Laporte said quietly. "It would be perfect. Too long to wait, but I can do it."

CHAPTER 37

NEW LOVE

Loch Lomond sparkled in the sunshine and welcomed Doctors LaPorte and Lingford for their weekend away. The Lodge was comfortable and quiet. Julius had booked two rooms overlooking the water. Elizabeth did not share any details with her friend, Jennifer, but allowed her to believe she was visiting Gordon House as she normally did several weekends during the year.

Butterflies in her stomach was an understatement. 'More like bats,' Elizabeth thought as she sat beside Julius in his sports car motoring the twenty-five miles from Glasgow to the Loch.

Settled into their rooms by eleven o'clock, the two doctors set off for a walk along the lakeside path. This is what they both desired, time alone together. They were silent at first, just enjoying walking side by side in the fresh air, both of them engrossed in their own thoughts. Past loves and future dreams occupying their minds.

As they reached a rustic wooden bench set in a grove of trees, they stopped to rest.

"Beautiful, isn't it?" Elizabeth said, gazing out across the rippling water.

"Yes, indeed," answered her companion, looking directly at Elizabeth, making her blush with the inference.

They talked about the happy times they each remembered. Elizabeth telling about her time at Oxford after the pandemic, when the colleges came to life again, and she met Elwyn. Julius told her about his time at Glasgow University, when life was one big party, where he made life-long friends.

They took a small sailboat out in the afternoon. Julius gave instructions as he steered into the wind and Elizabeth enjoyed learning to tack. They moored in a tiny inlet safe from the breeze and ate the scrumptious scones the Lodge had packed for them, washed down with a bottle of red wine.

Julius was relaxed and happy. He took Elizabeth's hand and drew her closer to him.

"It is time," he muttered, bending his head down to kiss her upturned lips.

A kiss, that is all it was. A kiss so sweet it stayed on their lips as they pressed body against body, arms wrapped around each other. Long ago memories sent fleeing. Only the present remained. Lips coming together again. This time apart and wanting more.

Julius had never felt like this in his life. The passion rose in him like a storm, catching him unawares and causing his breath to come in quick pants of desire. He held his love so close he could feel her breasts pushing against his chest and feel the bone of her pelvis making him crazy.

Elizabeth gasped for air as the kisses left her defenceless in their urgency. She opened her mouth wider to let him taste more of her and could feel his desire pushing against her. Lost in her own passion, she would have sunk to her knees and given herself to him right there, if he hadn't had such a firm grasp on her.

Julius stood very still, stopping himself with great difficulty from ravaging her. He held her to him gently now, drinking in the scent of her hair, the softness of her forehead against his cheek, and the wonder of feeling so much love for a woman, something he never imagined would happen.

"Julius," Elizabeth whispered. "It is good that we came away together. You have captured my heart, and your kisses have awakened my soul. I never thought I could want another man, but I want you, my dear Doctor LaPorte. I want all of you."

"Darling Elizabeth," Julius said, his eyes welling with tears. "You are beyond my wildest dreams."

He began to laugh. Tossing back his head and laughing out loud with pure joy.

"I am thinking that a boat is not the ideal spot to make love. Many hazards. We will find a better place, you and I. Although waiting for even a few hours may make me crazy."

It was late afternoon when they reached the lodge. Dinner was at 8:00pm, so they had ample time together before they dined.

"I am going to take advantage of the deep tub and have a luxurious bath," Elizabeth said as she headed for her room. "Will you wait for me?"

Julius nodded his agreement as he stood at the door to his room.

As she soaked up to her neck in rose-scented bubbles Elizabeth relived the afternoon on the boat and smiled. Too bad it was a shared bathroom with the whole second floor of the lodge, or she could have invited Julius to bathe with her. No matter. She would go to him freshly bathed and smelling of roses.

She returned to her room wrapped in the white bathrobe, which covered her from shoulders to ankles. Her hair was piled on top of her head, and little curls escaped around her face making her look like a young girl again. Julius was laying in her bed covered with a sheet, and watched her as she closed and locked the door. She untied the bathrobe and let it fall to her feet, completely at ease with his eyes on her. She pulled out the hairpins and let her hair cascade around her as she walked towards the bed.

"It has been a very long time Elizabeth," Julius admitted.

"Hush, my dear man," she said. "Let us enjoy this time together."

She pulled the sheet away from him so that she could see him. Julius was suddenly embarrassed. His experience in the past had always been in the dark, and well-covered with bed sheets and blankets. To be so exposed was something new. Elizabeth lay beside him, stroking him and kissing him until he almost lost control of his senses. As he slipped inside her, he was filled with such love for her it consumed him body and soul. This was where they needed to be. This was love.

They slept in the same bed that night, making love before they went to sleep and again first thing in the morning light. Their lives would never be the same. They had to be together somehow.

CHAPTER 38

JULIUS

J ulius LaPorte had a lot to think about as he travelled south the next day, leaving his beloved Elizabeth in Glasgow to continue her work.

He had fallen into a pace of life that suited him over the years since he became a widower. His work filled his days, and sometimes his nights. His home was efficiently run by Mrs Wheaton, the housekeeper, with daily help coming and going to take care of other duties like cooking, gardening, and cleaning. Mrs Wheaton took care of everything so that the doctor's home life was without stress. For Julius, time in the house meant listening to music on the newly acquired gramophone, reading a favourite book, or tending his collection of African Violet plants.

As a young man studying medicine at Glasgow University, he had fallen in love with Phylis Wright, a history student. They married after Julius had graduated and settled in Staffordshire, where Phylis' father owned a pottery factory. Their wedding present was the house he now occupied in the southern most town of Stoke-on-Trent.

With the help of his father-in-law's acquaintances, Julius had been given a junior position at The North Staffordshire Royal Infirmary. It was a general surgery job, covering a wide variety of operations, and he gained a wealth of experience as he watched and learned from experienced doctors. He was kept busy assisting with major, complicated surgeries, as well as working alone on the easier work.

He never forgot the cold March morning he was called to the operating room to scrub up and help with his first caesarean section surgery. The mother's pelvis was narrow and she had struggled for hours trying to birth the baby the natural way. She was exhausted and there was fear for the baby's life.

Julius had performed several appendectomies and bowel obstructions, so was confident he knew his way around the lower abdomen. He was amazed how different everything looked inside a pregnant woman. The uterus full of baby made the surgery a whole new experience. He helped Doctor Phillips cut through layer upon layer of skin, muscle and fat. Finally, there it was—pink, shiny and strong. Holding a tiny life inside it safe and secure. The final cut into the womb was the hardest layer to get through, but once it was made the baby was right there. Doctor Phillips put his hand into the opening and grasped the baby. A baby girl in full voice announced her arrival. Julius was enraptured.

After removing the placenta, Doctor Phillips left Julius to close the layers of tissue, which took a long time. He took his time, making sure the rows of stitches were secure and clean so that there would be less chance of infection or postpartum problems.

That first caesarean had been two decades ago, and since then Julius had lost count of the times he had brought a baby into the world that way. He had devoted his surgical practice to learning, developing and perfecting the life-saving operation. Mothers and babies had been lost over the years, but Julius celebrated every mother and baby who benefited from his expertise and thrived. He visited each patient every day during their hospital stay, not only checking her condition and surgical incision, but often picking up the baby and gently holding it for a few moments, in awe of the miracle of life.

Now, he was beginning a new phase of his life. He was to marry Elizabeth, and he pondered the many changes that would bring for both of them.

In Glasgow, Elizabeth's mind was in a similar turmoil. So many changes! So many things to consider! Yet nothing would deter her from the path ahead. Waking each morning with Julius beside her was what she wanted more than anything in the world.

It took a brief three months to put all the pieces in place. Doctor Julius LaPorte and Doctor Elizabeth Lingford would be married on September eighteenth, 1927.

The weeks before leaving Glasgow had been a whirlwind of planning as Elizabeth prepared for her wedding. Sir Kenneth insisted the nuptials be at her second home in Scotland, where she had put down an anchor.

"My dearest Elizabeth," Sir Kenneth had said. "Please agree to our offer to hold your wedding here at Gordon House. It would be the greatest gift to Jocelyn and myself. Having met Julius several times, we know he is the very best of men. Indeed he is also the very luckiest of men to have won your heart."

"You are like a father to me, Sir Kenneth," Elizabeth answered. "I will talk it over with Julius, but already know he will agree with anything that makes me happy.

"I would also be honoured to give you away in place of your Papa, if you would allow me."

Elizabeth answered him with a hug, kissing his rugged cheek, and whispering, "Yes please," into his ear.

Julius was delighted with the proposition of a wedding at Gordon House. He had an elderly aunt living in Wales who probably couldn't make the journey, but other than that he had no other family. Three of his close colleagues and friends would be his only guests.

Arrangements were made for the Lingford family to travel

from Suffolk, and stay at Gordon House. The family had grown in the past year to include another boy, born to Lydia, plus Carolyn's fiance Jacob Shaftsbury. Elizabeth invited Callum McCarthy too, but he declined her invitation due to his declining health and advanced age. Elizabeth wrote a long letter to him in reply, expressing her disappointment.

> *You are my oldest and dearest friend. I will miss you not being at my wedding. I so wanted you to meet my Julius LaPorte. You would like him. He is quiet and thoughtful and loves me more than I deserve. I also wanted you to see Sir Kenneth's stables here at Gordon house, and maybe ride with you. The trails are challenging and amazingly beautiful, with views of the ocean at every turn. My favourite mount is called Highland Lass. Appropriately named, don't you think? She reminds me of Silver Buttons. Same temperament!*
>
> *Oh, my friend, what trials you have seen me through. You have encouraged and supported me through the very worst of my days. I wanted you to see me on what will be the best, most happy of my days. I pray your health will improve, and I make you a promise that I will visit you as soon as I can after I am wed.*
>
> *Your ever devoted friend,*
> *Elizabeth*

The bride-to-be shed a tear as she sealed the envelope, and vowed she would keep her promise to see him soon.

CHAPTER 39

UNKNOWN FUTURE

T he final day at The Royal Glasgow was among the most difficult Elizabeth had endured. She walked with Doctor Hope through the wards one last time and embraced him on the steps, not able to utter a word except a choked "Thank you." She hugged each midwife and volunteer. Every one had earned Elizabeth's love and respect, and she shed a tear as she accepted their parting gift of a small stone mother and child carving, which she would treasure forever.

"I cannot bear the thought of you leaving the hospital," Jennifer cried as she clung onto Elizabeth. "My dear friend, I love you like a sister, and will miss you every minute of each day."

"More than sisters," she whispered, their tears melding on their cheeks. "Only the greatest love could have dragged me away from you. I will carry the memories of all we have shared for ever."

Gordon House was a profusion of fresh flowers for the wedding on September eighteenth. The gardeners had cut and delivered masses of hydrangeas, gladiolas, and dahlias, and a talented group of floral arrangers worked to create a beautiful display in the summerhouse, where the ceremony would take place. The last of the summer heather was gathered from the hill-sides around the estate to adorn the staircase in the hall, filling the air with its wild perfume. Bowls of roses sat on tables and in window ledges, showing off their array of colourful beauty.

As they waited for the ceremony to begin, Lady Lingford sat with Cousin Jocelyn in the midst of all the floral glory and drank in both the fragrance of the flowers and the atmosphere. Cousin Jocelyn was a gracious host, and the entire Lingford clan had been welcomed into Gordon House most generously. The entire upstairs west wing had been prepared for them, giving them ample and luxurious space during their stay. The two nannies accompanying the family were accommodated close at hand and took care of the four youngest family members with care and efficiency.

"Cousin Jocelyn," Lady Lingford said. "I must confide in you that I am extremely happy with the choice Elizabeth has made *this time*. A renowned surgeon, despite the age difference between them, seems to me to be a worthy partner. Of course, if Elizabeth had done as her parents wished, she would not have gone off to Oxford and pursued the career she chose."

"Cousin Maud," Jocelyn whispered in reply. "Sir Kenneth and I have met Doctor LaPorte several times, and hold him in the highest regard. He is indeed a perfect partner for our dear girl. Elizabeth is the daughter we never had and we couldn't have chosen a better life companion for her."

Sir Kenneth drew Elizabeth's hand through his arm and squeezed her hand.

"Ready?" he murmured.

"Yes," said Elizabeth, smiling up at him through her veil.

Sir Kenneth nodded to the piper, who stood waiting for his signal, and as he began to play they walked slowly down the aisle, filled with family and friends, towards Julius. The summer-house looked like a small church, with windows on every side and the sun gleaming through trees that cast flickering shadows onto the gathering. The bride's cream coloured silk dress was classic. No lace or embellishments, but it fit perfectly, the skirt flowing to the floor and rustling as she moved towards her waiting groom.

Promises exchanged, blessings given, register signed, and it was all accomplished in what seemed to Elizabeth a very short time. Unlike her first wedding, it was witnessed by her family and friends, and she etched every moment into her memory. She was Mrs. Julius LaPorte, and it felt so right.

The day passed in a swirl of happiness, a wedding feast only Cousin Jocelyn could have planned. The platters of venison, duck, beef wellington, and salmon were surrounded by trays of vegetables, fruits, cheese, and bread of every kind. Sauces, gravies, and a variety of wines added to the decadent fare. Plates for the children were specially prepared, with enough mouth-watering bites to tempt the most picky eater.

The guests chose from several richly decorated gateaux for dessert, served with fresh fruit and cream. After the tiered wedding cake was duly sliced by the bride and groom, Sir Kenneth presented them with the traditional quaich[1]–a two handled "loving cup" containing whiskey for them to share. Their union was considered sealed by the old tradition.

"Are you happy, dearest?" Julius whispered into his bride's ear.

"Happier than I ever imagined, my love," replied a radiant Elizabeth.

Toasts to the bride and groom were gloriously never-ending. The guests raised their glasses and drank to everyone, until every face was glowing with the effect of the wine and whiskey. Even Lady Lingford's usual stern countenance was transformed, as she laughed and burped and laughed again.

Everybody gathered on the front steps of Gordon House to wave farewell to the newlyweds. Elizabeth hugged her family

---

1. Ancient traditional Scottish drinking vessel. Gaelic 'coach' meaning 'cup'. Symbol of trust and unity.

and promised to visit Lingford Manor soon. She turned to say another tearful goodbye to Jennifer McPhee and Doctor Hope, with one more promise to stay in touch.

Saying goodbye to Cousin Jocelyn and dear Sir Kenneth was more difficult. Their eyes filled with tears as they drew her close.

"Goodbye my dear girl," Sir Kenneth choked. "These have been the happiest days of my life, since you came to stay. Thank you for giving an old man your friendship. I will miss you terribly, Elizabeth."

"I will come and ride with you whenever I can," Elizabeth promised kissing his wrinkled cheek. "You filled the void my father left, and I love you."

She ran down the steps to join Julius in the car.

She waved until she couldn't see them any more, and Gordon House faded into the distance.

CHAPTER 40

A HOUSE NOT A HOME

E lizabeth stretched and yawned, then reached for the
warm body beside her. He was laying on his side
facing the window, his regular slow breath telling his
wife that he was still sleeping. She moved behind him and slid
her arm around his body, holding him close, and pressed her
cheek between his shoulders. He smelled of Pears soap. He
stirred as he felt her presence next to him.

"Mmmm," he murmured. "What a lovely way to wake up."

The small hotel in the Lake District was isolated and quiet,
the perfect place for their honeymoon. In the life of two busy
doctors it was an oasis of comfort, somewhere to relax and rest
before they resumed their careers and jumped into medical practice once more.

Julius didn't roll over to face his wife, but reached to find her
with his left hand. She guided his hand between her legs and
raised her nightgown so that he could caress her. Adept fingers,
so experienced in surgery, touched her gently making her gasp
with pleasure. When she could stand no more, Julius turned
towards her, then over her and into her.

"Amazing," Julius moaned. "How was I ever lucky enough
to find you?"

"We found each other," Elizabeth whispered, her teeth finding his ear as he collapsed onto her.

They walked around lakes and trekked through the hills. They ate pot pie and drank beer in the local pub. They lay in the grass and watched the stars come out. They read books and made love in their cozy bedroom. Four days flew by too quickly.

A whole new chapter of their lives was about to begin. They headed south to Staffordshire to start life together as man and wife.

Surrounded by streets of dingy Victorian terraced homes, stood a big white house with double oak doors. The interior was elegantly and tastefully decorated, the rooms large and airy. The housekeeper, Mrs. Wheaton had her rooms on the top floor and, with the help of a daily cook and maid, kept the large house in perfect order.

The imprint of Phylis, the first Mrs. Laporte, was everywhere. Her ghost lingered in the rooms through portraits, ornaments, a handmade lap blanket on the drawing room sofa, perfumed soap in the bathroom, lace curtains at the windows. Everywhere Elizabeth looked was a reminder that she was the second wife.

Mrs. Wheaton seemed to consider the new mistress an intruder. Obviously younger by years than Doctor LaPorte, the housekeeper believed he must be infatuated with her beauty, and was convinced Elizabeth had wheedled her way into his life.

The atmosphere was claustrophobic for Elizabeth from the beginning, and she avoided any interaction with Mrs. Wheaton, and left her to manage the daily chores of running the house.

Doctor Julius returned to work at the hospital immediately upon their return, leaving his wife to settle in. Elizabeth hated having nothing to do except wander around the house. She desperately needed to have a purpose in her life. She missed the working and riding. A position at the hospital where Julius worked was out of the question, he had explained. Despite her experience in Glasgow, a woman doctor would not be allowed to practice at "The North Staffs", particularly when her husband was head of obstetric surgery.

"Julius, I have to talk to you," Elizabeth began. They had finished eating an excellent dinner prepared by the cook, Joan Turner, and served by the young daily maid, Bertha. Joan Turner liked the new Mrs LaPorte and enjoyed meeting with her to discuss menus. The difference of opinion about Elizabeth had caused a rift between cook and housekeeper, but Joan Turner stood her ground with the sour Mrs Wheaton, and made an extra effort to prepare Elizabeth's favourite foods.

"What is it, dear?" Julius responded. "You know you can talk to me about anything. Is something bothering you?"

Elizabeth rose from her seat at the table and beckoned her husband to bring his brandy into the adjoining sitting room. His brow furrowed into a frown as he followed her. She had been unusually quiet since coming to the house two weeks ago. They sat close together on the softly cushioned sofa.

"I want to begin by telling you how much I love and adore you," Elizabeth said. "Your house is beautiful. I can see why you love living here. But it's YOUR house. Yours and Phylis's. I may be over-sensitive, but I cannot stop imagining her in every room I walk into."

"Darling," Julius interrupted.

"No, no, please let me finish."

She kissed him on his mouth, and grasped his hand.

"Would you consider moving to another house? I know it has only been a short time, but I do not feel we can make our life together until we have truly begun again, in our own home. Try to understand, dearest. I want our home to be a place we both enjoy, full of the things we love. The furnishings from this house for instance, and my old pictures I have stored at Lingford Manor. What do you think? Is it too much to ask so soon?"

"Always ask, Elizabeth," Julius answered. "Never keep your

thoughts from me. You are part of me, and I want us to talk freely about how we feel and what we are thinking. Are you not happy, darling?"

"Happy being married to you," answered Elizabeth. "But can we begin our life together in a home we choose together? A home with no past history? Somewhere I can begin practicing medicine again. With no hope of working in a hospital, the only option is for me to begin my own surgery. Please say you support me in this, Julius."

"That is a lot to think about," Julius said softly.

He drew her into a standing position and put his arms around her, holding her close. He admitted to himself that he had given little thought to his wife continuing her medical practice. An absurd idea, now he thought about it. He had seen her absorbed in her work at the Glasgow hospital, and knew how much it meant to her. He squeezed his eyes shut and reprimanded himself for doing what just about every man in his position would have done—to expect his wife to stay at home and be a lady.

"We will begin again, my dearest," he said. "I apologize for not considering you. I blindly went ahead with my own life, not missing a beat, and expected you to fall in behind me. When all along you should have been by my side, not behind me. What an appalling lack of caring on my part. Forgive my ignorance."

"You are an amazing man," Elizabeth said, looking up into his beautiful eyes. "We were both swept away with love for each other, that we didn't stop to make decisions about the future, except that we wanted to be married so that we could be together forever."

He kissed the tip of her nose, and drew her close.

"If it's what you want, then I want it too," he said. "I am actually a bit ahead of you on this. I have had my eye on a property about two miles from here for a number of years. I almost made enquiries about it before we met, but never seemed to get around to it. I believe it belonged to a sea captain at one time, but it has been sadly neglected and unoccupied for some time. Let's take a drive so that you can see it for yourself."

Julius parked the car alongside a large red brick house on the corner of two tree-lined streets only a short walk from the hustle and bustle of the town's main road.

"Try to look past the obvious, darling," Julius said, as he helped his wife out of the car. "It has been empty for many years, but it is well built and in a great location. With a lick of paint and repairs it could be restored to its former glory. Shall we make enquiries and ask for a key to take a look inside?"

Elizabeth walked around the garden, looking up at the dirty windows and chipped paint. The broken steps up to the front door, and the pile of rubble at the side door where a small wall had collapsed. It was, however, an impressive building with three floors, large bay windows, heavy wooden doors, and a feeling of permanency about it.

"Why has nobody purchased it in all this time?" she asked.

"Probably the cost, I would say," answered Julius. "The factory owners all have homes outside the city now, and who else could afford a big rambling place like this?"

A key was procured from the agent in town, and, with some trepidation, Julius and Elizabeth returned to view the interior.

Julius put the key into the old lock and opened the door; the old hinges squealed their objection.

Dust filled their nostrils and scratched their eyes as they disturbed years of neglect. A ghostly scene lay before them. Cobwebs and dust clung to every surface in the empty, echoing rooms. A once beautiful curved wooden staircase led upstairs from the spacious front hallway. The three reception rooms had high ceilings and splendid fireplaces. The kitchen needed a complete overhaul as an old black cook stove, open fireplace with hob, and an antiquated cast-iron sink with a single brass tap, were the only fixtures.

Elizabeth raised her eyebrows and looked up at her husband, who returned her questioning eyes with an assuring smile.

"Let's keep going, dearest," was his only comment.

Three small rooms led from the kitchen, probably used for pantries or storage. Another small reception room with a fireplace and large window led to a hallway and door to the side of the house. Steps into the cellar were behind an interior door off the hall.

Leaving their footprints in the dust the two doctors made their way upstairs. The first floor landing led to four spacious and light-filled bedrooms, each with its own fireplace. Two water closets had been modernized somewhat, and had running cold water and flush toilets. The second floor, servants quarters, housed a cluster of small dark rooms, lit only by dormer windows under the eaves. Two water closets, furnished with commodes, wash basins and tin sitting tubs were placed in the centre of the corridor, appropriately labelled 'men' and 'women.'

They locked the wooden front door behind them and stood in the garden staring up once more at the old house.

"It needs a great deal of work," ventured Julius.

Elizabeth smiled in agreement. She could read on his face that he was hoping she would find something positive to say. She struggled to find anything.

CHAPTER 41

EXCITING PLANS

Julius purchased number fifty-eight Blackstone Road for a considerably reduced price, two weeks after they had been to see it. He was convinced it was the right decision, and that the splendid old house would be their permanent home. He spent hours telling his wife about his plans, winning her over by his enthusiasm.

"The sitting room at the side of the house would be perfect as a waiting room," he explained. "The two smaller rooms ideal for consulting, don't you think?"

Elizabeth smiled her agreement. It did sound exactly how she had imagined it.

Now they were at the point of no return. The house they now occupied had already been purchased by the owner of a building company, who was prepared to wait for occupancy.

Mrs Wheaton had given notice as soon as Doctor Laporte told her about the upcoming move, and she left without a word to Elizabeth. Joan Turner and Bertha both agreed to work extra hours to help pack and organize the contents of the house. With Julius in tow, Elizabeth went through each room, and tied a small blue ribbon to each item he wanted to keep. The rest, mostly purchased by Phylis LaPorte, was picked up by Louis Taylor's auction house.

A long list sat on the table in front of Elizabeth. She eyed it with dismay, attempting to put it in some order of preference. Written in her husband's impeccable handwriting, it listed the essential upgrades needed, the materials required, and the suggested tradesmen for the work.

Elizabeth scribbled notes beside each item on the list. Work was to begin the following week, when tradesmen would arrive at the house on Blackstone Road to transform it into a liveable space. Builders, carpenters, plumbers and interior decorators had been employed and Julius had found a foreman to oversee the proceedings.

According to the foreman, Albert Johnson, the house would be ready for occupancy by the following February.

Putting aside the list, Elizabeth thought about the promises she had made to two very important men. Autumn was rapidly turning into winter. They had already planned to travel to Lingford Manor for Christmas, where she could see Calum McCarthy, but there was only a small window of time for her to fulfil her obligation to travel north to ride with Sir Kenneth.

"Of course you must go," Julius said, when she asked him his advice that evening. "In fact, I will purposely make it my business to visit Doctor Hope in Glasgow. That way, I can drive you to Gordon House and back. There, it's all fixed up."

"My darling man," Elizabeth said. "I wish I could do something special for you."

"You do, every time we are together," Julius whispered huskily. "Being near you is all the 'something special' I could ever want or need."

Words were extinguished with kisses. With no housekeeper to consider, clothes were scattered to the floor. One of the sofas, destined for the auction house, provided a cozy spot for them to make love.

The renovations were left in the capable hands of Albert Johnson, and Doctor and Mrs LaPorte travelled north.

Sir Kenneth and Cousin Jocelyn welcomed them both with great joy.

"My dears, we have been counting the days since the wedding, and hoping you would return quickly for a visit," gushed Jocelyn.

"Indeed," said Sir Kenneth.

As he kissed Elizabeth on her cheek, he whispered "Are we riding tomorrow?"

Elizabeth smiled up at him, her eyes shining as she gave him a nod.

Julius left for Glasgow after dinner. He could tell by her countenance that his wife was already preoccupied thinking about her morning ride.

Three days of riding through the wilderness around Gordon House with Sir Kenneth at her side elated Elizabeth's spirit. Memories from the past flooded her mind as she drank in the smell of the straw in the stables, and felt the leather saddle between her thighs, the warm breath of Highland Lass on her cheek as she stroked her face, and the exhilaration of the wind in her face. She felt so alive. So free.

Julius joined them at Gordon House after three days working alongside Doctor Hope in Glasgow. He noticed immediately how radiant his wife looked, and promised himself that upon their return to the midlands he would seek out a local stable. Not for the first time he chastised himself on not seeing the obvious —Elizabeth needed horses around her; she needed to ride.

The first morning back at the hospital in Stoke, Julius sat sipping a much-needed cup of tea after performing a particularly difficult surgery: twin boys, who were tucked in together so tightly, it was a challenge to disentangle them and bring them both safely out of the womb. He looked around at the nurses and doctors gathered in the small tea room and smiled to himself. The usual chatter was about the surgery they had just been a part of, or the surgery yet to come, or the lack of sleep, or the longing for a plate of bacon and eggs with the local oatcakes[1] on the side. He broke the chatter with his question about nearby riding stables, and was rewarded with a quick answer.

According to one of Julius's colleagues, the small village of Endon was the place to find the best stables near the city. His daughter had a horse at the Granger estate, and spoke highly of the facility. He offered to set up a visit for Julius when he drove his daughter at the weekend.

"Where are we going?" Elizabeth asked. It was early Saturday morning and Julius had dispensed with the usual morning cuddles in bed, and thrown back the bed covers.

"Up you get," he shouted. "We need an early start."

After a quick breakfast of scrambled eggs and toast, they were now on their way.

"What's the secret?" Elizabeth continued to question.

"No secret. Just a surprise," grinned Julius.

The grimy streets were left behind and the countryside spread out before them. The narrow lanes between farmer's fields led to a small village, and from there to a rambling estate, where they turned into the tree-lined driveway up to an impressive white manor house.

"Who lives here? Are we visiting somebody?"

Julius drove around the house and parked in the spacious yard. A tall middle-aged gentleman appeared from a back door and strode over to the parked car. He introduced himself as Donald Martindale, stable master, and invited them to join him on a tour of the stables at the far end of the yard.

"What is going on?" whispered Elizabeth as they walked.

---

1. Oatcakes - Soft, yeasty oatmeal pancakes. Cooked on a griddle, size of a crepe. Eaten with savoury fillings.

"I thought you may like to ride regularly, so we're here to find you a horse," Julius explained. "I saw how much you enjoyed riding with Sir Kenneth in Scotland, and I wanted to surprise you. Horses have always been such an important part of your life, from a child, and it would give me the greatest pleasure for you to continue to enjoy your passion. Am I being too presumptuous?"

"You are incorrigible," Elizabeth said. "Of course I would love to ride, but you should have discussed it with me, darling. I have my own ideas of a good stable and an even better idea of a good horse."

"Nothing is set in stone, my dear," Julius told her. "This is only a visit to a very well renowned stable in close proximity to where we live. You will lead the way in this from here. It will be your decision whether or not it is a suitable stable, and you will certainly be in charge when it comes to selecting a horse."

Donald Martindale smiled to himself as he listened to the conversation behind him. He was confident that Doctor Elizabeth would find what she was looking for at his stables.

Everything about the Granger Manor stables impressed Elizabeth. They were similar to Lingford in so many ways. Decades of careful breeding had produced dozens of fine horses, many of which had gone on to race at the most prestigious race courses in the country. As Donald showed them around, Elizabeth stopped at several stalls to stroke the beautiful animals. Two young grooms led five horses into the stable yard for the guests to take a better look. Each horse was paraded in a circle, and then halted so that Elizabeth could approach, and examine them individually. They were all impressive specimens.

What would Callum think? How would he assess them?

Using the skills she had learned from her dear old friend at Lingford Manor, Elizabeth chose a young chestnut filly named Blue Shadow. She was lean with good muscle tone, and she responded when Elizabeth talked to her by nuzzling Elizabeth's neck.

With surprising ease Julius made the arrangements with the stable master for Blue Shadow's transfer of ownership, and room and board. Nothing would change for the mare, only the new rider, who she would come to trust and adore. Elizabeth became a frequent visitor at Granger stables, riding three or four days every week, despite the often times bleak weather.

As promised, Christmas was celebrated with the Lingford family, in the customary decadent way. Days of feasts and parties, attended by neighbours and friends from across the county. Lingford Manor bustled with the energy of the youngest members of the family, who seemed to never stop moving.

Elizabeth escaped to visit Callum McCarthy after two exhausting days.

She found him much changed. He was gaunt and grey-haired, and felt frail beneath her hands as she embraced him. The light still glistened in his eyes when she told him about Blue Shadow, and he shared his young mistress's delight as she described the beautiful mare.

"I would love to ride with you Miss Elizabeth," Callum said. "But these old bones are done with riding I'm afraid."

"Then come down to the stables with me, dear friend, and help me choose a horse that would suit me while I'm visiting."

"That I can do, and with pleasure," said the old stable master, rising to his feet and reaching for his warm jacket. "I know the very one. A fine older mare, who is still up to a good ride across the land. You may remember her. Sweet Charlotte is her name."

Tears welled in Elizabeth's eyes. Of course she remembered.

CHAPTER 42

HOME AT LAST

Riding Sweet Charlotte through the light dusting of snow on the ground, Elizabeth's life flickered in her memory like a much-loved book. So familiar, so wondrous, despite the tragedies along the way. Her face glowed and her eyes shone as she galloped under the trees with the wind whipping around her. Her heart ached for her Papa, so sadly missed on mornings like this.

Julius watched his wife striding across the stable yard after her ride. How beautiful she was. He was overcome with love for her, and so thankful that she had Blue Shadow near to home to, in some small way, replace what she had here at Lingford Manor.

During their stay in Suffolk, Elizabeth gathered together her belongings to send to Staffordshire. Pictures of Oxford and Venice, boxes of favourite books, including medical reference tomes, and her father's chess set. Hidden under a dust sheet in her bedroom was Elwyn's desk. How excited they had been when they had bought it. Now she would use it in her practice—a reminder of the wonderful man she had loved and lost. It didn't make her sad any more to think of him, and the sturdy wooden desk with all its drawers would serve her well in her new venture.

Julius visited the renovation site as often as he could, but Elizabeth didn't want to see it until it was complete. The image in her mind was of a dirty, dusty, cobwebby old building, not fit to live in. She wanted her first visit to transform that image. Even though Julius described what was being accomplished after every trip, she had a struggle imagining how it looked.

Everything was packed and ready to go by the end of January. Joan Turner, along with Bertha worked alongside their mistress to take care of the final details. Joan somehow prepared food despite all the chaos, carrying into the dining room shepherds pie or beef stew, accompanied by her famous scones. Julius and Elizabeth insisted that Joan and Bertha sat down with them to eat, and they had many happy times sitting around the table eating the delicious food and laughing about the mess they were in.

Joan Turner had been widowed for several years, and although she was now close to forty years of age, she agreed to move to the new house as a live-in housekeeper and cook. Bertha too was delighted to be given room and board with the two doctors. The eldest of eight siblings, she looked forward to having her own room, and regular meals. She felt more a part of Elizabeth's family than she did her own.

How could Elizabeth ever have imagined anything on the scale of the renovation to the house on Blackstone Road. She walked from room to room in a daze, wondering to herself if this was the same house she had walked through three months before. Nothing was the same!

From the entrance hall with its mosaic tiled floor and refinished magnificent oak staircase, to the high-ceilinged reception rooms painted in the palest blue. Joan Turner had been consulted at every stage regarding equipping the kitchen, and Elizabeth gasped in surprise when she saw the finished product. The tiled black and white floor reflected the light from the new wide kitchen window. Everything Joan had dreamed of had a place: a beautiful black gas stove, a Welsh Dresser for all her baking supplies, a shiny kitchen sink big enough for the largest pots, a sturdy wooden kitchen table with four chairs, hanging racks for pots and pans, cupboards and shelves to store everything they owned.

Upstairs the four bedrooms each had their own colour scheme with plush carpets and velvet drapes. Elizabeth had chosen a pale green for their bedroom, and it took her breath away to see the finished room. The bathrooms had been refitted with the very latest tubs and wash basins, complete with mirrors and shelving for toiletries. Two lavatories, equipped with a pull flush, were located beside the bathrooms. The top floor was inviting and light, with newly painted walls and doors. Light sconces had been installed between each room, giving the long hallway a comfortable warm glow. Instead of eight small rooms, there were now four lovely double rooms, each furnished with two single beds, bedside tables, a small wardrobe and a desk and chair. Each room had a fireplace with a small armchair beside it, which made it feel cozy and homely. The water closets and bathrooms had been updated to the highest standard.

The furniture Julius had chosen to bring with him fit perfectly into the drawing room and dining room. The rest of the house, including the bedrooms, had been outfitted with new furnishings, chosen by Elizabeth and Julius. Their personal collections of art and ornaments completed the sense of belonging they both imagined.

The doctor's surgery and waiting room was ready for Elizabeth to set up. The only piece of furniture in the space was Elwyn's desk, which stood in her consulting room, ready for her to use. She imagined what it would look like with an examining table, filing cabinets, chairs, pictures on the walls, and a fire burning in the grate. There would also be an area where children could play or look at a book while they waited. She couldn't contain her excitement!

Julius waited expectantly for his wife's reaction, and when she joined him in the hallway, he hurried towards her.

"Well, darling?" He said, his brow furrowed as he looked into her eyes.

Elizabeth flew into his arms.

"It is more than I ever dreamed," she whispered, as she held him close. "I am completely overwhelmed with everything. How on earth did you pay for it all?"

"Shhh! Cost is not an issue. It was all covered from the sale of my house. There is money left for you to equip your doctor's quarters. This is our new beginning, Elizabeth. I knew I would love this house the first moment I set eyes on it. To share it with you is beyond my wildest dreams."

He held her face between his hands and covered her face with kisses.

"Thank you, Julius," Elizabeth said. "I am the happiest woman on earth, married to the happiest man. We will fill this house with our love, and it will become our refuge, our home."

"It already is," murmured Julius.

CHAPTER 43

BLACKSTONE ROAD SURGERY

F ires burned brightly in the fireplaces at the house on Blackstone Road. Joan Turner and Bertha were both settled into their rooms on the top floor, along with Phillip Bagnall, a young man hired by Julius to keep the house in good repair and tend the garden, which had been left to go wild.

The smell of apple pie floated through the rooms from the kitchen where Joan was busy baking. She couldn't have been more delighted with her situation, and she hummed a tune as she took the two pies out of the new gas oven and placed them on the table.

Doctor Elizabeth's rooms were almost ready. Chairs stood around the cheery waiting room, along with a table covered in periodicals, newspapers, and children's books. Phillip lit a fire in both the waiting room and consulting room every morning to take the chill out of the air. As Doctor Elizabeth told him, "People who are sick always feel a little chilled, despite the outdoor temperature."

Advertisements were placed in the local newspapers and posted on the town hall notice board that the new doctor's surgery on Blackstone Street was open for business at competitive rates. Elizabeth had her full name printed on the advertisements and posters so that there would be no misunderstanding that she was a female doctor. She knew that if a gentleman was to seek medical advice he would turn on his heel and walk away when he saw her.

Her first three patients were all women referred by coworkers of Julius. Each had minor problems with their health, and came more out of curiosity and a sense of support for the lady doctor. It was a generous gesture, and Elizabeth asked them to spread the word among their friends and family. It would be difficult to build up a practice of local people, especially in an area where every penny coming into a household was spent on rent and food. Little was left over for the luxury of medical care.

A loud banging on the front door wakened both doctors at 4:00am. Before Elizabeth had put on her dressing gown, she heard Phillip running from the top floor down the back stairs to open the door. A man's voice echoed through the house, reaching Elizabeth's ear as she hurried down the main staircase.

"Need a doctor," the man panted, the sweat rolling down his face as he spoke. "Wife is bad. She won't stop screamin' and moanin'."

"Come inside," Elizabeth ordered calmly. "Give me a few minutes to dress and I will come with you."

"No," he yelled in a panic. "Told ya, we need a doctor."

"I am a doctor, good sir," replied Elizabeth. "I will accompany you to your home and tend your wife. Now wait here until I am ready."

Then, turning to Phillip, she gave him instructions to pour the distraught man a glass of brandy.

She was ready in record time, with Julius helping her get into her clothes.

"Let me go, dearest," he offered. "It's so early and who knows what you will be heading into."

"No, Julius. I need to do this. If I ever want to gain the trust of the people living close by, they need to know they can rely on me."

Julius hurried to the consulting room to get his wife's medical bag, and thrust it into her hand as she followed the man into the empty street.

"What's your name," Elizabeth asked as they almost ran down a maze of narrow roads.

"Ronny, Ronny Deakin," he panted.

"And your wife's name?"

"Alice."

Ronny stopped at a terraced house in the middle of a row of such homes, and pushed the old, battered door open, with a thud. The screams hadn't subsided, and they hurried up the winding, dark staircase off the kitchen, and into one of the two bedrooms at the top of the stairs.

A brass bedstead held a thin kapok mattress, covered in a thin grey sheet. The screams were issuing from a young woman lying on the bed with her hands gripping the brass rails of the bedstead above her. Saliva ran out of her mouth, tears poured out of her eyes, and sweat covered her body as she writhed in agony.

This was Elizabeth's wheelhouse. She had experienced the scenario many times during her stay at Glasgow's Royal Maternity Hospital—a young undernourished woman terrified out of her mind by unbearable labour pains. The panic on the young girl's face intensified as another contraction swept over her, forcing her head back and inducing another guttural scream.

"Well now, Mrs Deakin," Elizabeth said calmly, taking the girl's hand in her own and looking into the frightened eyes. "My name is Doctor Lingford. Let's see what's going on shall we."

Conditions were just about as bad as they could be in the tiny room. Hardly any light, dirty linens, and cold and damp. Elizabeth gently examined the mother, who, although distraught, had a strong pulse and good breathing. The baby was in a good position, with head well down. She felt inside, and found the cervix well dilated, but the mother's pelvis was small, something indicative of the working poor no matter what city.

"You are doing splendidly, my dear," Elizabeth encouraged. "Your baby is well on its way. You have to be brave and work very hard for a while longer. I want you to breathe slowly and calmly if you can. I am going to help your baby through into the birth canal. It will be painful, but once done you will be able to handle the rest of the labour."

"I just want you to help me," yelled Alice. "I'm going to die. I know it."

"No, you are not going to die," Elizabeth reassured her. "Let's get on, shall we? Now, Mr Deakin, I have work for you to do," Elizabeth said. "Bring your wife a drink of water first. Then light a fire. Next get some light in here, so that we can see what we are doing. We need clean linens, and clean towels or cloths. I also need water and soap, so that I can wash my hands. If you don't have them, borrow them from somebody. Don't stand there gaping at me. Go, go."

Ronny scurried down the stairs to run the errands, quickly returning with a tin mug full of water, which Alice gulped down. He returned with sticks and coal to build a fire and a merry flame was soon burning in the grate. Two oil lamps were brought in and placed on an old chest of drawers. Lastly, Ronny carried in a bowl of warm water with a small bar of carbolic soap floating in it. He set the bowl on the floor and placed a ragged piece of towel beside it.

"I'll have to go knock Mam up to ask for sheets and stuff," Ronny said. "She's got some baby things ready. Just 'elp Alice."

With the lamps and firelight, Elizabeth went ahead with helping the baby.

She scrubbed her hands, before beginning, and explained to Alice what she would attempt to do. Pushing the rim of the cervix over the baby's head would be painful, and if Elizabeth wasn't careful it may rip the tissue. She had performed this procedure a number of times in Glasgow, and she took her time being as gentle as she could to help Alice and her baby. Slowly the taught skin eased over the baby's head inch by inch, helped by a lubricant from Elizabeth's bag.

Once the head was at last in the birth canal, Elizabeth coached her patient with each contraction, so that the birthing process could progress. Alice stopped screaming and followed the doctor's directions.

Within minutes of leaving Ronny returned, with his mother in tow, carrying a bundle of sheets and towels. Mrs Deakin took off her coat and pulled up her sleeves. She took one of the clean sheets and folded it neatly before helping Elizabeth to replace the sodden, stained linen beneath Alice.

"There, there, duck,"[1] clucked Mrs Deakin, as she wiped Alice's forehead. "It'll all soon be over. We've all been through it, ducks. You just keep listening to the doctor."

It was the hardest work Alice had ever had to do. The baby barely fit through her pelvis into the outside world, and the young woman was at the point of exhaustion. Elizabeth smiled with relief when the worst was over and the baby's head lay in her hand.

Ronny was long gone. It was no place for a father at such a time. His mum gave him orders to keep the kettle boiling on the hob, ready for a cup of tea once the baby had arrived.

"Now, Alice," Elizabeth said gently. "No more pushing until I say so. Baby is about to be born, but we need things to go slowly. That's it! You are doing really well."

A few minutes later the baby slid into Elizabeth's waiting hands, screaming his arrival as he took his first breath.

"Well done, Alice," Elizabeth said. "You have a beautiful baby boy."

Overcome with tears, Alice nodded and smiled at the doctor and her mother-in-law.

"Would you look in my bag for scissors and cord please, Mrs Deakin," instructed Elizabeth.

---

1. Term of endearment used frequently in North Staffordshire to this day

"'Ere you go doctor," Mrs Deakin said, handing the requested items to the doctor. "You know your business, you do."

Mrs Deakin handed over a soft cotton blanket to wrap the newborn. Soon he was snuggled into his mother's arms, warm and content.

"Is there anything more beautiful than a new baby, doctor?" Mrs Deakin asked. "'E's a right little smasher, 'e is. Can I shout for our Ronny now?"

"Let's just wait for the placenta, then you can call him. We don't want him fainting do we? Some men have a problem with blood."

Once the all clear was given Mrs Deakin called her son.

Ronny crept into the room, his face whiter than the bedsheets. He fell on his knees beside the bed and stared at the tiny face of his son. Tears spilled down his cheeks unchecked. He kissed Alice on her cheek and lifted the baby into his arms.

Mrs Deakin rummaged in her bag and drew out all the things the baby would need: swaddling blankets, nappies, undershirts, nightgowns, and knitted hats, matinee jackets and a blanket. A bar of baby soap and a small soft towel made up the layette.

"I'll go downstairs and get a nice bowl of clean warm water, doctor," she said, making her way to the door. "I'll wash the baby first, then Alice next. Mr Deakin will be 'ere soon with the baby crib. It's been passed 'round the whole family, but it's clean and comfy. I've brought a nice crusty loaf, baked yesterday, so we can have some of that, with a nice cuppa. Alice must be hungry after all she's bin through. Eeeee! What a day! I'm that excited I can 'ardly speak."

Elizabeth laughed out loud. She wasn't needed here any more. This family would thrive under Mrs Deakin's care. She packed up her bag, took one more look at mother and baby, and put on her coat.

"I'll see ya out, then," Ronny said, handing the baby back to his wife. "Thank ya Doctor. Thank ya. 'Ow much do I owe ya?"

A worried frown appeared on his young face. Doctors were

expensive, especially when called in the middle of the night. Night visits always cost more.

"Don't you worry, Ronny," Elizabeth answered. "Alice was my very first patient in town. Allow me to offer my services as a gift this time. I'd be happy for you to spread the word about my new practice though. That would be a great help. Better than any payment, I believe."

With that Elizabeth shook hands with Ronny and walked home.

CHAPTER 44

LIFE IS SO GOOD

Word spread quickly throughout the neighbourhood about the new lady doctor, and how she had helped Alice in her time of need. As a result the seats in the waiting room at the new surgery began to fill each day from nine to eleven o'clock.

"I wouldn't bother ya doctor, if it wasn't important," Jenny Watts murmured. She held a new baby tightly in her arms, and wouldn't meet Elizabeth's eyes as she spoke. "Baby's got a bad rash. Can't seem to clear it up no matter 'ow much lard I use on it."

Elizabeth gently took the baby from Jenny's arms, and lay her on the examining table. Unwrapping the swaddled infant, she saw a rash she'd seen many dozens of times in Glasgow, and smiled at the young mother.

"A bad nappy rash," Elizabeth announced. "Nothing to worry about, but you were right to bring her in. She needs careful handling, and it will soon clear up."

It was the usual education of the mother that counted most in such circumstances, and Doctor Lingford explained the regime of changing the nappy[1] regularly, cleaning the baby with soap and water, airing out the affected area, and using a freshly laundered nappy. She also gave Jenny a tin of cream containing zinc and castor oil, which was a tried and true recipe for healing nappy rash.

Elizabeth had invented a sliding scale for payment for service before opening the surgery. To charge the going rate of one pound, ten shillings[2] for a visit was out of the reach of patients like Jenny. Even ten shillings was a stress on most families, as the average wage for a worker in the pottery factories or in the mines was only one pound per week. Although to Julius the small amount was laughable, his wife began her fee scale at two shillings all the way up to two pounds for the known affluent clients.

"Thank ya, doctor," Jenny said, re-swaddling the now screaming baby. "I'm ever so grateful."

Jenny pressed the two shillings into Elizabeth's hand before returning to the waiting room to nurse her baby to calm her screams.

The two hours were filled with women patients from all walks of life, with various ailments and complaints. She put three stitches into a cut hand, bandaged a severely swollen ankle, prescribed a poultice for pleurisy, gave out a salt water recipe to three patients with sore throats, syringed ears, and confirmed a pregnancy. It was a busy morning!

"Well, darling," Julius said, as he sat down to a steaming shepherd's pie at dinner time. "How was your day?"

"Oh Julius, it was so good," answered Elizabeth. "All women patients, of course. The whole surgery went very smoothly, and the patients were from all walks of life. I am so happy to be back at work. News spread quickly about my home visit to Alice, and just about every woman I saw mentioned it to me. I believe my

---

1. Diaper
2. There were twenty shillings in a pound.

practice will be a resounding success. Although I will have to work on understanding the dialect."

Elizabeth tucked into her dinner with a relish.

"I'm proud of you, my love," grinned Julius.

He raised his wine glass and toasted his wife.

"Doctor Elizabeth Lingford, the finest doctor in town!"

Elizabeth's eyes sparkled as she returned the toast.

"Doctor Julius LaPorte, the finest surgeon in town!"

Bertha came to clear the table, smiling at her employers as she caught their happiness. The clean plates told her the meal had been enjoyed, and she walked jauntily back to the kitchen to report to Joan Turner.

"They loved the shepherd's pie, Mrs Turner," Bertha said. "They were laughin' and toastin' each other when I went to clear. Lovely couple, they are. I'm so 'appy workin' 'ere."

"We're both lucky, Bertha," smiled Joan. "We've landed on our feet all right. Good people are 'ard to come by, and that's no mistake. Especially rich folks. Most are snobby and look down their noses at the likes of us. Not the doctors though. They're the best."

The two women chatted and laughed together as they set the table in the kitchen for their own dinner. Joined by Phillip, the three of them tucked into the second shepherd's pie. Joan Turner always gave young Phillip the lion's share of the meal. He worked very hard most days, tending the garden, sweeping the walkways, painting and repairing. He always had a project to work on; building a tool shed was his latest venture, and he was very proud of the way it was turning out.

"Thanks, Missus," Phillip said, smiling at the cook. "Grand pie is this. I can't ever remember eating food this good in my whole life. Yer a great cook, and I am grateful, believe me."

Joan gave the young man a big smile as she piled more of the potatoes and meat on his plate, with a good helping of carrots and peas and gravy.

"You get that inside yer, lad," she laughed. "Watching you eat the food I've cooked is thanks enough for me."

It was a happy household, and all who lived under its roof knew how fortunate they were.

As the evening quiet settled on the home, Joan climbed the stairs to her room to sit in the twilight and do her knitting. Bertha set out to visit her sister who lived a short walk away. Phillip met his mates for a pint at the local pub.

Elizabeth sat next to her husband with her head on his shoulder on the cozy sofa in the living room, until closeness became overwhelming and they scurried upstairs to strip off their clothes and climb into bed.

"The best part of my day," murmured Julius as he took his wife into his arms.

"Mine too," Elizabeth whispered back.

CHAPTER 45

GOODBYE DEAR FRIEND

T he months flew by with ease. Life had never been so comfortable and rewarding for Elizabeth. She enjoyed every day of her medical practice, and cherished the weekends when she drove out to Granger Manor to ride Blue Shadow.

A shadow fell on their lives, suddenly and without warning. Elizabeth and Julius drove to Scotland immediately. Her friend and confidante, Sir Kenneth, was dead. He had refused to allow his wife to write to the family about his illness. He didn't want them rushing to Gordon House to visit a dying man.

He wanted Elizabeth in particular to remember the good times they had shared, riding in the early mornings, watching the sea churn below them. He wanted her to remember the discussions over dinner, the drives into Glasgow, the comfortable silent walks in the twilight. He hoped she knew how much he loved her.

The smell of heather drifted through the open bedroom window, greeting Elizabeth as she stretched and yawned. Elizabeth turned over in the soft warm bed and snuggled into the back of Julius who lay sleeping beside her. Tears formed in the well of her eyes as she remembered not only Sir Kenneth, but the other strong, quiet men in her life who she had lost: her brother Henry, her father, and Elwyn.

She clung to the strong, quiet man beside her, so thankful for him, and the love they shared. Julius turned over and wrapped his arms around her, words of comfort unnecessary; she knew his heart.

Elizabeth's brother, Percy, arrived on the early train into Glasgow, and was picked up by the chauffeur. He was at Gordon House by mid-afternoon, with apologies from his mother, Lady Lingford, who was unable to travel due to her declining health.

"No need to apologize, dear Percy," Cousin Jocelyn sighed. "It is enough to have you, Elizabeth and Julius here. You are a great comfort to me."

Sir Kenneth had requested a quiet funeral in the local Presbyterian Church. Every pew was filled with neighbours, friends, and kindly locals who had known Sir Kenneth and served him over the years. It was a simple, short service, and included scriptures chosen by Sir Kenneth and read, at his request, by Elizabeth.

A small group of close friends gathered with the family for lunch at Gordon House, where stories were shared about Sir Kenneth, and condolences offered to his widow. It was all over by mid-afternoon.

Suddenly the house was quiet, and loneliness settled on the family as they sat wondering what to do next.

Elizabeth took the opportunity to escape the despair she felt, and ran upstairs to change before she walked to the stables. The stable master greeted her with a grim nod.

"Would you saddle Red Clover for me, please Robertson?" Elizabeth asked.

"Certainly, Miss," Robertson replied. "It would be my pleasure. We're all feeling down, you understand. Not quite sure what will happen to the stables now Sir Kenneth has gone."

He gulped as he hurried away to prepare the horse.

As the young stable hand led Red Clover out of the stable, Robertson appeared behind him leading Sir Kenneth's horse.

"If you don't mind, Miss," Robertson began. "I would like to ride along with you today. These two horses are used to riding together, as you know, and it would mean a lot to me and the horse to accompany you."

"Of course," Elizabeth answered quickly. "You remind me of the stable master at Lingford Manor, where I grew up. You both seem to have a sense to know what is helpful, indeed what is really needed. For you to ride with me today would be both of those."

It was a silent ride, as were many rides with Sir Kenneth. Elizabeth appreciated the company of the elderly stable master more than she could say. The wild countryside calmed her spirit, and helped ease the dull ache she had in her chest. She felt the presence of Sir Kenneth riding beside her, and somehow knew he was enjoying being with her. She smiled down at the sparkling sea, and turned the horse around to head back to the house.

Sir Kenneth's lawyer came to the house two days later to read the will. Percy and Julius arranged to return home once the will was read, but Elizabeth was to stay with Cousin Jocelyn for one more week.

The reading was short and precise, as everybody expected. Jocelyn was already aware of its contents, so there were no surprises for her. Having no children to inherit, there was a list of bequests dividing a large portion of his riches between several beneficiaries:

Trust amounts for the children of Percy, Carolyn and Lydia; generous sums to staff at Gordon House; a staggering amount to The Royal Glasgow Maternity Hospital, much to Elizabeth's delight; and charitable contributions to a variety of local organizations.

"Lastly," the lawyer read in his mundane deep voice. "Lady Cunningham will remain at Gordon House with all living expenses provided for the rest of her life. Gordon House itself, and the balance of Sir Kenneth's fortune, he leaves to Doctor Elizabeth Lingford."

The silence in the room was broken as Jocelyn clapped her hand with delight. Everybody began talking at once, except Elizabeth who sat in her chair stunned and silent.

"Just as we planned," Jocelyn exclaimed. "Just as it should be."

She walked over to where Elizabeth sat and enclosed her with her generous warm arms.

"Darling," she cried, the tears flowing down her round cheeks. "You are the nearest we came to having a daughter of our own. Sir Kenneth loved you very much. You gave him so much pleasure, and he wanted you to take care of our beloved home, and particularly the stables. He knew you would make sure the horses would remain here in good care. It was of the utmost importance to him as his health failed and the end drew ever nearer. Elizabeth, you made us so happy when you came to stay with us. It is our dearest wish that you will make Gordon House your home for the rest of your life."

After her heartrending speech Jocelyn plumped down into the big easy chair next to Elizabeth and gasped for breath, dabbed her eyes, and beamed from ear to ear.

CHAPTER 46

INHERITANCE

The Gordon House housekeeper, Mrs Campbell, had gathered the indoor staff in the drawing room, as instructed by Lady Jocelyn. Robertson, along with the stable hands and outdoor workers were also asked to be present. Most of them had been in service with the Cunningham family from a young age, and regarded Gordon House as their home. They stood in two quiet rows awaiting the news they dreaded to even think about now Sir Kenneth was no longer with them.

"Firstly, thank you for your kindness and care over these past months," began Jocelyn. "It has not been easy for any of us, and I could not have managed without each one of you. Now that the estate is settled, I will leave it to Doctor Lingford to explain."

Elizabeth had said goodbye to her husband and brother two days ago, after long conversations about the future. They had agreed on a short-term plan, and deferred future decisions for a later date, when their minds would be clearer and emotions steadier.

"I feel I know you all well," began Elizabeth, facing the anxious staff and smiling reassuringly. "I think you have been informed of the bequests Sir Kenneth has left each of you."

Elizabeth paused to catch her breath. The hardest announcement was yet to come, and she chose her words carefully.

"With Lady Cunningham's blessing, Sir Kenneth has left Gordon House to the person he considered his adopted daughter. In fact, to me!"

An audible gasp echoed through the room. Every eye turned to Jocelyn.

"I could not be happier," she said, smiling at her beloved care-givers. "As Elizabeth said, it was my dearest wish, and has my blessing. Now, listen to what she has to tell you regarding the future."

The eyes reverted back to Elizabeth.

She gulped down a glass of water before continuing.

"My husband and brother, along with Lady Cunningham, have had several conversations over the past few days, and we all agreed on how to move forward. Sir Kenneth, of course, made it clear that Lady Cunningham should remain at Gordon House, and that the house should run as it always has. In fact, nothing will change for any of you."

An audible sigh of relief circulated among the staff.

"It will be my pleasure to visit as often as I can. There is much still to discuss, but for now I intend to treat Gordon House as my beloved holiday home. Nothing revives me more than a visit here to walk, ride and spend time with Lady Cunningham. I promise to keep you all up to date with any future plans. For now, please continue to follow Sir Kenneth's wishes and take care of all the things he loved."

"Thank you, Doctor Lingford," Mrs Campbell said on behalf of the staff.

"Please, Mrs Campbell, call me Miss Elizabeth, or just Elizabeth, as you always have." Elizabeth replied. "That goes for the rest of you. It would make me feel very uncomfortable to have you call me anything else."

With a nod to Elizabeth, Mrs Campbell ushered the indoor staff out of the drawing room. Robertson touched his forehead and smiled at his young mistress as he followed the stable hands and groundskeepers out of the room.

"Oh, my dear," Jocelyn said as she held out her hands to her young friend. "I think that went very well. It has put their minds at rest."

Elizabeth was tired. She made sure Jocelyn was content before she headed into Glasgow to meet Jennifer. She needed to talk to her wise friend about the inheritance. Not only the bequest to the maternity hospital, but the unexpected personal inheritance she had received.

The two friends met in their favourite tea shop and ordered their tea and fruit tarts.

Elizabeth broke the news that Sir Kenneth had left a large bequest to the hospital. More money than Jennifer could have imagined, and she stared at her friend in disbelief.

"Do you have any idea what this means for the hospital?" Jennifer gasped. "It will keep us going for years, and pay for improvements and staff we so badly need. I am flabbergasted! Wait until I share this news with Doctor Hope and the rest of the staff."

Not able to keep her seat any longer, Jennifer jumped up and grabbed Elizabeth into a strong hug, causing other customers to smile at her excitement.

After settling back into her seat and taking a long drink of tea, Jennifer looked at her friend with anticipation. She knew there must be more to tell.

"Jen, there is more," Elizabeth continued. "Sir Kenneth left me Gordon House along with an incredible fortune."

"Wow! Elizabeth," Jennifer gasped as she heard the news. "What will you do with it all?"

"That is the big question, Jen," replied Elizabeth. "I am totally unprepared for something like this. I have to think it all through. Lady Cunningham will continue to live there as usual, but I do have to consider a plan for the future. Any ideas?"

"You could become a lady of leisure and live at Gordon House."

Elizabeth stared at her friend across the small table in the tea shop where they sat, until Jennifer dropped her eyes and laughed.

"I know you too well," Jennifer said. "You wouldn't even consider it."

They drank their tea and ate their tarts as they laughed and talked about the various scenarios the inheritance could be used for.

Even though they reached no resolution, Elizabeth considered Jennifer's wise counsel as she travelled south to Staffordshire, and her uncertain future.

Julius picked up his wife from the train station, and put his arm around her shoulders. He could see how tired she was, and he hurried her to the car. He knew they had a lot to talk about, but now was not the time. Elizabeth needed to rest, and he intended to make sure she had some quiet days ahead.

Joan Turner ensured her mistress was not disturbed as she bustled around the house baking favourite recipes, brewing tea, and diverting any would-be patients to Doctor Morrison's surgery a few streets away.

Julius was anxious about the discussion they needed to have. Life was so sweet at the moment. His work was rewarding and he loved working at the North Staffs Hospital. Elizabeth had begun her own practice, and was enjoying building relationships with her patients. The house was comfortable and cozy and was a culmination of the two of them working together to make it a home. Joan, Bertha and Phillip were like part of the family. Julius wanted everything to stay just as it was.

The question hung in the air between the two doctors every day, with both parties avoiding the conversation they needed to have.

Plans to drive out to the stables on Saturday morning to ride Blue Shadow fell through when Elizabeth awoke and heard the wind driving sheets of rain against the bedroom windows. Trees bent, their red and orange leaves flying off the branches, as October announced its arrival.

Bertha had lit fires in the dining room and sitting room, filling the air with warmth and comfort. Julius smiled at his wife across the breakfast table as he nibbled on his toast, smothered with home-made raspberry jam.

"Let's just take the morning to relax," he said. "We will take our tea into the sitting room and cozy up on the sofa in front of the fire, watch the rain beat against the windows, and do absolutely nothing."

They carried their tea into the sitting room as Julius suggested, but Elizabeth knew by the knot in her stomach that this was the time for the discussion they had been avoiding.

CHAPTER 47

SAVING GORDON HOUSE

Elizabeth stared into the flames dancing in the fireplace as she sipped her tea.

"Well, darling," Julius began as he reached for her hand. "Are we ready to face the elephant in the room?"

"Are we?" asked Elizabeth "Ready or not, we have to give it a shot."

They began by talking about all the things they loved about their life together. Things they treasured most: time spent together, the home they'd built around them, jobs they loved, family they visited.

Elizabeth reiterated that the life of a "lady" had never interested her. She had been born into a privileged world, part of a privileged family, and had chosen a different path for herself. She admitted she was afraid of the inheritance Sir Kenneth had left her. It raised questions she didn't know how to answer.

Julius held her close and kissed her gently. They looked into each other's eyes and said at the same time, "We don't want anything to change."

A myriad of ideas were discussed over the next few hours. Joan, realizing serious business ensued in the sitting room, brought in a fresh pot of tea and oatmeal biscuits to sustain her dear employers.

"Are you happy with our decision?" Julius asked his wife.

"I am, my love," Elizabeth replied. "Gordon House will be preserved, which was Sir Kenneth's dearest wish. The stables will continue to be a vibrant part of the estate. I couldn't be happier."

"There it is then," stated Julius. "We will write it all out and the lawyers can draw up the legal side of things. Gordon House and estate will be donated to The National Trust, with an endowment fund from the inheritance to cover expenses. Furthermore, a trust specifically for the stables needs to be created, giving details regarding their use for the underprivileged. That way the stables will remain active and the staff employed."

"It sounds perfect," Elizabeth smiled. "Particularly the plan for the stables. I couldn't bear to think of them empty and unused."

Julius pulled Elizabeth to her feet and spun her around. Why had they been so scared to talk about all of this? It hadn't been difficult to reach a decision that they were both happy with. Their lives wouldn't change. They could continue to live and work and love each other.

A month later, Elizabeth journeyed north once more to tell Cousin Jocelyn about their decision.

"I had imagined you would live here, my dear," Jocelyn said with tears in her eyes. "That was Sir Kenneth's intent."

"I wouldn't hurt you for the world," Elizabeth said. "This plan will ensure Gordon House is kept just as it is now. We will come often to visit, I promise. The estate will be a lively active place, with people coming and going enjoying the beautiful house and grounds, and riding the horses. I believe Sir Kenneth would have loved the idea."

Jocelyn dabbed her eyes and smiled.

She would learn to live with Elizabeth's decision. For now,

she would enjoy her home and not worry about what would happen after she was gone.

"Then you need to meet with the staff once more to explain this all to them. I'm sure they will be relieved to hear their positions at the house are not in jeopardy."

Elizabeth told Robertson about the National Trust before she met with the rest of the staff. They were riding together before dinner, wrapped up warmly against the cold weather, and had stopped to admire the majestic view of the shoreline from the cliffs bordering the Gordon House estate.

The elderly stable master smiled when he heard about the plan for the stables.

"I knew you would come up with something special to ensure the stables remained in use, Miss Elizabeth. I knew you'd never let them go unused and uncared for now the master has gone. It's a grand plan, it is. I can already think of a number of folks in the town who will jump at the chance to organize such a venture."

As she turned her horse towards the house, Elizabeth glowed with happiness. Robertson's approval meant so much, and it made the announcement to the rest of the staff after dinner that evening so much easier.

Applause broke out after her short speech, followed by numerous questions, which Elizabeth did her best to answer. Gordon House was dear to them all, and they were elated that they would continue to live and work there to keep it in good order.

As the wind whistled around the house and the rain pelted the windows in her bedroom, Elizabeth snuggled into the warm cozy bed and thought of Sir Kenneth. Her memories of the dear quiet man tumbled through her mind, and she smiled as she thought about how he had transformed from a silent, distant, solitary man into a most beloved friend.

She would return home in good spirits, convinced she had

made a good decision about her legacy. It was time to return to Julius, and continue with her medical practice and the life they were building together.

CHAPTER 48

JULIUS TO THE RESCUE

Winter appeared earlier than usual, with traces of snow on the ground in November and a biting wind that never seemed to ease.

Phillip lit fires in the house, surgery, and waiting room every day. Patients were grateful for the warm, welcoming atmosphere awaiting them as they scurried inside. All of them women; some with babies, children clinging to them, some older, weary and dragged down with the hardships of life, even bent old ladies who struggled to walk upright and whose breath came in short gasps. Every week there were more of them, until the surgery hours were extended to three hours, so that Elizabeth could see them all.

"She's a grand doctor, she is," the women of the neighbourhood declared. "A real treat to 'ave a lady looking out for ya."

"No nonsense, mind ya. She don't waste time. All business, but always kind with it."

"Me mam was at death's door when Doctor Lingford came out to see 'er. Like a tornado she was, comin' into the 'ouse. Don't know 'ow she walks on them 'igh 'eels. Anyroad, me mam was up and about it no time once she got medicine."

"Same with our little Jack. Never 'eard a cough as bad as 'is.

Up all night, every night, I was. Thought 'e'd cough up 'is lungs.
She came out three days runnin' to see to 'im. Told us what to
do, and even brought medicine with 'er and a poultice. Put it on
'is chest 'erself, she did. I can't say enough good things about
Doctor Lingford."

"Nor me neither. Ya'd never get a man doctor taking such
care. Most don't 'ave time for women and kids."

As the women filed into the surgery each day, they smiled
shyly at the other patients in a knowing way. They had found a
good doctor.

Their collective experience with male doctors had been less
than pleasant. Women were not listened to nor given any sympathy. Advice of any kind was never forthcoming, particularly
pertaining to 'women's issues,' or parenting. As a result it was
usually the last resort, when every other alternative had been
tried, for a woman to seek medical help. Babies and children
were all treated at home, with remedies of warm water mixed
with a few drops of brandy and sugar for upper respiratory
problems. Kaolin Poultices[1] were made to ease painful and
congested chest infections, and sore knees and elbows. A
mixture of baking soda, salt, and sugar was used for stomach
ailments, prunes for constipation, Sal Valatile for fainting spells,
a hot water bottle and warm blanket to cuddle into for period
cramps. These were the home-made remedies, handed down for
generations.

Elizabeth's days were full and satisfying. The women she met
never ceased to amaze her with their fortitude amidst the
harshest of environments. Like the women of Glasgow's inner
city, they survived through the worst life could throw at them.
Each day they trailed through the surgery with their stories of
life as they knew it. Often desperate, many would cry as they

---

1. Kaolin Poultice BP possesses emollient properties. It provides heat and mois-
ture locally to relieve pain and draw pus, if present, from a wound.

    Kaolin is a soft white clay that is an essential ingredient in the manufacture of
china or porcelain.

told about the realities they endured on a daily basis. Yet there were times of joy to balance the despair; health was restored to young women with small children depending on them, babies thrived after a poor beginning to their lives, and youngsters with scabies and impetigo were treated. A myriad of patients simply felt better because somebody listened to them.

At the end of each day, Elizabeth sat with her husband after dinner, and exchanged stories about the patients they had met that day. They never tired of listening, even if many stories were the same. Their lives had a rhythm that they enjoyed, and even on the frequent occasions when one or the other doctor was called out after hours, they supported and encouraged each other.

"I'll keep the bed warm for you, darling," Julius whispered, on one such night.

"I may not be back soon," yawned Elizabeth as she hurried to get dressed. "It's a first baby for Rose Morgan, and the midwife needs help. I probably won't see you until dinner tonight."

"Good luck," Julius groaned, as he turned over, pulled the blankets over his head and began to snore quietly.

Steven Morgan was waiting at the front door for her. They hurried through the cold night together, the puddles splashing their boots, and the misty rain clinging to their clothes.

Elizabeth didn't mind these night-time jaunts. It was by far the favourite part of her job; to welcome a new baby into the world. She soothed the soon-to-be new father's concerns as they walked.

"Try not to worry about Rose," she said. "First babies always take their time. Everything will be fine. I've delivered many babies in my time. All will be well."

Rose was screaming so loudly they heard her from the top of the street. The midwife met them at the front door and ushered Elizabeth into the small parlour, where the young woman lay writhing on the thin mattress by the wall.

Elizabeth wished she could have taken back the words she

had spoken to Steven Morgan. "All will be well" was a grave distortion of the truth. All would not be well, as was evident after a brief examination.

"How long has she been labouring?" asked Elizabeth

"Since about two o'clock yesterday afternoon, doctor," answered the midwife. "She's not progressing like she should. That's why I called for you."

"Right," Elizabeth said to the distraught midwife. "The birth canal is too small for the baby to descend. We will need to get her to the North Staffs as soon as possible. Now listen carefully Steven. You need to do exactly as I say."

"Yes doctor. Anything you say," Steven muttered. "Just help Rose."

"This is highly unconventional, but it must be done," Elizabeth said, her voice taking on its no-nonsense tone. "Go back to my house and wake my husband, Doctor LaPorte. Tell him I need him to bring the car to your house to pick up Rose and take her to the hospital. He will not argue with you. He will know what to do. Go now, Steven. Run all the way."

There was little to be done for Rose while they waited. The midwife applied cold cloths to her forehead and Elizabeth reassured the frantic young mother that help was close at hand.

Steven and Julius arrived less than half an hour later. Julius, was unshaven, with his hair sticking up, and no collar—so different from his usual immaculate self. He moved quickly towards Rose, as he listened to his wife telling him what was wrong, and carefully wrapped the labouring woman in the only blanket. He carried her out to the car with Steven's help and transferred her to the back seat with her husband beside her.

"Jump in, Elizabeth," Julius yelled to his wife. "This is going to have to be a very fast drive."

The North Staffs Hospital was not nearby, but Julius pushed the big powerful car to its limits and covered the miles in record time. He yelled instructions to the startled staff as he burst through the emergency entrance and lay Rose on the first wheeled stretcher he could find. People flew in all directions to help Julius transport his patient to the emergency operating room, where he scrubbed his hands and flung on a white chin to floor apron.

Elizabeth stayed with Rose, who was by now not even aware of where she was or what was happening to her. Julius waited for the anesthetic to do its job before skillfully making the first incision to rescue the baby and the mother. He worked quickly, with the knowledge that it may already be too late to save them both. He pulled the baby girl from her nest inside her mother's body, and gently held her head down. Everybody in the room held their breath as the lifeless child dangled in Doctor LaPorte's grasp. He snatched a towel held out by one of the attending nurses and rubbed the tiny body, as he prayed for a reaction. A small choke, then an almost inaudible wisp of a breath, then a cry like a tiny kitten. A uniform sigh of relief echoed through the room, as each person in attendance smiled at the miracle of new life.

All attention was now on Rose, whose torn body lay before them. Elizabeth confirmed her heart was still beating and she was breathing. The team now gathered around her, carefully closed her uterus and the layers of muscle and tissue covering it, finally stitching the skin back in place and dressing the wound. All they could do now was wait for Rose to awaken.

The baby was doing well after such a traumatic birth. She was gently cleaned and wrapped in a soft white blanket before Elizabeth carried her out of the operating room to show her to her dad.

Steven sat with his head in his hands on a small stool just outside the door. He looked up as he heard footsteps approach.

"Look at this beautiful baby girl, Steven," Elizabeth said. "She is perfect. Here take her and hold her. She is yours."

"Oh my God!" whispered Steven, taking the tiny bundle into his arms. "It's a miracle. That's what it is."

He pressed the tiny forehead against his lips and then held his daughter's face against his.

"I don't want to hurt her, doctor," he said.

"You can never hurt a baby with love," Elizabeth said.

He suddenly remembered his wife, still fighting for her life in the room beside him.

"Rose?" he questioned, as he looked straight into Elizabeth's eyes.

"The doctors and nurses are working with her now. They know what they are doing. She is in good hands."

This time Elizabeth didn't make any rash statements like "All will be well," but looked steadily back at the young father, and hoped he was reassured.

Julius came out to join them, looking exhausted and elated at the same time. He smiled as he walked up to Steven and took his unoccupied hand.

"Looks like Rose is out of the woods," he announced. "You'll be able to see her once they've moved her into a side ward and cleaned her up a bit."

"Thank you, thank you both. You saved both their lives." Steven sobbed.

"It's what we do," Julius said. "We are both very happy it turned out so well."

The two tired doctors headed for the door, and back to their bed.

CHAPTER 49

MAKING MEMORIES

C ousin Jocelyn travelled to Lingford for Christmas that year. It was a happy reunion for Lady Lingford, whose health continued to decline, and who was now confined to a wheelchair.

Elizabeth and Julius had mixed feelings about the trip. Delighted as they were to visit family, and particularly spend time with their nieces and nephews, who seemed to fill every room with their rambunctious presence, they rarely found time to be alone together. Only late at night, when the house finally settled down, did they fall into bed exhausted by the day's activities. Even a quick cuddle ended with one or the other of them snoring.

Lady Lingford demanded much of Elizabeth's time during the day. Despite her cousin's visit, she wanted her eldest daughter to hear all about her various medical problems and discomforts. Even Christmas Day festivities were interrupted several times with calls from Her Ladyship for Elizabeth to attend her as she felt faint.

Julius sympathized with his wife, but took every opportunity to be away from the drama, preferring to find the youngest members of the family to enjoy. Having no children of his own, he took great pleasure in rolling around on the floor among the toddlers, playing with their Christmas gifts, making them laugh, and delighting in the affectionate cuddles he received.

The wonderful atmosphere of Lingford Manor at Christmas was always memorable. From the towering tree in the hall, decked out in red and silver, to the sumptuous feasts prepared by the dedicated kitchen staff, and served in the formal dining room, whose table was decked out in yuletide opulence. The family shared memories of past years, told funny stories from their childhood, listened to the younger members tell about their adventures, and ate until they were so full it was hard to breathe.

Elizabeth managed to slip away after breakfast on Boxing Day to visit McCarthy in his small residence in the stable yard. Delighted to see her, he rose slowly from his armchair by the fire.

"Miss Elizabeth, come in," he greeted. "How grand to see you, Miss."

"McCarthy, my old friend," Elizabeth said, as she took both his hands in hers and looked into the wizened old face she knew so well. "It's so very good to see you. Are you well? Is there anything you need?"

"Getting old, Miss," answered the old stable master. "Past my best. But I have no complaints. I have this lovely little place where it's warm and cozy, enough to eat, and wonderful memories to keep me company."

"Some of our memories are probably the same," smiled Elizabeth. "Mostly involving horses, I would imagine."

"You're right there," laughed McCarthy. "About you too, Miss. I remember all the times you helped birth a colt, when you were just a slip of a girl. How you loved to ride more than anything in the world, especially with His Lordship by your side. You were always a fine horsewoman."

It was hard for Elizabeth to drag herself away from the old man. She realized it might be the last time she would see him. Signs of the end of life were evident: noticeable weight loss, laboured breathing, blue tinged lips, and a strong smell of urine indicated incontinence. She would make arrangements with the house staff for somebody to care for him, and make sure he had all he needed to make him comfortable.

She held him close to her as she said goodbye, trying hard not to cry. Her old friend knew how she felt, and looked into her eyes for one last time before collapsing into his chair, a radiant smile on his face. It was enough that they had been able to spend the time together.

"I will be back at Lingford before too long, Julius," Elizabeth said as they travelled north after Christmas. "McCarthy doesn't have long to live."

It was only two weeks later when word arrived by telegram that McCarthy was gone, and Elizabeth journeyed south again. She was grateful to have spent time with him, and for a chance to have had the opportunity to talk about the memories they had shared. Grief for the old stable master was wrapped in the grief of losing Sir Kenneth and included losing her father, so long ago. The wonderful strong men she had known and loved, now gone.

The small chapel in the village was filled with members of the Lingford family and staff. Others from the village joined them for the simple service of remembrance. Two of the Lingford horses pulled the carriage carrying McCarthy's coffin from his home on the Estate to the village. The stable hands were pall bearers and carried his coffin with reverence into the Chapel. Elizabeth read scripture and Percy shared a brief monologue about the stable master, and his dedication to the Lingford family during his lifetime.

Elizabeth threw herself into her work with a new vengeance. To enhance the memory of the two men who had recently died, she made a commitment to ride every weekend, despite the winter weather. Tossing her head and galloping to the fence, Blue Shadow greeted her owner enthusiastically each time Elizabeth arrived at the Granger Manor stables. It felt good to ride out in the cold wind, with the warm horse beneath her. Always at peace when riding, she benefited physically and mentally from her weekend jaunts.

Springtime soon became evident on such rides, as the first crocuses peeked through the cold earth, and the sun's warmth brought the earthy smell of new life into the woods and dales.

Life was back to its usual, reliable, unchangeable rhythm.

CHAPTER 50

UNEXPECTED GIFT

Her head over the toilet bowl for the third morning that week, Elizabeth faced the extremely unlikely possibility she may be pregnant.

How is it possible? she asked herself.

She had convinced herself that she was barren when the years with Elwyn had not produced a child. She had shared her conviction with Julius before their marriage, and he had assured her that, at his age, parenthood was not something he desired. In fact, Julius suspected that his childless first marriage was his problem. They had both entered their marriage content in the knowledge that parenthood was not in their future.

Now everything was turned upside down.

Elizabeth would be considered an 'older mother' at the age of twenty-nine for a first baby. She knew from her experience in midwifery that young women aged eighteen to twenty-two were at their prime for birthing babies. Many were a good deal younger, and many were much older, adding to their families on a yearly basis until they were worn out.

Julius was considerably past the age when the majority of men became fathers for the first time. He had turned forty-seven in the new year. His colleague at the hospital was the same age and had just welcomed his first grandchild into the world.

The toilet bowl became a regular companion every morning, as Elizabeth lived with a secret she didn't know how to share with her husband. Once the morning ritual in the toilet was over, the rest of her day was perfectly fine. Julius always left for the hospital early, so never witnessed his wife's distress. At the weekends, she was careful to wait until Julius was downstairs before attempting to get out of bed. She hid soda crackers in the drawer beside her bed, and nibbled on them until her husband was safely out of the way.

Hiding this incredible news from her husband felt wrong, and Julius was aware almost immediately that his wife was struggling with some unspoken issue. In bed at night, he held her close and stroked her head, hoping she would feel comfortable to share what was troubling her.

After two long weeks, Elizabeth decided to confess her secret to her worried husband. She came downstairs on Saturday morning and joined him in the dining room where he was finishing his breakfast.

"Are you riding today, my dear?" Julius asked.

"Not today," Elizabeth answered.

She sat facing him and poured herself tea from the china teapot covered in a colourful knitted warmer. She sipped the tea slowly, not taking her eyes off the rim of the cup.

"What is it darling?" Julius continued. "What is troubling you?"

Tears spilled down Elizabeth's cheeks, although she was smiling at the same time.

"I don't know how to tell you, Julius," she spluttered.

He took out his handkerchief and wiped her face.

"How bad can it be?" he questioned.

"It's not bad. It's good," Elizabeth said between sobs. "It's terrific in fact. It's a miracle, an unexpected miracle. Something we never even dreamed of."

"What are you talking about, darling?" Julius asked.

Elizabeth walked around the table and put her arms around her husband's neck from behind.

"I believe I am pregnant," she whispered in his ear.

They stayed in that position, not moving, hardly breathing, like statues made of stone, until Julius disentangled himself from his wife's arms and rose from his chair. His face was ashen grey, and his hands shook as he reached out to grasp her to him. He buried his head into her hair, then tenderly kissed her forehead.

"Is this real? Are you sure?" he finally choked.

"It is very real," Elizabeth said. "I have been hiding my morning sickness for a few weeks, until I was convinced of the cause of it. Now my menstrual cycle has not happened. I am very sure. We are going to have a baby."

"Joy oh joy!" yelled Julius, not caring if the house staff heard. "I can barely bring myself to believe such news. Oh my love, my dearest wife, this is a mountain top moment in my life. I am to be a father! A father!"

Julius danced around the dining room, throwing his arms up in the air, and laughing and crying all at once.

"It is too much," he babbled on, grabbing Elizabeth once more and twirling her around with him. "I gave up hope many years ago. I believed it was a low sperm count on my part that prevented Phylis from becoming pregnant. We never discussed it. We never discussed it, but were content with our childless marriage."

"I too, imagined I was not able to have children," Elizabeth said. "And was completely content to share with you alone, my lovely man".

But now!" Julius laughed. "We are to be three. Oh Elizabeth, this is the best news I have ever had."

Elizabeth joined in his laughter, as they clung onto each other.

"Mrs T, Mrs T," Julius called loudly, bringing their house-keeper running from the kitchen.

"Bring more tea, please. Also some of your delicious muffins. We are celebrating, Joan. We're going to have a baby."

"Lord help us, Doctor LaPorte," Joan said, pulling her apron up to her face and staring at them both. "You surely are joking?"

"He is not joking, Joan," laughed Elizabeth. "Please don't spread the word just yet. We are in the very early stages of the pregnancy."

"Well, dear me," Joan continued. "Let me be the first to congratulate you. What a joy it will be to have a baby in the house."

Joan bumped into the door on her way out to get more tea.

It would take some time for the household to come to terms with the news, and how it might change their peaceful lives.

CHAPTER 51

WELCOME ALICE

J oan Turner hurried into town the next day to buy yarn to begin knitting. Keeping her promise to keep the news a secret, she told Bertha she was knitting for her niece.

Like magic, Elizabeth's daily encounter with the toilet bowl ceased three months into her pregnancy. She felt and looked a picture of health and happiness. Even though her waistline had not yet noticeably changed, her sensitive women patients knew instinctively what was going on.

With nods and winks to each other in the waiting room, they whispered their suspicions.

"Doctor's in the family way."

"She's got a bun in the oven."

"First baby, at 'er age!"

"I've 'eard the 'usband's a lot older."

"I'm worried she won't carry on as our doctor."

But carry on she did! Elizabeth continued seeing patients and making house calls. She had never felt better, and the only change she made in her routine was to her riding on the weekends. Trusting Blue Shadow's quiet, gentle character, she rode until the sixth month, mostly at a slow, steady pace. For the last trimester, she visited the stable frequently to walk her horse and be around the smells and atmosphere in the stable. It was her sanctuary—the source of long-ago precious memories.

Julius spoiled and pampered his wife during the time of waiting. He planned the nursery, with input from Elizabeth about soft furnishings. He instructed Phillip to wallpaper the bedroom next to theirs, having chosen a paper covered in baby animals on a sunny yellow background. A new carpet was installed, along with a cradle, chest of drawers, rocking chair, and a sturdy table for bathing and dressing the infant. The drawers were soon filled with necessities, including the knitted items lovingly made by Joan.

"You should probably come to the North Staffs for the delivery," Julius suggested. "I can make arrangements for you to have the very best of care."

"Absolutely not," Elizabeth retorted. "I have had a perfect pregnancy, and I will give birth here at home, like every other mother. I have already talked to Winnifred Beardmore, who is an excellent midwife, and she will attend me when the time comes."

Julius raised his eyebrows, and opened his mouth to argue the point, but decided against it, seeing the determined look on his wife's face.

"Very well, as you wish," he said. "I will be here too, of course. I do have some experience."

"Oh, darling, you will be right with me," Elizabeth consoled her husband. "I wouldn't bring our baby into this world without you beside me."

It all went according to plan, and Winnifred Beardmore arrived when Elizabeth's contractions became more frequent, and Julius assessed the timing was right.

How different to be patients instead of doctors!

The midwife assured them continually that all was well, as the long labour of a first baby born to a woman at thirty years of age, progressed ever so slowly and painfully.

Joan, Bertha, and Phillip sat in the kitchen brewing pots and pots of tea as the hours slipped by. Joan took cups of the steaming brew into the bedroom at regular intervals for Julius and the midwife, along with cool fresh water for Elizabeth.

Phillip fell asleep with his head to one side on the kitchen table, his mouth open. As he snored softly, Joan was too tense to relax and, with fingers flying, continued to knit the fan and feather lacy shawl she had almost finished. Bertha busied herself washing the tea cups, refilling the kettle, and listening at the bottom of the stairs for a call from the midwife that supplies were now needed.

It had been quiet for so long, Bertha sat down on the bottom stair and laid her head against the strong wooden stair rail. She jolted with a start when she heard Mrs Beardmore's voice from above.

"We need the supplies now," she called. "Warm water, cloths, towels. Bring everything upstairs."

Joan and Bertha hurriedly filled the jug with warm water, collected the items needed, and ran upstairs, hearts fluttering with excitement. The midwife smiled a greeting and told them where to put everything.

"Better put the kettle on again," Mrs Beardmore said. "This new mother is going to need a cuppa very soon."

The two women flew back down the stairs to refill the kettle and tell the now awakened Phillip that things were on the move.

"'Bout time!" he said with a grunt.

"One more push, Doctor Lingford," urged Winnifred.

"I can't," yelled Elizabeth.

She clung onto Julius' hand as her body did the work of pushing the baby into the world. A baby girl with a mass of dark hair slid into Winnifred's waiting hands, and announced her arrival with a hearty cry.

The cry was heard downstairs, and the boiling water was poured into the teapot immediately; the cuppa for Doctor Elizabeth was on its way upstairs before the baby was five minutes old.

Elizabeth and Julius had witnessed the birth of a baby, if not hundreds, of times, yet nothing could compare to the birth of their own daughter. Both doctors were unprepared for the trauma and distress they had experienced.

They both cried, then laughed, then cried again. Julius took the tiny girl and laid her on her mother's naked breast, so that she could suckle.

Efficient Winnifred Beardmore had everything cleaned up in no time, and took the baby to bathe her in the warm water. Dressed and swaddled, she now slept comfortably in the crook of her father's arm, while his tired wife enjoyed her tea and scones, with Joan at her side beaming from ear to ear.

"I should have had more sympathy for the women I attend-ed," Elizabeth said between mouthfuls of the delicious scones. "That was the hardest most painful work of my life."

"But the most rewarding," glowed Julius. "Darling, you were marvellous. I don't think I've ever been that scared in my life."

Winnifred nodded and smiled at the two of them.

"You're no different than every other new mam and dad," she said. "We're all born the same way. Doesn't matter if you're rich or poor, educated or not, young or old. It's always a miracle, no matter what."

They named her Alice Victoria, and she was doted on day and night by both her parents, and the live-in servants. Bertha took on extra duties taking care of the baby during the day, so that Elizabeth could rest and eventually begin to see a few patients each day. The baby thrived on all the attention, and delighted everybody who met her with her dimpled cheeks, curly black hair, and steel grey eyes.

CHAPTER 52

JOY BEYOND MEASURE

In the thirty years of Elizabeth's life she couldn't remember being so happy. Her future seemed settled and the years of change were behind her. Alice's arrival, although completely unexpected, cemented everything she held dear, giving new meaning to her marriage, her work, and her future.

For both parents, Alice brought a joy they had never imagined. She was the centre of their existence, and as they watched her grow into a little girl, she filled their home with her exuberance and energy.

Julius pared down his surgery hours, taking Fridays off each week, to spend more time with his daughter. Elizabeth opened her practice three mornings each week, and arranged with Doctor Morrison to take some of her house calls. Fortunately Julius had arranged to have a telephone installed at the house, which made communication so easy. A morning phone call to her colleague, and Elizabeth could let Doctor Morrison know about the patients who needed a home visit, although she still preferred to attend the midwifery cases herself.

The family at Lingford Manor were overjoyed with the news of the baby, and when Julius, Elizabeth and Alice finally made the trip to visit, they were greeted by a group of boisterous children, all wanting to play with Alice. The family had increased over the years, with Percy, Lydia and Carolyn adding more offspring to their families. The grandchildren of Arnold and Maud Lingford now numbered ten. The old manor house was alive with noise and activity, as a steady stream of youngsters chased each other, tumbling over the furniture and rolling around on the floor.

Alice, being an only child and from a quiet adult household, stared in amazement at all the chaos and sat on her father's lap. It took a few hours of observance before she was confident enough to take the hand of Percy's eldest daughter, and join in the fun. Her cousins were gentle with her, and took her to play with the doll's house in the nursery, while the adults had afternoon tea and chatted about the time when they were children.

Lady Lingford had deteriorated still further, and stayed in her room seated near the window where she could look out over the garden. She no longer communicated, except to nod and smile when she had a visitor. She didn't recognize Elizabeth or any of her other children. She was in her own world, consisting of a window and a garden.

"Poor Mama," Elizabeth said to Carolyn as they sat beside their mother. "She isn't really old, yet she has withdrawn from the world. How sad that she has missed so much of life with her grandchildren."

"I don't think she suffers, Elizabeth," Carolyn said. "She is well cared for, and content, I believe. We tried to include her in family gatherings until she became so distraught with the children around her, that we decided it was better she stayed in her room where she is comfortable."

"I'm sure that losing Henry and then Father had a far greater impact on her than any of us imagined," Elizabeth said. "Grief, particularly hidden beneath the veneer Mama always had, can destroy the soul, and have long-lasting effects on the mind and body."

Elizabeth kissed her mother before leaving, and received a

nod and smile in her direction. It was the last time she would see her.

Lady Lingford died a month after their visit, and the LaPortes travelled south once more for a funeral. It was quiet and restrained. The family had mourned the loss of their mother for years. Her death was only a final expected step.

After the funeral, Elizabeth took her leave of her brother and sisters and their families with a light heart. Mother's illness over such a long period had been a strain on them all, and in many ways she was relieved it was over for them. She felt guilty that she had lived away from Lingford during those years and borne none of the anguish. She held each one of them close before turning away to climb into the car next to Julius.

"Take me home, my dear," Elizabeth whispered.

As soon as Alice turned three years of age, she accompanied her mother to the stables at Granger Manor. She was instantly delighted with the horses she saw running around in the fields, and when she was introduced to Blue Shadow at close quarters, she almost tumbled from Elizabeth's arms as she tried to get closer.

The horse was suspicious of the tiny person at first, but eventually relented to Elizabeth's gentle persuasion, and allowed Alice to stroke her nose and feed her the carrot she offered. They were soon firm friends; Blue Shadow nuzzled the curious little girl on her neck, sending her into fits of laughter.

"I love her, Mummy," Alice laughed. "Can I ride on her back?"

"She's much too big for you, darling," Elizabeth said. "You can begin riding on a small pony though. I will make arrangements with the stable master. You are going to love riding as much as I do."

Every day Alice begged to go back to the stables. She began

her riding lessons on a gentle pony named Buttons, with her mother keeping careful watch. Saturday mornings were the highlight of the week for both mother and daughter. A custom from Elizabeth's childhood that brought back a flood of happy memories.

CHAPTER 53

WALKING OUT

C hange was inevitable. Although Julius and Elizabeth clung desperately to their lives staying the same, it seemed a new surprise was always on their doorstep.

"Can I 'ave a word, Doctor Laporte?" Phillip asked. The two men were working in the garden together. It was a sunny Saturday morning and Elizabeth and Alice were riding at Grange Stables.

"Of course, Phillip. What is it?" Julius responded, getting up from his kneeling position to give the young man his attention.

"Well, it's like this, sir," Phillip began. "I've been walkin' out with a young lady for the best part of a year now. I want to ask 'er to marry me, but I need to find a better position so I can provide for 'er."

"I see," Julius said. "Thank you for talking to me about it. I am happy for you. Finding somebody to be your wife is no easy task, and you are a fortunate young man. Can I persuade you to stay with us for now? At least give us time to think how we may help with your future plans."

"Of course," Phillip replied. "The last thing I want is to leave you and Doctor Elizabeth. You're like me family. That's what's making it so 'ard."

"Leave it with me then. I'll talk to my wife about it tonight. She's the one with the best ideas."

Phillip had no family close by. His parents had both died when he was a boy and he had been brought up by an older sister, who had since moved to Yorkshire to marry a farmer. He considered himself lucky to have found his position with the LaPorte family, who had given him a home as well as employment. Joan Turner was like a mother to him, and Bertha like a sister. He never went without a meal, or a comfortable bed to sleep in, and if he hadn't met Vera at the local Chapel, he would have been content to stay where he was forever.

"We have to think of some way we can keep him here with us," was Elizabeth's first reaction to the news. "He's too old to begin an apprenticeship, and he could probably only find work as a labourer on a pottery factory. He's a good lad, hardworking and conscientious."

"I agree," said Julius. "We have to consider what would be best for him and his future though. Are we doing him any favours by holding onto him?"

They both kept their ears to the ground in the community, hoping a solution would present itself, and miraculously it did.

Mrs Griffin hobbled into the surgery, her face screwed up in pain.

"Good morning, Mrs Griffin," greeted Elizabeth. "How can I help you?"

"It's this blasted knee, Doctor," she rubbed the offending leg. "Giving me some gyp, it is. I can't even stand up for a few minutes without it giving way. I've been rubbing it with horse liniment every night, but it's doing nothing."

"Let me take a look," Elizabeth said.

Easier said than done. Mrs Griffin removed her shoe, her woollen over sock, her lyle stocking, and several feet of bandage before the knee was ready for examination. She winced as the doctor carefully moved the joint.

"You have arthritis very badly in this joint," Elizabeth told her. "No amount of liniment or bandages will help, I'm afraid. You will need to keep the pressure off this knee. That means rest as much as you can. It also means a cane or even a crutch to help support you when you stand or walk. There is no easy answer to this, Mrs Griffin."

"How am I going to manage the shop?" she cried. "With Billy gone, these last three years have been hard enough. We never had a family, and I can't afford to get somebody in to run it for me. This will be the finish of me."

The old lady sat sobbing quietly.

Elizabeth's mind was racing. The little hardware shop was just in the next street, a few minutes away. It stocked everything from nails, wood, screws, saws, plumbing pipes, to kitchen utensils, clothes pegs, mangles, and everything in between. It had served the community well for more than thirty years.

"Dry your tears, Mrs Griffin," Elizabeth said. "I will send Phillip home with you to give you a hand. He will get you settled and write a note to put on the front door to say the shop will be closed for a few days."

"I can't do that," gasped Mrs Griffin. "I've never closed the shop, except for two days when Billy died."

"Well, you need to get some rest right now. I will come on home visits for the next few days to see how you are getting on. You let Phillip know what food you need and he will shop for you. Now, no more arguing. We will just take this a day at a time."

Elizabeth couldn't wait for Julius to come home. She gave Alice her tea, and settled her at her little play table in the dining room, giving her blocks and colouring to occupy her. Bertha served dinner to the two doctors, smiling at Julius as she knew it was one of his favourite meals—roast pork, potatoes, carrots, stuffing and apple sauce, with lashings of gravy.

"I think a small miracle might have happened today," began Elizabeth. "Maybe the answer to our prayers regarding Phillip."

"I want to hear all about this miracle then," Julius grinned.

Elizabeth went on to tell him all about Mrs Griffin and the hardware shop, watching his face for his reaction.

"And?" he questioned, his mouth full of pork and potatoes. "The miracle would be?"

"Isn't it obvious?" Elizabeth asked. "It's the perfect shop for Phillip to run. It sells everything he is most interested in and knows so much about."

"Mmmm! How would this work, darling?"

"Julius, we could buy the shop from Mrs Griffin. She can't continue to run it. I've thought it all through, and it would work so well for everybody."

Her husband's frown deepened as he continued to listen.

"Mrs Griffin could continue to live there, of course. She would be invaluable in helping Phillip get used to things. Phillip could still live with us, along with Vera—there's plenty of room for two in his bedroom and we could convert one of the other rooms on that floor to a small sitting room for them, so that they had some privacy. Don't you think it's a perfect plan.?"

"I can see some imperfections, to be honest," Julius retorted.

"What?"

"A newly married couple moving in with us. Not exactly how I would imagine they intended to begin life together. I'm sure they would prefer their own accommodations."

"Then who would help us here?" asked Elizabeth

"Ah! Well! That is the question, isn't it."

CHAPTER 54

MRS GRIFFIN TO THE RESCUE

Phillip was excited about Elizabeth's idea. His young lady, Vera, worked in a haberdashery store in the town, and he thought she would jump at the chance to work in the hardware store instead. Before he mentioned it to her, he promised to wait until Doctor Elizabeth had been to visit Mrs Griffin, who was a vital part of the equation.

"Come in, Doctor," greeted Mrs Griffin. "Come through to the living room."

She hobbled ahead of Elizabeth, introducing her on the way to Pamela, who was looking after the shop.

"She's my friend's granddaughter," Mrs Griffin explained. "She's married to a nice young man, with a good job, and they're expecting later this year. She was happy to help out for a couple of months, while I make some decisions about the shop."

Elizabeth poured the boiling water from the old blackened kettle simmering on the fire hob, and filled the teapot, already prepared with the tea leaves. She carried the tray, with cups, sugar, milk, and a plate of shortbread cookies over to the table.

"Here we go," she said, pouring a cup of the steaming brew. "I've come to put a proposition to you concerning the shop and your future plans."

"Dr Julius and I would be interested in purchasing the premises, as an investment. You would, of course, continue to live here for as long as you need to. We would also like you to consider allowing Phillip, and his young lady to take over the running of the shop. We haven't worked out all the details yet, but we are very fond of Phillip and hope to find some way of keeping him involved at our property."

"Well I never," gulped Mrs Griffin. "You've surprised me with your plan, and no mistake. I don't know what to think. I took an instant liking to young Phillip. Ever so kind, he was, helping me home."

"Please take some time to think it through, Mrs Griffin," Elizabeth said. "Phillip wants to ask his young lady to marry him, and doesn't feel he can pop the question until he has better employment. I believe this move may be the answer he's looking for."

The old lady looked up at her doctor with tears in her eyes.

"I understand," she said. "You have his best interests at heart, and God bless you for that. I have nobody to answer to—just myself and the good Lord. He probably struck me with this bad knee so I had to make a new path in life. If that path means helping young Phillip, then I'm all for it. Sounds like I wouldn't have any hardship anyhow, staying in my own place, and having him here to help out. What does he say about all this? When does he want to get married? Does his young lady know about the plan?"

"Hold on," Elizabeth replied. "The first thing we needed to do was to talk to you about it. I don't want you to make a snap decision. I want you to really think about it."

"I've never had to sit on a decision for long in my life. I make my mind up fast, I do. The one big question I have really is …"

"Well, what is your big question?" Elizabeth asked.

"Do you think young Phillip and his lass would consider living here with me? There's a lovely big bedroom upstairs, and now I'm so handicapped, I stay down here. I have a little bedroom at the back, just off the kitchen. It suits me just fine. Close to the loo and the kitchen. If Phillips's young lady has experience working in a shop, she'll do well here. It would leave time for Phillip to still go over the road to your place and do his work there."

There it was, the whole plan laid out. A perfect plan that would work for everybody. Not only would the young couple have somewhere to live, but Vera would have work and Phillip would still tend to the maintenance and grounds at the doctors' house as part of the LaPorte household staff.

"Mrs Griffin, I believe you have solved every problem," laughed Elizabeth, gulping down the last of her tea. "Why don't I come back to visit once Phillip has talked to Vera."

Phillips's face turned scarlet when his employers explained what Mrs Griffin had proposed. It was a splendid solution to his dilemma, and he was especially elated that he could still work for them. He asked if he could leave early that afternoon to wait for Vera to finish work, so that he could tell her everything.

Phillip came back to the house that evening shining with happiness.

"I asked her to marry me today," he laughed. "And she said 'yes'."

"Why didn't you bring 'er back with you?" Joan asked. "We all want to meet your young lady. Invite 'er for tea on Sunday. The doctors will both be home, and I'll make a special treat for us all."

Vera was nervous about meeting Phillip's "family." She dressed in her best frock, and fussed with her blond curly hair— finally deciding to hold the curls in order with a blue satin ribbon. Phillip went to her house to pick her up, and they walked the fifteen minutes to Blackstone Road hand in hand.

"Don't be scared, Vera," Phillip said. "They're all lovely people. Joan and Bertha will make you feel right at home, and the doctors and little Alice will do the same. They're all longing to meet you."

The young couple were greeted warmly by Joan and Bertha, putting Vera at ease right away. Tea was laid out on the kitchen table, with enough cakes, scones, and savoury sandwiches to feed a small army. The doctors and Alice joined them in the kitchen and sat around the table in the comfortable atmosphere. They chatted and laughed, and all made a fuss of Alice, who declared the tea "The best I've ever had".

Plans for a quick wedding ensued. With somewhere to live and a job for each of them, Phillip and Vera saw no reason to wait.

Vera chose a simple dress with pink rose buds in her hair. Her two younger sisters were bridesmaids, and wore matching blue dresses. Alice was asked to be in the bridal party too, and a pale pink organza dress was bought for her. Vera's dad proudly walked Vera down the aisle in the small Wesleyan chapel. He was a hard working potter, and one of the few who didn't drink. Despite a family of five to support, he had scraped together enough savings to buy dresses for his three girls for this special occasion. His beaming face showed how delighted he was.

Julius and Elizabeth invited guests to their house after the wedding ceremony, where Joan and Bertha had been preparing a luncheon for days. The house was buzzing with happiness, as the bride's family joined with the groom's adopted family to celebrate.

With the newly married couple settled into their new home at the hardware shop, and Mrs Griffin content and happy with the arrangement, Elizabeth looked forward to a comfortable, peaceful life.

CHAPTER 55

1939

The dining room looked festive with the table set for ten. The best china surrounded by crystal glasses, linen napkins, floral centrepieces and candles, was perfectly placed. In the kitchen Joan Turner was busy putting the final touches to a pink and white birthday cake. Bertha stood at the stove stirring a pot of gravy, and keeping an eye on the other bubbling pots.

"Is everything going well?" Elizabeth asked as she peeked around the door into the kitchen. "Do you need me to help in any way?"

"It's all under control," Joan answered. "Don't you worry now. Dinner will be served on time."

Julius poured drinks for their guests as they arrived. Two families who they had come to know as friends chatted and laughed with each other in the living room. Alice's best friends were among them, along with their parents. Four girls all together, who ran upstairs with Alice to look at her newly decorated bedroom.

"I can barely believe we are celebrating Alice's eighth birthday," Julius laughed. "Elizabeth and I are delighted you could join us. It means the world to our daughter to have her friends here."

A wonderful meal of favourite foods was served by a beaming Bertha and Phillip: cheese and onion soup with crusty buns, followed by fried chicken, baby potatoes, and peas. Lastly, the pink and white cake was carried into the dining room with eight candles burning brightly.

"Happy Birthday" resounded around the room, while Alice blushed and giggled before blowing out the flames.

Eight years of watching their daughter grow, years when life was so sweet and abundant for them. Each Christmas they travelled to Lingford and again in the summer to ride, relax and enjoy family times. Late August, they always drove north to Scotland to spend time with Jocelyn at Gordon House, where they showed Alice the beauty of the western coastline and the surrounding countryside.

Jennifer McPhee, Elizabeth's colleague from Glasgow Hospital, had married a poet from Aberdeen, and moved there with him to open her own practice. She made the trip to Gordon House every year when the LaPorte family were there to spend a few days with her dear friend.

Jocelyn remained in surprisingly good health, and enjoyed watching all the activity as people from the town came to use the stables each day.

Alice became a proficient rider, and accompanied her mother to Granger Manor each Saturday, but most of all she loved to ride the ponies at Lingford and Gordon House. She inherited her love for the outdoors from Elizabeth, and was never happier than when riding through the countryside under the trees at Lingford, or galloping through the heather towards the sea in Scotland.

Phillip and Vera worked hard running the shop and taking care of Mrs Griffin. Vera gave birth to a son in the first year of their marriage, with Elizabeth attending her. He was a big baby and the birth was not without difficulty. Phillip closed the shop and sat beside his wife, holding her hand through the hours of labour, while Elizabeth popped back and forth between home and shop, keeping an eye on her patient. Since Alice's birth, Elizabeth had a new respect and empathy for the birthing process, and encouraged Vera to be brave and strong each time she checked on her progress. Eventually the baby made it into the world, greeted by tears of joy by his parents and doctor.

They named him Noah. A year later, and with a lot less trouble, Margaret was born.

Despite the hustle and bustle of life with two babies, Vera and Phillip seemed to manage their lives with very little fuss. Mrs Griffin loved nothing more than watching over the sleeping babies while Vera worked in the shop, and even managed to hobble out of her room to serve customers when Vera was busy with her family. Phillip was always on hand when deliveries arrived or if Vera needed more time with the babies. The arrangement worked very well for them all.

The whole community went on living their lives, but everybody in 1938 had one ear tuned to the news on the radio, or an eye on the daily newspapers. Surely not! Not again! Rumours of war with Germany was the issue of the day. People clung onto the words of the Prime Minister, who told them not to worry, he had signed a peace agreement with Germany. There would not be another war. Still, the rumours persisted.

Julius and Elizabeth, like many of their peers had already lived through one world war. The memories from that time were imbedded in their minds. There were no happy memories, only recollections of sorrow, destruction, pain and anguish. How could this happen again so soon?

The following year, they cancelled their trip to Scotland in August, preferring to stay at home to await the outcome of more negotiations, as the tension in Europe grew.

On September 3rd, a pleasant Sunday morning, the whole of Great Britain came to a standstill.

"Make a pot of tea please, Joan," Elizabeth said as she walked into the kitchen. "I think we're going to need it. Bring it through to the living room, and ask Bertha to join us."

The five of them gathered around the radio at eleven o'clock to listen to the Prime Minister. The streets of the town were silent and empty as every family gathered to listen, praying they would hear good news.

It could not have been worse. Neville Chamberlain announced that the government had given Germany an ultimatum to withdraw their troops from Poland. No such action had occurred, and Britain was now at war with Germany.

The small group in the LaPorte house sat in stunned silence, each holding their cups of tea. Alice looked from one to another, searching for a sign from one of the adults that it was not as bad as it sounded.

After the initial shock, tears spilled down Bertha's face, and Joan put her arm around her young friend to comfort her. Julius did the same with Elizabeth and Alice, enclosing both of them in his strong arms and kissing each forehead.

"What does it mean?" asked Alice anxiously.

"War," her father answered with one word. "Something we thought could never happen again in our lifetime. What utter fools."

Julius jumped up to pace the floor, angry that such a decision had been reached. His mind flooded with visions of young men in battle, hurt and dying. Of the women left at home to struggle on their own, not knowing if they would see their husbands, sons, and brothers again. He pushed his lips together and closed his eyes to blot out the images, and to stop himself from saying anything else in front of his precious nine-year-old daughter.

The pleasant, peaceful life they had enjoyed since Alice was born was about to disintegrate, not only for their family, but for every family in the United Kingdom and beyond.

CHAPTER 56

NO QUICK FIX

E
lizabeth had been fourteen years old when the great
war began. She remembered those days vividly. Her
two brothers had left to join all the other young men
ready to fight for their country. Elwyn Thomas had said goodbye
as he packed his few belongings and headed home to join a
Welsh regiment. The small community of Lingford had been
suddenly bereft of young men, with women having to keep the
estate running. The war that they thought would be over by
Christmas had lasted four long years, and Elizabeth had grown
from girl to woman during that time.

Now, at almost forty years of age she knew, from past experience, that war was never a quick fix. How many months or years
would this one last? How many men would die? How many
families would be ripped apart? What would happen if
Germany defeated them?

When Alice was finally in bed and assured everything would
be all right, Elizabeth joined Julius in the living room and sank
down on the sofa beside him, resting her head on his strong
shoulder.

"Will we survive another conflict with Germany?" she asked
quietly.

"We must," Julius replied. "Anything else is unthinkable. I cannot begin to imagine what the battle will be like this time. Vastly improved arms of every kind: tanks, mortars, machine guns, grenades. The aircraft nowadays are beyond anything we thought possible—fast and deadly fighter planes, bombers that can carry a load of bombs enough to destroy a city. The incredible armada of ships we will need, from huge battleships to destroyers and convoy escorts, to defend the oceans is mind-blowing."

"Maybe peace can still be achieved, somehow," Elizabeth sighed. "I keep remembering the soldiers at Lingford coming back from the front. It was all so horrible, Julius. So many killed and maimed. Surely it won't be as bad!"

"My darling, you are so precious," smiled Julius. "You keep thinking that way. I saw my fill of horror during the three years I served as an army surgeon to last me several lifetimes. I, like many others, have spent the past twenty years trying to eradicate some of those memories. I have a feeling this war will be much worse."

An ice cold chill filled Elizabeth's body. She sat very still beside her husband, not daring to ask her next question.

As they sat in silence, she gathered her courage. She had to know.

"Do you think you will be called up again?"

"No, I do not," Julius replied, trying not to look at his wife. "I am far too old now to be considered, even as a volunteer. A great pity, because I could, and would willingly contribute my experience in a battlefield medical facility."

Julius sat gazing into space, wishing he was younger. Despite all he would leave behind, he wanted to serve his country as he had done before. It was difficult for him to accept his lack of youth, which would confine him to his safe position at the North Staffordshire Hospital.

Julius pulled his wife into his arms and held her close.

"I hope and pray that this conflict will be over soon, and that there will be few casualties. I can't bear to think of a repetition of the last war," Julius said softly. "My greatest consolation is that I will be here with you and Alice. You are both so precious to me that I cannot imagine leaving you behind."

"So many of our patients will be in that very situation," Elizabeth muttered. "Babies will be born without their fathers even knowing. Mothers, sweethearts, sisters and daughters, will all feel the despair and worry of their loved ones fighting in a foreign land, waiting and hoping that the telegram they dread will never be delivered."

"We will be on our own front line right here, won't we?" Julius said. "Left to comfort and support the families who will try their best to live through this incredibly stressful time."

Elizabeth cuddled closer to her husband, thankful that he would be with her for the duration of this second war with Germany in their lifetime.

Nobody could talk of anything other than war. The whole town was buzzing with it. Every patient Elizabeth saw, no matter the ailment, wanted to have their say, especially those who had lived through it all before. The women mourned the loved ones they had lost more than twenty years before and cried in anguish thinking about the ones they may lose in the second war.

All men between the ages of eighteen and forty-one would be conscripted, and were required to register with the National Service. Within a few months, more than one and a half million young single men, including volunteers, had been absorbed into the army. Conscription continued until the villages, towns and cities of Britain were noticeably devoid of young men.

As Christmas approached, nobody felt like celebrating. Many households were without husbands, brothers, and sweethearts, leaving the women to put on a brave face for the children.

"Come on, Mrs T. You too, Bertha." Julius announced as he strode into the kitchen on December 21st. "We are not going to let

Hitler dictate to this family. We are all going to Lingford for Christmas, including the two of you, if you are willing."

"Oh Doctor Laporte," smiled Joan, "What a lovely treat that would be. Are you sure me and Bertha won't be in the way?"

"Not at all, my dear," answered the doctor. "In fact, there is a hidden agenda. Would it be possible to rustle up some Christmas baking before we leave? Mince pies or a nice pork pie or two? We are leaving on December twenty-third. Can you manage a miracle like that in a couple of days?"

"You can count on it, sir," answered Joan Turner. "We'll have it all ready to go, won't we Bertha?"

"Of course we will," said Bertha, smiling up at her employer. "Me mam won't mind me not goin' 'ome. She's got me auntie and 'er three boys stayin' over Christmas. Too many folks in one little 'ouse."

"Then it's all settled," Julius said with a smile.

Two days later the family, along with Joan Turner and Bertha, loaded up the car and set out for the journey south. If this was to be the last Christmas together, they were determined to enjoy it.

CHAPTER 57

CHRISTMAS AT LINGFORD

The Laporte family did not regret their decision to spend Christmas at Lingford. Alice enjoyed the company of her cousins immensely and loved the freedom the vast estate allowed her.

The household staff welcomed Joan and Bertha into their midst. They were happy to have extra help, particularly because the household had increased in numbers when three evacuee children from London had arrived two weeks before. Two brothers and a sister, whose ages ranged from eight to twelve, were now part of the Lingford family.

They missed their mother desperately, and had spent most of their days in tears, not wanting to eat much or talk to anybody. Alice, being a similar age, made it her mission to befriend them and before long had them laughing and eating. Once she had persuaded them to go to the stables with her and pet the horses and meet the stable hands, they were won over. The only horses they had seen in London were either police or military, and the three children were fascinated by everything they saw in the cavernous Lingford Stables. They moved from stall to stall, tentatively at first, looking up at the huge animals towering above their heads. Alice handed out carrots to the children, assuring them that the horses would not bite off their hands along with the carrots. They were soon happily stroking the smooth warm necks and giggling at the wet hairy noses exploring their ears and heads.

"They're luvly, aren't they?" The eldest boy said. "Big and scary at first, but not any more. What would mam say if she could see us now?"

"She'd laugh and laugh," smiled his brother. "She'd say we were lucky to be livin' in such a place."

"Come on," Alice said, "Let's go and ask Tom if he can take us for a ride.

Tom Anderson was the new stable master. He had big shoes to fill, but had worked with McCarthy for more than ten years, and knew every detail of running the stables, as well as every inch of every horse.

He gazed at the young mistress with a smile on his face.

"You want a ride do you?" he asked. "Well, I don't know about that Miss. Maybe I should check with Miss Elizabeth first. If she gives the go-ahead, we could hitch up old Barnaby here and go for a trot around the estate."

He walked with the children back to the manor and waited while Alice found her mother. Elizabeth was all for the idea, of course.

"Give me ten minutes, Sam," she said. "I think I'll join you. What fun! I'll grab blankets to keep us all warm."

Covered in warm blankets, the four children sat in the open carriage as one of the young stable boys trotted the horse around the estate park. They came back rosy-cheeked and hungry. Making up for the lack of food in previous days they demolished the Cornish pasties served for lunch, washing them down with fresh milk, followed by cook's special chocolate pudding.

"Thank you, Alice," the eldest boy, Mark, said. "It's bin a cracking day. We don't feel so 'omesick any more."

His brother, Jim, and sister, Diane, nodded in agreement, their mouths so full of pasty they couldn't answer.

Despite the circumstances, Christmas turned out to be an unexpected pleasure at Lingford Manor. The whole family joined them for Christmas dinner, with the older cousins supervising all kinds of hilarious activities for the afternoon. The three children from London were dragged into games of charades, hide-and-seek, hunt the thimble, and blind man's bluff. It was noisy, chaotic and so much fun.

The two hay wagons were hitched up after tea, and everybody bundled up in their warmest clothes before climbing aboard for the hayride. They sang carols and funny ditties, pushed each other off the back of the wagons, fed the horses apples at the end of the ride, and tumbled back into the house for hot chocolate and Joan's mince pies.

Mark, Jim, and Diane were sad to say goodbye to their new friend, Alice, when the LaPorte family packed up to head north. They were, however, feeling much better about their life in the country, and they were all looking forward to going to school in the village after the Christmas break. Alice made them promise to visit the stables every day, and she talked to her Uncle Percy about riding lessons for them. She hoped it would take away some of the heartache of leaving their home and family behind.

CHAPTER 58

NOT ENOUGH TO EAT

A new reality hit Britain in the new year. Rationing of food and other essential items came into force, challenging everybody to review and reduce their basic meal choices. Ration books were issued to each family, supposedly providing sufficient calories to survive. The threat of German Uboats targeting merchant ships in the Atlantic Ocean forced the government to recognize that food transportation from North America was in jeopardy, and the people of Britain could face serious starvation.

At first only bacon, butter, and sugar were rationed, but other foods were quickly added as the year went on. Women shared recipes with each other, with suggestions of how to spin out the meagre quantity of ingredients they had to work with.

Families with children were given an extra stamp each week for luxury items such as one egg, two ounces of cheese, and one orange per child, which were deemed essential for growth. Big families faired better than those with fewer children. The meagre extra rations for children could be spread a little further.

The basic diet for the average working class people became canned corned beef, potatoes, and canned sardines. People lined up at the butchers' shops to be first in line to buy a few links of sausage. Tinned milk sandwiches became a popular lunch in Staffordshire, or meat paste of some kind—whatever was available in the grocery shops.

Mrs Plant was one such mother, known to Elizabeth. She lived in one of the poorest streets in town, and struggled every day to feed her family.

"Mam, I can't eat another sardine," whined Betty, as Mrs Plant shared two small tins of the tiny fish between her brood of five children. "Why does dad get sausages?"

"Because 'e works all day long, and deserves a good tea."[1] Snapped her mother. "You'll eat your sardines without another outburst like that."

"Can we have some of dad's chips then?" asked Billy, who at ten years old was always hungry.

Before his wife could answer, Mr Plant carefully shared his chips with the children, giving each child three chips. He winked at each child as he deposited the wonderful deep fried potatoes onto their plates.

"You soft old bugger," his wife said, but with a smile on her face. "Y'd give your arse away and shit through your ribs if you thought it would help yer little 'uns".

She laughed out loud, joined by her family, and placed a big loud kiss on her husband's forehead.

"Eee though," Mr Plant said quietly. "I wouldn'a say no to an oatcake or two smothered in bacon and cheese."

Everybody did their best in dire circumstances, and looked for small ways they could support each other and make life a little easier.

Phillip was exempt from National Service because of his flat feet. He was desperately disappointed, and was determined to do everything in his power to help with the war effort. He joined the Home Guard, working several nights each week on street

---

1. Tea. The common word for dinner or supper.

patrol, to ensure no lights were visible, and report any suspicious or dangerous activity.

He and Vera tried to offer a variety of available foods in their little shop, but the shelves often stood empty when the convoys bringing food across the Atlantic didn't arrive on time, or worse still were sunk during their hazardous journey.

Phillip was inspired to dig up the flower beds at the doctors' house and, with permission from Julius and Elizabeth, he planted vegetables instead. By the end of summer he was able to harvest potatoes, cabbage, carrots and turnips to offer to his customers. Many households followed his example, and grew what they could on any spare patch of earth, although it was rare to find anywhere in the industrial town that wasn't paved.

Further afield, out in the countryside, the land army girls worked tirelessly to provide fresh produce, which was snapped up by the city folks at the Saturday markets. The Government created the land army to help farmers while the young men who normally worked on the farms were fighting. These hard-working girls worked throughout Britain helping produce food for the population.

At Granger Manor every spare plot of land was put into use to aid the plight of the hungry. Each week when she returned from her ride Elizabeth brought back enough vegetables to fill the boot of her car. Phillip and Vera stocked their shelves with the precious food, and the families waiting outside the shop were able to exchange food stamps for the fresh food.

The living conditions of the people in North Staffordshire deteriorated quickly. Old men drowned their sorrows nightly at the pub. The women struggled on, trying to keep food on the table for their families, and taking on part time jobs at the factories to help replace the young men. Houses remained neglected when there were not enough hours in the day to do more than the bare necessities. Children learned to fend for themselves, the oldest taking care of the younger ones. They became used to running to the chippie[2] for tuppence[3] worth of chips for the family to share. Mothers and grans would send their oldest, often only eight or ten years of age, to the market on Saturday nights to buy broken biscuits, dinged apples, or any other food that the vendors may be getting rid of for a few pence. Somehow they managed to survive, despite the lack of any kind of comfort.

Young women were called up to war work, most of them to the munitions factory in Swynnerton, or a smaller percentage to the land army. A few, who had the skills required, joined the army, airforce, or navy as nurses, drivers, or office workers.

Through it all Elizabeth kept her practise going. Babies were born, arriving nine months after their father's military leave. Women were troubled with poor health from lack of good food, as well as long laborious work days. Every mother was malnourished in some way. Monthly menstruation often stopped, constipation was prevalent, and the constant worry on all their minds was whether or not their men serving in the armed forces would make it home unscathed.

Everybody worked. Everybody scrounged for food. Everybody was hungry.

Julius sank down into the soft cushions of the sofa in the living room, exhausted from a long day which had begun at four in the morning. It had not been an easy day. A mother in her forties had struggled to give birth to her tenth child, who was stillborn. Julius had been called in for a consultation after the poor woman did not recover well after the birth.

Julius took the woman's hand in his and looked into her eyes.

"My name is Doctor Laporte," he said gently. "I am here to help you. I am so sorry you lost your baby. Try not to be scared, I will examine you and will decide what is best for you. Is that all right with you?"

---

2. Chippie. Fish and Chip shop
3. Tuppence. Two pence

Mrs Price nodded in agreement and closed her eyes, letting the tears ooze down her ashen cheeks.

It had been obvious to Julius, after the examination, that Mrs Price needed surgery quickly. Her uterus was worn out and there was no way to stem the tide of blood. She needed a hysterectomy if she was going to survive.

"You need an operation," Julius explained to his patient. "Rest assured that I will take great care of you, and you will be healthy and strong after you've had a rest. Now you lie back and let us look after you."

"Hello, darling," Elizabeth greeted her tired husband, handing him a small glass of sherry. "Tough day?"

"Thank you," Julius sighed. "You could say that. The sherry is most welcome."

He paused after sipping his drink, before finding his wife's eyes with his own.

"It was a tough day, but nothing nearly as tough as being an army surgeon during the great war. I have thought and thought about little else since our troops were rescued from Dunkirk in June. The Germans could have invaded at that time and won the war in a matter of weeks. Why didn't they? Britain had nothing to fight back with after leaving just about every scrap of military equipment in France."

"Maybe because the German Luftwaffe[4] are so superior, they believe they can accomplish their victory over Britain by bombing our cities every night. The news today was horrifying. London was bombed again, and Coventry has been reduced to a pile of rubble. The RAF is doing its best with what fighter planes they have, but there are so few pilots trying to hold off such a tremendous force of German bombers."

"If we survive this onslaught somehow, there will be plans for an invasion sometime in the future. I only wish I was eligible to volunteer. 'Too old' the army said when I enquired. What a

---

4. Luftwaffe. German airforce

load of stuff and nonsense. I feel I would be a great asset to any military hospital. Look at all the experience I have. Am I to sit at home and let other men do my job?"

Julius jumped up and paced up and down the room with his fists clenched and his eyes flashing. At fifty-eight years of age he was appalled to be written off as "too old."

"My poor brave darling," Elizabeth consoled him. "The army is at least making this woman a happy wife. I couldn't bear to lose you, and you are desperately needed here at home. The war will be over soon, I think, and we will welcome our men home with jubilation. In the meantime, you and I are challenged to keep their loved ones safe and in good health. It is a noble role that we shouldn't take lightly."

Julius bent to kiss his wife's upturned face and smiled down at her. She always looked for the positive in every situation, and he loved her for making him feel needed and loved.

CHAPTER 59

SURVIVING AGAINST
ALL ODDS

I n July of 1940 the Luftwaffe began attacking Britain with a vengeance, bombing port cities, factories, and centres of population. For more than three months the Royal Air Force fought in the skies, and against all odds defeated the German Air Command. Winston Churchill's quote regarding the bravery of the RAF fighter pilots became an iconic phrase all over the free world: "Never in the field of human conflict was so much owed by so many to so few".

Britain continued to recruit servicemen, who trained, marched, obeyed orders, and prepared themselves for the call to arms.

The Americans entered the war effort after Pearl Harbour was bombed by the Japanese in December 1941, and US troops began arriving on British soil at the beginning of 1942.

Weeks turned into months and months into years. News from Europe was full of doom and gloom as Germany invaded country after country. Rumours of atrocities against anybody who was not supportive of the Third Reich were extremely disturbing.

Elizabeth watched Alice grow into a gawky twelve-year-old, who loved horses as much as her mother, with Vera and Phillip's youngsters coming a close second in her affections. She babysat the two energetic children after school most days while both sets of parents were busy. There were always treats in the kitchen baked fresh by Joan, despite the lack of real ingredients—scones with home-made jam, rhubarb or apple tart, molasses biscuits, oatmeal biscuits, or a favourite called war cake, when Joan could get a few raisins.

Elizabeth's days were always filled, with morning surgery hours treating patients with the usual ailments of coughs, colds, earaches, bronchitis, skin rashes, and so on. The afternoons were often more of the same, but with patients who were too sick to leave their beds and come to the surgery. She knew each household had made a special effort to tidy up for the doctor's visit, and she was well aware of the stares she created when she turned up at the door in a tailored suit, silk blouse, high heeled pumps, and makeup. She refused to "dress down" to make people feel more comfortable. She was who she was, and her patients trusted her completely despite her "posh" persona.

She would fling her overcoat onto a chair as she entered the house.

"Where is the patient?" was always her first question. "What seems to be the trouble?" was her second. Sometimes the sick person was lying on a sofa in the parlour, sometimes up a narrow winding staircase leading to a bedroom with an old bedstead or a mattress on the floor. There was often more than one sick inhabitant, especially when there was a family of children involved. Childhood ailments like measles, chickenpox, and mumps spread like wildfire through the small, cramped houses, and in infected homes there would be a row of small, pale faces staring up at the doctor as she entered the bedroom. If one child came down with something contagious, the mother would put the other children in the same bed so that they could all get it together.

A doctor's visit was expensive, so she wasn't called unless there was a real concern. Mothers or Grans knew what the diseases looked like, and just got on with taking care of their children while they were sick. When the doctor visited, it was usually because something had gone wrong, like a high fever that would not break, scabs from chickenpox that were infected, no appetite, or very lethargic. Whatever the reason, Elizabeth dealt with each situation with efficiency and caring, assuring the mother that she had done well, and prescribing medication to ease the discomfort.

Many of the problems were caused or made worse by the lack of proper hygiene. This was not the fault of the mother, but because most homes had only a cold water tap in an outside kitchen and a toilet detached from the house and often shared with another family. Prescribing a soothing soda bath in clean lukewarm water to ease the sores of chickenpox was something that was never going to be possible. Bathing each child with a clean cloth was as much as they could do. Keeping bed linens clean was impossible with as many as five children in one bed, some incontinent. Laundering sheets was a huge task at the best of times, and Elizabeth became used to the smell of dried urine that permeated the rooms of the sick.

The doctor was rarely called to tend the elderly. They were taken care of by family members as they aged and grew frail. Even when death was near, and Elizabeth was asked to call she, more often than not, found the old man or woman fully dressed and propped in an armchair. They were tough people, raised to suffer in silence and not bother others with their petty grievances.

Elizabeth tossed her coat onto a chair by the door of a tiny tenement house in the shadow of a large bottle kiln in the middle of town. She had to squint in the darkened room to see the old lady sitting in the corner.

"She's on 'er way out," whispered the daughter. "Won't eat a thing. Won't talk. Won't move. 'Asn't even been to the lav. Mind you doctor, she's a good age. Seventy-two, she is."

"Well, well, Mrs Johnson," Elizabeth greeted the old lady. "Let's take a look at you."

Mrs Johnson scrunched up her eyes and bent her head to her chest. She clasped her arms even tighter around her chest.

Elizabeth felt her pulse, despite the obvious displeasure from her patient.

"Open your eyes, please," Elizabeth said sharply, but not unkindly.

The old lady was so shocked to hear the command, spoken in such a posh[1] accent, that her eyes flew open and she stared at the image in front of her. Not what she'd expected! Elizabeth's red lipstick and black hair came into focus, and Mrs Johnson blew out a loud raspberry with her tongue.

"That's better," Elizabeth said. "Now we are getting somewhere. Open your mouth."

A quick medical examination, with not a word from the old woman in disagreement, was soon performed.

"Well done, Mrs Johnson," Elizabeth complimented her patient. "I'll pop in to see you again tomorrow, if that's all right."

As she gathered her coat, Elizabeth turned to Mrs Johnson's daughter. "You are quite right," she whispered. "She is near the end of her life. Her heart is barely beating, and her breathing is laboured. Keep her as comfortable as you can. Don't worry about food or toilet issues. She is way beyond that now. I expect she will pass away in the next few days. I'll see you tomorrow, but call me if you need me before then."

"Thank you doctor," said the weepy daughter. "She's been a grand mam. I don't want 'er to suffer."

As well as the regular afternoon home visits, babies were born—usually at night. Still Elizabeth's first love, she never tired of being called out to a birth. Whether it was a first baby or a

---

1. Posh – Originally an acronym: Port Out, Starboard Some. A nautical term used by the very rich who would pay more for cabins facing the sun on trips to and from India from England. Came to mean 'from or acting like the upper class'

tenth baby, the miracle was still the same. Whether born on a layer of newspaper in a potter's poor home, or born on silk sheets in a pottery owner's mansion, the joy was there.

Despite the additional war-related problems, bringing a baby into the world was still the most rewarding part of Elizabeth's practise, and her hope for whatever future they were all facing.

CHAPTER 60

THE TIDE IS TURNED

Phillip ran across the street to the doctors' house as soon as he heard the news. The invasion had begun. It was the sixth of June, 1944.

"It's started," Phillip shouted out as he burst through the kitchen door. "The day we've all been waiting for. Our troops have invaded France."

Joan and Bertha couldn't help smiling at their friend's enthusiasm.

"We heard it too Phillip. Just like you, everybody's been tuned into the radio all day. The King's giving a speech tonight. After all this time waiting, now at last something is happening."

Elizabeth popped her head around the door, having just finished surgery.

"I gather you heard the news?" she said. "Pray for all those young men landing on French soil today. I fear for them."

The others nodded their agreement, all quiet for a few minutes as they thought about the fight ahead for the allied forces.

Nobody could have imagined the battles that lay ahead before the final defeat of the Nazi regime. So many lives would be lost. So many would suffer life-changing injuries. So many hearts would be broken.

The world Elizabeth and Julius had hoped would never change had been plunged into turmoil and chaos, and nothing remained constant or dependable in their lives. Throughout the month of June every day brought more news of the desperate battles along the coast of France. The allied armies, led by General Dwight Eisenhower, suffered incredible losses, but bravely fought their way inland, mile by treacherous mile.

Julius listened to the radio and read the newspapers with increasing despair. He felt so useless! If he couldn't be on the battlefield, maybe he could help in some other way. As the weeks passed, he grew more and more agitated, and looked for ways he could somehow be more involved in the war effort.

The last day of June was plagued with dark skies and persistent rain. The streets around the doctors' house became filled with rivers of grey water. If the people living in those streets needed sunshine to lighten their lives a little, it was not going to happen on this day. Thunder crashed overhead as Elizabeth drove down steep, God-forsaken, narrow streets to the worst part of the community, where terraced houses were crammed together. It was late into the night, and she had been called out by a midwife. A young boy, no older than ten years old, had ridden his uncle's battered bicycle through the storm to bring the note. Elizabeth had to follow the boy on the bicycle because the blackout turned the darkest night into an eerie inky blackness. Without streetlights or car headlights, it was nearly impossible to find the way around.

There was barely room for a car in the narrow lane and Elizabeth had to inch her way slowly to number thirty-three, where the completely sodden boy stood pointing. Another thunder clap announced her arrival as she banged on the door.

"About bloody time," mumbled the elderly old woman as she threw open the door. "Mrs Moore sent for ya ages ago."

"Well, here I am," Elizabeth replied. "You can wait in the

kitchen now." The old woman scowled as she was dismissed to the back room.

Elizabeth threw her wet macintosh onto the back of an old horsehair sofa, and scanned the tiny room.

The parlour was used rarely, set aside for special occasions like a visit from the vicar, or landlord, or other important folks. It was also the room where a coffin would lie before a burial so the neighbours could pay their respects, and could be used to tend to the sick, the dying, or, as in this case, for birthing babies. A narrow bed took up most of the room, and this is where a young woman lay, her ashen face covered in a film of perspiration.

"Well, well, Mrs Podmore," Elizabeth said as she quickly moved to the bedside. "Let's see what we can do to help bring this baby into the world shall we?"

Elizabeth had seen this young woman before on several occasions before she had married a young guardsman, and also during her pregnancy. As with most of the women in the area, Dorothy was undernourished to the point of skeletal. Pregnancy took an enormous toll on mothers who did not have enough to eat, and who lived and worked every day in such impoverished conditions.

"I've bin 'ere all day, doctor," Mrs Moore informed Elizabeth. "She's suffering. Fost babby, I know, but still, it's takin' it's time."

"You did the right thing sending for me, Mrs Moore. Baby is quite small, but so is mother's pelvis. I'll try and get things moving, but it's still going to take a few hours before we have a baby."

Dorothy screamed in agony as the doctor manipulated the baby's head into a better position, and broke the water that surrounded the tiny body.

"I'm sorry, my dear," Elizabeth said. "You are being very brave. Your work is not over yet, but you'll find it a little easier to bear now that your baby is in a good position to push its way out. I will leave you in Mrs Moore's capable hands, and pop back to see you in a few hours."

"Thank you, Doctor," murmured Dorothy. "I thought I was going to die."

Elizabeth smiled at her patient kindly.

"Nothing new in that! Most first mothers feel exactly the same, including myself."

The storm raged all night, and when Elizabeth awoke with a start as another crash shook the house, she jumped out of bed still in her clothes from the night before, and hurried to the car to drive back to Edward Street.

It was 5:15am and the morning was dreary and grey. The rain pelted on the car and there were a few rumbles of thunder still stubbornly hanging over the soaked streets. She grabbed her bag, along with one of the small packages of baby clothing she kept at the ready, and headed into the comfortless house.

"Good morning," Elizabeth greeted. "It looks like I'm in time for the big event of the day."

Dorothy's eyes were glazed with exhaustion and distress. Mrs Moore smiled at the doctor and nodded her head. It had been a long, difficult night.

Elizabeth checked the baby's heartbeat, and held her patient's hand.

"It's time,' she said. "You need to work very hard to help your baby."

Somehow, mothers manage to find the strength, after hours of pain, to push their babies into the world. Dorothy was no exception. She mustered every scrap of energy she could find in her frail body to help her baby.

A tiny girl was born as the morning light seeped into the dark parlour.

"She's beautiful," Elizabeth said, smiling at the mother. "I will leave you in Mrs Moore's capable hands, and see you and your baby in two weeks at the surgery. Now rest and recover"

CHAPTER 61

A FAMILY AGAIN

Julius was restless. Ever since the war began, he had thought he was wasting his time at the hospital delivering babies, when he needed to be with the wounded men and women who were fighting for his freedom. He called Doctor Finlay at the Manchester Royal Infirmary early in July to ask how he could be involved in serving the wounded.

"My dear fellow," Doctor Finlay said. "Come and join us here. We are in desperate need of surgical help. Come immediately if you can."

Julius told Elizabeth that evening about his conversation. He was so animated and excited at the prospect, that Elizabeth could only add her blessing. Manchester was not that far away. Julius would be able to come home regularly for visits, she thought.

Julius temporarily moved to Manchester later that month. He was thrust into the middle of chaos with servicemen from the battlefields of France, Belgium, Africa, Italy—men who had been patched up in a field hospital and evacuated home, a journey filled with immense discomfort. They often arrived in Manchester in a deplorable state, after being transported from trucks to trains to ships, before arriving on English soil, only to wait for another truck to take them to the hospital closest to their home.

Elizabeth became like many of the women around her, living without her husband. She wrote letters to Julius every few days, keeping him in touch with what was going on at home, and particularly news about Alice. They both missed him terribly, and dreamt about a time when he could return home to be with them forever.

The dream would have to wait though, as the war raged on and Julius was overwhelmed with the number of casualties. Soldiers, sailors, pilots, even civilians from the badly bombed areas filled every available space, including corridors and waiting rooms. Doctors, nurses, and orderlies worked long days and nights. Julius hardly had a moment to write to his wife and daughter. He missed them terribly and ached to lie in Elizabeth's arms. He lost track of the time he had been away from them, and wept into his pillow on nights when he was too tired to sleep. Even though he was only a short forty miles from his family, there was never an opportunity to take time off to see them. He couldn't leave his colleagues while they were so inundated with desperately sick victims of war.

Families waited anxiously for news of loved ones, and dreaded a knock on their door where an army messenger would tell them their husband, or son would not be coming home. Others read telegrams saying their family member was being treated in a hospital. No news meant their men were still fighting somewhere. All they could do was pray for their safety.

The summer months were unusually hot and humid. The women sat out on their front steps and watched the children play hopscotch on the street. They helped each other through the long days, shared food, shared endless cups of tea, minded young babies, and told stories of their men at war.

In the doctors' big house, Alice sat reading a book in the rocking chair by the open window at the front of the house, where an occasional wisp of breeze found its way inside to cool her hot face. She heard the crunch of gravel on the path outside and froze in place. It wasn't that she hadn't heard dozens of footsteps on the gravel before, but these sounded different. Familiar!

She was in his arms the instant the door opened.

"Daddy, it's you!" she gasped, holding the tall thin man around his waist and wetting his thin shirt with her tears.

Julius closed his eyes and drank in the pleasure of seeing his daughter.

"Look at you, my darling," he finally managed to say. "Where is that little girl I left here just a few months ago?"

They both laughed as they made their way towards the kitchen.

"Mum's out doing her rounds," Alice explained. "She will be home soon, and will be so delighted to see you. Why didn't you tell us you were coming?"

"I wanted to surprise you both, and I never know if a planned visit is going to be cancelled at the last minute. I barely got away, even so."

"Doctor LaPorte," shrieked Joan and Bertha in unison. More hugs were exchanged, and the kettle was soon whistling on the stove ready for tea.

They all heard Elizabeth's car pull up to the side of the house. Julius put his fingers on his lips and walked out of the kitchen to greet his wife.

Elizabeth's hands were full. She carried her medical bag, two bags of groceries, a newspaper, and a plate of scones made by one of her patients. When she saw her husband open the side door, she dropped everything and ran to him. He smothered her in kisses and wet her with his tears. How long he had dreamed of being with her again?

"Julius, is it really you?" Elizabeth gulped between sobs. "I can't believe it."

"It is really me," her husband laughed. "Back from the purgatory known as The Manchester Royal Infirmary. We have two days. Isn't it marvellous?"

It was marvellous! The family went to the park for the after-noon and lay on the soft grass in a row, holding hands, watching the fluffy clouds float across the sky, and pretending there was no war. Julius rowed his two loves around the small lake, never taking his eyes off them as they sat opposite, dipping their fingers in the water, and laughing at the children splashing on the shore. It was pure joy to be together.

Joan and Bertha pulled together the best meal they could manage with their meagre supplies, and invited Phillip, Vera, and their rambunctious children for dinner. The nine of them sat around the table in the dining room feasting like royalty on sausage, mash, and cabbage. Julius found a hidden bottle of wine in his study and Joan made very diluted orange juice for the children using a bottle of concentrate supplied by the government.

They made no mention of war, telling stories about happier times. After dinner they sat outside in the little patch of garden at the back of the house, and watched the three youngsters playing "Crazed, cracked, chipped, or broken", a favourite ball game everybody knew.

Julius fell into bed, remembering the comfort of the soft pillows and clean sheets. He turned to watch his wife as she climbed in beside him, a radiant smile on her face. This was not the efficient doctor everybody else saw, but a beautiful woman, dressed in the finest pale pink silk nightgown, her hair cascading over her shoulders, her lips moist and lush, and her eyes on his as he enfolded her in his arms.

"So long!" Julius murmured into her hair. The silk nightgown was quickly removed, as were his pyjamas. It was like the first time; every sense heightened, every touch sensual, every kiss deeper, until all the love they had for each other spilled over. Afterwards, Elizabeth lay in her husband's arms drinking in the closeness of him.

"Can we stay like this forever?" she said.

"Sadly, no," Julius replied. "But we will make love as often as we can tonight, through the night, and tomorrow. I just want to remember this time with you, when I'm back in Manchester."

The two days leave was an oasis in a desert of despair. The family managed another two days in December, but not during Christmas. It was the first time they had been separated for the holiday season, and they were overcome with sadness. Julius was too busy to really notice the difference in the day, apart from a choir from a local church who made the rounds of the wards singing carols. Elizabeth and Alice missed him dreadfully, but had the companionship of their dear friends to share a simple meal with. There were even a few presents under the tiny spindly tree for Alice to open.

After five years of war, maybe 1945 would be better! Surely the war would be over soon. The allies were making great strides in Europe and the far east. Hitler's days were numbered and the German army in retreat.

Battles took place all over the world during the final countdown to victory. Cities were destroyed, thousands dead and maimed. Brave men and women continued the fight against tyranny. War had become the normal way of life. The people living through it every day thought it would never be over. Yet in May of 1945, war with Germany did come to an end. The war with Japan would not be resolved until September when the Americans dropped two atomic bombs on Hiroshima and Nagasaki.

Elizabeth looked out over the crowds gathered in the street outside their corner house, waving flags, singing, crying, and laughing. Now the men and women who had survived would come home to their families. Most six years older than when it all began. Most damaged in some way. Many not able to work. Many not able to sleep, their heads full of nightmares of what they had seen and done.

Julius stayed in Manchester until the end of August. He looked ten years older, worn down by too many surgeries, not enough sleep, not enough to eat, and by the thousands of men he had seen who would not be returning to their families healthy and strong. He had, however, made good friends during his time there. Other doctors and nurses who worked together through every imaginable difficulty. They were a close team—all of them dedicated to serving the battle-weary, injured, and maimed young soldiers, airman, and sailors that streamed through their doors every day.

Julius had thought he could be of no service during this war if he wasn't at the front in a field hospital, but he had changed his mind. Despite the cost to himself and his family, he never regretted the work he was able to do. He had been of service, and that mattered a great deal to him.

"He's here!" shouted Alice from her perch at the front bay window."Dad's here."

Julius barely made it through the door before his sixteen-year-old daughter flung herself at him. She was tall and elegant like her mother, and was thrilled to have her father home to stay.

"What a welcome!" Julius laughed.

His friend, Donald, had driven Julius from Manchester, and he now stood on the doorstep with his arms full of boxes and bags.

"Shall I drop them in here then, Jules?" he asked cheerfully.

"Oh sorry, old chap. Let me help with the rest of my things." Julius said. "By the way, this is my daughter, Alice."

Donald grinned and nodded his head towards the young girl. "Nice to meet you. I hope you know what a great dad you've got?"

Alice beamed in response. Of course she knew how great her dad was.

When all the luggage from his long stay in the rainy city was piled into the hallway, Julius looked around for his wife.

"She's out delivering a baby," Alice said.

"Well, that comes first," Julius smiled. "Let's find out if there's a cup of tea in the kitchen shall we?"

By the time Elizabeth returned, the piles of luggage were

cleared away and a wonderful smell of apple pie permeated the air. She paused before going in search of her husband, taking in the moment. He was home to stay! Life would somehow return to what it had been before the war. They were a family again, and she felt the tears spring into her eyes at the very thought of it.

CHAPTER 62

PRECIOUS PEACE

Nothing was as it was before the war. It would be years before even a semblance of the daily life the people of Britain had known returned. Food was still rationed, jobs were scarce, and poverty ruled in every working-class area of the land. In the big cities, thousands of families whose houses had been destroyed by bombs, had no home to go back to, and continued to live with family or friends or anybody who would give them a roof over their heads. Over five million troops were scattered all over the world at the end of the war, and it would take almost two years to demobilize them all. After the initial celebration of Victory in Europe Day, the women, yet again, had to wait for their young men and women to come home. For those with loved ones involved in the war with Japan the wait was even longer.

The LaPortes knew they were among the lucky ones, and they worked hard to make life better for the people in their community. Julius went back to the North Staffordshire Hospital to continue his work in obstetrics, whilst his wife expanded her practise, hiring a young doctor who had worked alongside Julius in Manchester. The extra help gave Elizabeth some extra time at home.

Busy as they were, they agreed to take a break at Christmas and travel to Lingford to reconnect with family. Cousin Jocelyn was making the trip from Scotland, which was another reason for Elizabeth to be excited about the visit. She had only communicated with Cousin Jocelyn through letters and a very occasional phone call.

Lingford Manor had once more been used to house injured soldiers. At Lord Lingford's insistence, the last of them had been moved into cottage hospitals closer to their homes, so by the time Christmas arrived, the Manor was able to accommodate the festivities.

It was a joyous celebration to be all together again. The grand old house was filled with laughter and gayety, as the four families merged into one, to remember old times, and catch up on the lost years. It seemed incredulous to the four Lingford siblings that there were ten young people to carry on their legacy, some now with partners of their own.

"How would Father have coped with all of this?" laughed Percy, as the youngsters played a game of charades with great gusto.

"He would have stood by the window, in his favourite spot, and watched them with great delight," Elizabeth said.

"I fear Mama would not have been as delighted," Carolyn chimed in, producing a peel of laughter from the grown ups.

"Well, as I am the only person here from their generation," Cousin Jocelyn began, "I must say I am enjoying every minute of watching my fine young great nieces and nephews. I even have a mind to join in with the game."

Elizabeth sat beside her aunt and gave her hand a squeeze. What a grand old lady she was to make the long journey from Scotland to be with her family. She was frail now, and used a cane when she walked, but was still enthusiastic and kind. She asked Elizabeth to visit her in Scotland as soon as she could in the new year.

"I want you to see the stables, my dear. You will be impressed with the work they are doing there, and the full roster of local people who have riding lessons. It's everything you wanted, despite the war years, when we were so short of stable hands. Girls from the village came to help with the horses though, and they are indispensable now. Not all of the young lads are coming home, you see, so the girls will continue to do their work."

"I will make time to visit, I promise," Elizabeth said. "I cannot imagine a more wonderful place on this earth than Gordon House and its surroundings."

Alice was having the time of her life with her cousins. Most of them were years older than her, but Percy and his wife had added two children to their family later in their marriage, so Fiona and Michael were also in their mid teens. The fun never stopped! After charades, they dressed in warm clothes and all went for a hike up to the woods, stopping along the way to chase each other around the trees, and gather horse chestnuts and pinecones.

Christmas dinner was a festive affair, with everyone gathered in the dining room. Jacob Littlejohn had slaughtered two pigs from the farm and, with the help of the land army girls, there was already a plentiful amount of potatoes, carrots, turnips, and cabbage in the storage barn, apples from the orchards, and cream and butter from the dairy. It was a feast indeed.

Percy's wife, Phoebe, now Lady Lingford, had talked to the housekeeper and cook about the menu. She was concerned about the amount of food needed for a houseful of people. Phoebe's main concern was that all the indoor and outdoor staff would have the same meals as the family.

"Don't you worry M'Lady," Sally Thompson told her. Sally had taken over from her mother as cook many years ago, and she couldn't have wished for a better or more considerate mistress. "There will be enough for everybody. Some of the land army girls have helped with the baking and preparation. Hard working girls they are."

"I must thank them personally," Phoebe said. "Also the entire staff for their extra work to make these few days so wonderful for all of us. I'll speak to them all on Boxing Day."

Nobody had tasted food quite so delicious for many years. As Percy had said in the blessing before the meal, they were incredibly fortunate and most grateful to have so much when most of the country was still in turmoil.

Early the next morning Elizabeth and Alice walked down to the stables together. Tom, Callum McCarthy's successor, greeted them in the stable yard. He was well know to Elizabeth, having worked at the Lingford stables from a young boy.

"Good morning, Miss Elizabeth," Tom greeted her. "I have two horses saddled and ready for you. Two gentle mares, who will suit you both perfectly I think." He paused and smiled at them. "They were both sired by a favourite of yours M'Lady. Black Diamond."

"How marvellous," Elizabeth laughed. "Good old man. I remember him with great affection, although he and I got into a bit of trouble now and again."

Their mounts were strong and powerful, proving the worth of their famous stud father. Alice loved riding with her mother, and relished the chance to explore the Lingford property. They followed all the trails Elizabeth had ridden with her father a generation before, and despite the cold didn't return to the stables for more than an hour.

"Thank you Thomas," greeted Elizabeth. "Wonderful memories of long ago flooded back to me while I was riding. Memories of my father and of McCarthy. Now I have a new memory to add to them. Alice riding with me this morning was something I will treasure forever."

"I'm happy for you," Tom said, taking the reins of her horse. "Your daughter takes after you. She has just as good a seat as yourself at her age."

Alice blushed with the compliment, and smiled her thanks at the stable master. Like her mother, she would treasure this morning's memory.

CHAPTER 63

MEMORIES

Several years later, Elizabeth smiled to herself as she remembered that Christmas morning ride with her daughter, and the numerous other rides with her father, Callum McCarthy, and Sir Kenneth.

She gazed down at the rugged coastline from her vantage point on the headland of the Gordon House property. The horse beneath her stood quietly, sensing his rider's need to absorb and enjoy her surroundings.

Cousin Jocelyn had died peacefully in her bed a month ago, and Elizabeth had stayed after the funeral to deal with all the paperwork involved in Gordon House becoming the property of the National Trust. It would take a few months for everything to be settled, but the whole process was easier than she had anticipated.

The family would retain living accommodation at Gordon House, and many of the present staff would be hired to maintain the property. Every effort was made to make sure the dedicated people who had worked for Sir Kenneth and Lady Jocelyn, could stay if they so desired. Once the house was opened to the public, a luncheon would be offered every day, giving cook and the kitchen maids plenty to keep them busy. When the family were in residence, extra help would be hired to accommodate their needs.

Of course, the stables, were already a very successful part of the wider community, and would remain so. There would always be a horse ready and waiting for Miss Elizabeth.

Alice had been tutored at home for two years, and was now in her third year of studies at Oxford. Much to her parent's delight, she had decided on pursuing veterinary medicine. Once her mother's dream, Alice didn't veer from her chosen path. After she achieved her Bachelor of Science from Oxford she planned to apply to The Glasgow Veterinary College, where she could be close to Gordon House.

As Elizabeth turned her horse to head back to the stables, she thought of all the changes in her life. She, who had wanted "everything to stay the same" so many times!

"Nothing stays the same, dearest," Julius had reminded her many times. "We must live through each of the changes without regret."

Dear Julius, she thought, he is the "constant" in my life.

She rode into the stable yard, and thanked old Robertson, who took the reins as she dismounted.

"Thank you, Miss Elizabeth, for all you've done to keep the old house and stables going. It means a lot to all of us."

"No thanks are required, Robertson," Elizabeth smiled. "This is your home, and I am so grateful for your dedication. I plan to visit often, and our daughter, Alice, will hopefully be studying in Glasgow in September. I know you will take care of her, and make sure there is always a good horse for her to ride when she's staying here."

"No worries about that, Miss," replied the old stable master. "It will be my pleasure to take care of Miss Alice. Sir Kenneth would be proud of how everything has turned out, I know that."

As she packed her bag for the trip home the next day, Elizabeth's heart was filled with love for the second home she had found here in Scotland. During the dark days after Elwyn had died, she would never have imagined where life would lead her. Julius was right, life was full of changes, and she embraced the adventure ahead, realizing she had little control over the twists and turns in the journey.

Alice fulfilled her dream and, after studying in Glasgow, decided to stay in Scotland, joining a well-established veterinary practise in Dumbarton, where she met and married the love of her life, Malcolm Stewart, a co-worker at the clinic. After their second child was born, they moved to Gordon House, and began their own veterinary practise. Alice's life revolved around keeping the horses healthy, and Malcolm made a name for himself in the surrounding countryside and farmlands, as well as operating a small animal clinic in town.

Julius retired the year after their second grandchild was born, to enjoy life at a slower pace. He enthusiastically agreed to travel to Glasgow University twice each year to lecture on obstetrics, which gave him an opportunity to visit his daughter's family. He delighted in his small grandsons, Graham and Duncan, who followed him around like two happy puppies. Together, they explored every corner of the vast estate, finding new and exciting adventures along the way.

Elizabeth joined her husband in Scotland whenever she could find time to get away from her practise, and she continued to work for several more years.

She had delivered hundreds of babies, visited hundreds of homes, attended the dying, and seen thousands of patients over the years. It was time for the next step on her journey.

She envied Julius spending so much of his time at Gordon House, playing with their grandsons, developing a deeper relationship with their dear daughter, Alice and her husband, Graham. He came home with tales of walking on the land around the house, visiting the stables, eating with the family, and waking each morning in the middle of the rugged, beautiful land.

"Julius, I have made a decision," Elizabeth said, as they

walked together on the country lane beside the stables at Granger Manor. "It is time for me to end my practise and officially retire."

Julius stopped mid-stride and faced his wife in surprise.

"I have wondered so many times how long it would be before you made this decision. I could not be happier, my dearest. It will be wonderful to have you beside me when we go to Scotland, or Lingford, or The Lake District, or anywhere else we feel like being."

Elizabeth smiled up at him, her eyes glistening.

"I don't want to just retire, but move permanently to Gordon House. I have already missed so much of the babies growing up. Let's begin a new journey, darling man."

"Yes, oh yes," grinned Julius.

He took her into his arms and kissed her, cementing their future together.

News of Doctor Lingford's retirement spread rapidly through the streets of the town, and gathered momentum every day.

"Did ya 'ear about Doctor Lingford?" Norma Johnson called to her neighbour as they were cleaning their steps. "She's retirin'."

"Go on with ya. Who says?" Jean shouted back.

"Mrs Plant, at the shop. Says she'll be gone at month's end."

"What's that?" yelled Doreen from two doors away.

"Doctor's leavin'" replied Jean.

"Well, I dunner know what we'll do. Can't replace a Doc like 'er."

"You can say that again," Norma chimed in. "The best of the best."

A crowd gathered in the street, their step-cleaning forgotten, as they all shared stories about the posh lady doctor they had all come to love.

"I'll put the kettle on. We need a cuppa." Jean said. "Come in, all of ya."

The women filed into the small kitchen at the back of the terraced house. Cups of tea were handed out to each of them.

"We should do something nice for 'er before she goes." Doreen suggested.

"Like what?" the other women asked.

"'Ow about a collection of stories about 'er being our doc?" Jean said.

"I'd need 'elp with that. I'm not good with writing." Shelley Smith confessed shyly.

"We'll all chip in and 'elp each other." Jean said.

They agreed it was a lovely idea and they all helped spread the word around the narrow streets. The stories poured in, with Norma and Jean collecting them all. Some on scraps of lined paper, others on card, some with pencil, others neatly written in ink. It didn't matter, they took each story and had them bound together at Thompson's Stationery in town.

Elizabeth stared at the book in disbelief. A group of the local women were standing in her office, after presenting her with their gift, waiting to see her reaction.

Never emotional in front of her patients, Elizabeth bit her lip to gain control. As always she was dressed elegantly, her hair coiffured, make-up immaculate, and wearing her trade-mark high heels.

"I am lost for words," she began. "This is the most wonderful gift I have ever received. Thank you all. I will treasure it forever. I have learned so much from all of you over the years. It has been my utmost privilege to be part of your lives. Your courage and resiliency during the most dire circumstances has always amazed me, and I will carry memories of you all for the rest of my life."

A few sniffles and sobs echoed around the small room, as the women nodded and smiled at each other.

"More than sixty women gave us their stories, Doctor," Norma said. "And we're still getting more and more. We may 'ave to do a second edition."

Everybody laughed, including Elizabeth.

She shook hands with each of them, thanking them again. This was goodbye! She wouldn't see these women again. When the door closed behind the last woman, Elizabeth sat at her desk with the book in front of her, and allowed the tears to overflow, some of them dropped onto the cover of the book, entitled "The Best Doctor Ever."

CHAPTER 64

HOME

L eaving her home in Staffordshire was difficult on many levels for Elizabeth. Her memories were etched into every room. The surgery and waiting room where she had begun her medical practise, and treated hundreds of women and children. The kitchen where Joan and Bertha had cooked the most delicious meals, and where they gathered as a family to enjoy each other's company. It was where they had listened to the Prime Minister's speech declaring war with Germany, and where, after almost six years of unending misery, they wept together as Winston Churchill declared VE Day. The living room painted pictures of happy family times, and Alice running around playing chase with Julius. The bedroom full of memories of love and intimacy. The bed where she had given birth to Alice.

Some decisions had already been made. Elizabeth and Julius knew from the moment they had decided to move to Gordon House that Joan and Bertha would remain at the house. It was their home.

Age had forced Joan to give up most of her duties. She was content to potter around the kitchen, preparing vegetables, baking pies, and keeping Bertha company. The stairs had become unmanagable, so the doctors had converted the surgery and waiting room into a cozy bedroom and sitting room for her.

Phillip and Vera still ran the grocery shop across the street, although their living conditions were very cramped now the children were growing.

"Julius, we need a new plan," Elizabeth said.

She sat beside her husband in the cozy living room and placed her cup and saucer on the table beside her.

"I am all ears, my love," Julius smiled.

"Moving to Gordon House permanently will not be easy for us. There are loose ends here we need to deal with before we go."

"I thought all your patients knew you were retired. What else is there to do?"

"Our *family*, Julius!" Elizabeth said. "Joan, Bertha, Phillip, Vera, Noah and Margaret."

She counted them off on her fingers as she said their names, her eyes opening very wide as she looked at her husband intently.

"Darling," Julius replied. "They are not our family. Well, not REAL family."

"How can you say that?" replied his indignant wife. "They are as much our family as they can ever be, and I need to make a plan that includes their well being into the future. I will not rest until it is done. Indeed, I will not be able to move to Gordon House unless they are settled and happy."

"Point taken," assured Julius, taking his wife's hand in his and kissing her finger tips. "What do you have in mind?"

"This house has been and still is a wonderful family home. Needless to say Joan and Bertha will always have a home here. I think we should offer Phillip and his family a home here too. The tiny rooms above the shop are so cramped. Here, the children could each have a bedroom, Phillip and Vera could have our room, and it would be the best possible situation for them all. Joan and Bertha would love it, and Mrs Griffin would still be taken care of with Phillip and Vera being there most of the time during the day. What do you think?"

"Well, I must say you've really thought it through, haven't you?" Julius laughed. "As always, my dearest, your proposal is flawless. If everybody is in agreement, there will be details to sort out, but I don't see any big obstacles."

Elizabeth hugged her husband, and planted a kiss on his lips.

"You are the dearest man I know," she pronounced.

A meeting of the "family" was called for seven o'clock that evening, and they all settled around the kitchen table, with cups of hot tea and slices of Joan's apple pie in front of them. Noah and Margaret were already tucked into their beds, with Mrs Griffin on baby-sitting duty.

After outlining the plan, they all sat in silence. Joan began to cry. Vera began to cry. Bertha tried to comfort them both, while Phillip just sat looking stunned.

"Well, what do you think?" Julius asked, beginning to feel uncomfortable.

"Do you know what we are all thinking?" Phillip finally said. "We're thinking you two doctors maybe angels in disguise. We're thinking how did we get so lucky to be part of your lives. We're thinking how do we ever say thank you or repay you for what you have done in the past, and what you're proposing now for all of us."

The three women nodded, smiled and cried their agreement.

"We are the ones who are grateful and thankful for the four of you," Elizabeth said. "You are our family. You have taken care of us, and our home for all these years with loyalty and love. We can't move to Scotland until we are sure you are settled and happy. This would be a gift for us. Please say you agree."

"I don't say much these days," began Joan Turner. "I'm an old lady now and not capable of doing much of anything. To continue to live here, with Bertha and Phillip's family is the best I could hope for."

"You know how I feel about you," Bertha joined in, looking

from one doctor to the other as she spoke. "You are my family! I would be overjoyed to live here, where I've been so happy. What a joy it will be to keep the house going. I vote a big YES!"

Vera smiled shyly and looked at her husband, who nodded his encouragement.

"It's too much for us to hope for really," she muttered. "But my mind is already whirling with excitement. I'll be able to help Bertha with the house and cooking, and the children will have all this room to play and grow. I'm just overwhelmed."

"Then, it's settled," exclaimed Elizabeth. "I couldn't be happier."

"Not all settled though," said Phillip. "We must contribute towards the cost of living here."

"Details we will work out together," Julius insisted.

The doctors both knew they did not need money, but also realized Phillip in particular would not be comfortable with free accommodation. With all the input the four of them would have in keeping the house and gardens well maintained, a minimal charge would be worked out.

It turned out to be the best plan for all concerned. All the furnishings would remain, so very little had to be transported to their new home.

The day they left was full of mixed emotions. Excited for the future, and sad to say goodbye. Promises were made to visit, and telephone often to stay in touch, but Elizabeth knew Joan's days were few, and she clung onto her old friend as she wished her well.

Gordon House was prepared and ready for Julius and Elizabeth's arrival. Alice, Malcolm and the two boys were there to meet them, filling their arms and hearts with love. The staff, so familiar and dear to Elizabeth, lined up in the great hall to welcome them "home". Elizabeth thought about her first visit so many years ago. Sir Kenneth and Cousin Jocelyn would have been delighted with their decision to make this their home.

The next morning the sun streamed into the bedroom as

Julius drew the curtains to look out onto the rugged surroundings. Elizabeth stirred as the sun flooded the room with light. Mornings at Gordon House were magical. The sound of the wind in the trees, the glorious spacious land spreading in every direction, and the glimpse of the distant sea beyond the headland.

A light tap on the door announced the arrival of Sheila carrying a tray with tea and fruit.

"Good morning, Doctor," Sheila said quietly. "Is there anything else you need?"

"No thank you," Elizabeth said.

This was now the life they would have. For both doctors it was an alien life, where there was no hurry or rush; Nobody waiting for attention.

After a leisurely breakfast, they had time to play with their small grandsons, and take a walk around the gardens. Elizabeth wrote letters to her brother and sisters. Julius met with the estate manager for an update on the workings of the public visits at the weekends, and the stable programme.

Half way through the morning, Elizabeth could wait no longer and changed into her riding clothes and headed to the stables.

Robertson had retired as stable master, but still lived in his home on the property. The new stable master was a younger version of Robertson, a man who had worked beside the old master for most of his life. Elizabeth asked where she could find him, and was directed to the stable comfy room, where staff gathered to have their breaks.

"Good morning," Elizabeth called as she walked through the archway into the comfy room. The four stable hands jumped to their feet with caps in hand to greet her.

"Relax, please," she said. "I'm here to meet the stable master and hope to go for a ride, if one of you could saddle a good horse for me."

She walked towards John Wallace and held out her hand.

"Nice to see you again John," she said. "I was delighted to hear that you are stable master. You've worked alongside Robertson for many years, and I know the stables are in good hands with you at the helm."

"Thank you, M'Lady," John said. "I hope to follow in his footsteps and run the stables with the same high standards. We have a lovely, spirited mare named Jenny Wren for your to ride. I think you will enjoy each other."

"I just have one more request, John," Elizabeth said. "For you to join me on my ride. I always enjoyed the company of Robertson, or Sir Kenneth."

"It would be my pleasure M'Lady," John Wallace said.

Jenny Wren was a perfect choice for Elizabeth, and as she led her out of the stable yard and onto the moor, the wonderful familiar feeling filled Elizabeth with joy.

Memories flooded her, as she thought about riding throughout her life. The horses: Black Diamond, Sweet Charlotte, Silver Buttons, Lucky Lady, Red Clover, Blue Shadow, and Highland Lass. The men she had ridden with and trusted with her precious horses: her father, Callum McCarthy, Tom Anderson, Sir Kenneth, Robertson, and now John Wallace.

She galloped across the heather until she brought Jenny Wren to a standstill facing the sea. The waves churned beneath her, and the wind whipped her face, as a smile slowly grew, and she felt a tear trickle down her cheek.

This was where she belonged. This was home.

AUTHOR'S NOTES

As I enthusiastically began writing my fourth novel, Lady Elizabeth's story led me down paths I had not imagined. Days of research turned into months as I explored each era of Elizabeth's life. So much was new to me: country life in a manor house, horses, world wars, 1918 pandemic, education at Oxford University, Lady Margaret Hall, Glasgow Maternity Hospital, general practise. I was fascinated by it all, and wove all I learned into the story.

The life of a young girl born into the aristocracy was in itself a perfect place to begin my research. Who hasn't been inthralled with the Downton Abbey series? It was important to find out about the workings of a large country estate, so I delved into the land, the money, the organization, the workforce, and all the creative ways the gentry had persevered in their attempts to keep their inherited properties.

HORSES

Horses were a whole other difficulty for me. I knew nothing about horses!

I do love animals, however, and I relished the idea of finding out all I could about these dearly loved creatures who captured Elizabeth's heart. Most of my limited knowledge was gained from hours of tracking down stories of stable masters, stable hands, vets, stud farms, racing thoroughbreds, and the impact these magnificent animals had on every day life in the early part of the twentieth century. I even gathered up my courage to watch videos of a number of foals being born. A big thank you to Diane Dominy for reading through my "horse" chapters.

My dad loved a "flutter" on the horses. I remember him picking out his horses in the Saturday morning newspaper and walking down to the bookie who lived in the next street. Dad would then settle himself in front of the TV on Saturday afternoon to watch his horses win or lose. He never spent much money, but he was thrilled if he picked a winner. Researching the famous New Market Racecourse took me back to those early years with my Dad. I couldn't believe it had been around since 1636 when King Charles I was on the throne. His son, Charles II, introduced the Town Plate in 1671, and was the only reigning monarch to ride a winning horse. How cool was that![1]

OXFORD AND LADY MARGARET HALL

Oxford University research took up several weeks of my time as I delved into the history of women's acceptance into the famous bastion of a thousand years of educating men. In 1860 a small group of innovative women persuaded prominent scholars to tutor the first nine young students, but It wasn't until 1879 that Lady Margaret Hall became the first women's college. Named after Lady Margaret Beaufort, mother of King Henry II, a new building was erected in 1894 to accommodate twenty-five female students. Before 1920 women couldn't earn degrees, and the courses offered were very limited.

---

1. See *The Daily Telegraph Chronicle of Horse Racing*, ed. *Norman S. Barrett*, *Guinness Publishing*, *1995*.

I thought it was a fun fact to read that J.R.R. Tolkien began tutoring a few students; his daughter would go on to attend Lady Margaret Hall 30 years later. 1920 was a huge landmark, and between 1920 and 1921 1,159 women matriculated from Oxford University. However, it wasn't until 1957 that quotas restricting women undergraduates was finally removed.[2]

"SPANISH FLU"

I really knew little about the "Spanish Flu" epidemic, so the research was again fascinating. In March 1918 the first case was reported, not in Spain, but in the state of Kansas, USA. It spread quickly and April saw cases in France, Germany, and the United Kingdom. Over the next two years, one third of the world's population had been infected, with estimated deaths vastly fluctuating between 20 and 50 million, making it the deadliest pandemic in history.[3]

ST. MARY'S CHURCH, BURY SAINT EDMUNDS

Old churches have always drawn me in. I've visited many during my lifetime, in England and Italy mostly. They have a peace and tranquility about them that fills my soul and leaves me in awe of the history they hold within their walls and the hundreds of thousands of people who have worshiped there.

St. Mary's Church, Bury Saint Edmunds is such a Church in Suffolk, England. The ancient stones have been there since 1290 and were once part of an abbey. It happens to have the second

---

2. *Lady Margaret Hall Website: https://www.lmh.ox.ac.uk/*
3. *There are many sources for details on the 1918 Flu Pandemic. This short article by Ben Johnson on the Historic UK Website is a good primer: https://www.historic-uk.com/ HistoryUK/HistoryofBritain/The-Spanish-Flu-pandemic-of-1918/*

longest aisle and the largest west window in England. Can you imagine a wedding in such a church?[4]

HOSPITALS

The most involved, most difficult, most fascinating research was by far The Royal Glasgow Maternity Hospital. What an incredible journey it was to search through the historical data, the newspaper articles, and the personal experiences of the Glasgow women and their families.[5]

My three children were born in beautiful modern hospitals. One baby in St. Boniface Hospital, Winnipeg, Manitoba, Canada, and two in The North Staffordshire Birthing Centre, Stoke-on-Trent, Staffordshire, England. Two births were attended by doctors and one birth with midwives. The care was second to none, with caring and considerate staff around me, clean, modern facilities, and great post natal care. What did I know of giving birth back in the 1920s in Glasgow?

Maternity Hospitals (known as lying-in hospitals) have been around in the UK since the 18th century. The Glasgow Hospital was opened in 1834 and made the controversial decision to allow unmarried women as patients, causing uproar in the community. Situated in Rottenrow, one of the oldest streets in Glasgow, by 1880 it was so overcrowded with poor and destitute women that it was demolished and new premises were opened in 1881 on the same street. Being a voluntary hospital it relied on charitable donations for its upkeep. It is unrecorded how many patients passed through RGMH, and how many lives were saved. From testimonies of countless women, it was the difference between life and death for themselves and their babies.

In 2002 this historic hospital was demolished and Rottenrow

---

4. *Detail of the church can be found at St. Mary's Church website: https:// stmaryschurchbse.org/*
5. *An excellent source for information and stories are the countless articles found in the British Newspaper Archive: https://www.britishnewspaperarchive.co.uk/*

Gardens now stands in its place. Researching the history of this remarkable hospital, I was filled with admiration for the doctors and nurses and volunteers who worked under the most difficult conditions to bring comfort to those in such desperate need.

Thank you to Elaine Labdon for reading through the "maternity" chapters. Have to say I have such admiration for the midwives of our time.

248 miles south of Glasgow is the city of Stoke-on-Trent where I was born. The hospital where Julius LaPorte worked no longer exists. In 1804 the Wedgwood family partially funded the first small hospital in Etruria, mostly to serve their employees, and vaccinate against the dreaded smallpox disease. As more of the general public began to use its services, the hospital was moved to a bigger premises in 1819. The big relocation to Hartshill was in 1869, where it was named the North Staffordshire Infirmary. Following a visit from King George V in 1925 the "Royal" was officially added to the hospital name.

The North Staffs, as locals called it, served a vast area in Staffordshire, alongside its sister hospital The City General. I remember visiting patients at the North Staffs: my husband, David, who broke his leg playing football (soccer) when he was nineteen years of age, and, more seriously, my dad after he suffered a massive heart attack when he was forty five years of age (I was twenty years old at the time). Over the years, many of my family and friends were patients there, and I look back with thankfulness that we all had access to a publicly funded medical system.

A decision to amalgamate the two hospitals was made in 2007, and came to fruition in August 2012 when the Royal Stoke University Hospital was opened.[6]

---

6. Details of The North Staffs can be found on the history page on the *North Staffordshire Medical Institute Website:* https://nsmedicalinstitute.co.uk/our-history/

SICK BABIES AND CHILDREN

At the time Doctor Lingford began her medical practise the general population rarely saw a doctor and, only in dire circumstances, would a doctor be asked to make a house call. The working class in the UK just couldn't afford the fees. Elizabeth would have relied on a few private patients to provide some of her income. National health didn't begin until 1948 when the NHS (National Health Service) was made available to all citizens, paid for by taxes and administered by the government.

Even as late as 1945, when my husband David was a baby, his Mam mixed hot toddies (warm water, brandy and sugar) to relieve his bronchitis. She kept him near the only source of heat in the house, which was the living room fire, smothered him in Vicks VapoRub, and tended him day and night until he was better. When one of the seven Brough children caught chickenpox my mother-in-law put all seven children in her double bed—four at the top and three at the bottom, so that they would all catch the disease at the same time. I valued my mother-in-law's opinion when our children were small, knowing there was very little she hadn't experienced.

As a mother, I was not that smart! Our three children caught chickenpox one after the other, with a full three weeks incubation period between each of them. So it took about ten weeks before all three were clear of spots.

I have to say I am most grateful that we have lived in two countries, Britain and Canada, that both provide a national health service.

∾

Lady Elizabeth, M.D., was a joy to work on. It was a constant reminder of my own early years, and of all the stories my mum and gran told me. The research was fascinating, even though I did tend to go down "worm holes" to find out more and more that really had nothing to do with my story. Thanks for reading my novel. I sincerely hope you enjoyed it.

I'm always happy to hear from my readers. Several people have reached out to me from as far away as Australia, Hong Kong, Germany, as well as North America, and the United Kingdom.

Ann Brough
annb@cmds.ca

ALSO BY ANN BROUGH

THE BITTER SWEET LIFE OF ANNIE JENKINS

The early twentieth century in the heart of the English Potteries, where the lines between upper-class owners and poor factory workers were set in stone…

a saga of forbidden love, raging obsession, agonizing loss, and a candy shop that saves one woman's life.

THE PRUSSIAN CAPTAIN

Based on a true story, spanning half a century, this sweeping tale takes you from upper-class English society, to New York, Boston, and the wilds of the Napa Valley. But life and love may be found in the most unlikely places—the poverty-stricken streets of Neck End.

THE WELSH GUARDSMAN

An historical family saga, based on a true story, filled with tragedy, love and loss. Readers are calling it an emotionally gripping must-read and a triumphant sequel to *The Prussian Captain*.

ACKNOWLEDGMENTS

It's always an exciting journey to write a novel, and I am so grateful for those special people who have encouraged and supported me through this fourth story.

Once again, I am indebted to my sister, Christine Podmore, for her tireless research and advice. She digs up so many interesting facts and goes far beyond expectations. Thanks a million Christine.

My daughter, Tracey Silagy, always takes the time to sit down with me for several days to go through the manuscript, page by page. We work together to change, tweak and move words, sentences and even paragraphs around to greatly benefit the novel. Thank you, my dearest girl, for all your input and support.

The research for this novel was formidable, and I spent many many months reading and studying everything from horses to women studying at Oxford in 1920, to obstetric practices through the 1920s to 1940s. I am so grateful to Elaine Labdon, a practising midwife, for proof-reading and checking facts regarding the birthing experience.

I knew little or nothing about breeding horses. I enjoyed all the research, over many weeks, to learn enough to give it a shot. Many thanks to Diane Dominy for proof-reading the 'horse' sections. She breeds horses in Alberta, and I so appreciated her time helping me with this.

To my husband David, who read chapter by chapter, despite

his distaste of some of the more graphic passages, and encouraged me to keep writing. He brought me tea and made lunch, and kept me going. You are my star.

Thank you Matt, for your fantastic publishing skills. Without you there would be no book.

ABOUT THE AUTHOR

In her early seventies, Ann Brough wrote her first novel, *The Prussian Captain*, and followed it up with *The Welsh Guardsman*, *The Bitter Sweet Life of Annie Jenkins*, and now *Doctor Elizabeth, M.D.* Each of her books are set in England between the late nineteenth to the mid-twentieth centuries.

Born and raised in Stoke-On-Trent, England, Ann immigrated to Canada in 1967 and again in 1978, with a seven year residence in England during that time. She currently lives with her husband, David, in a quiet and beautiful community called Lester Beach, situated on the shores of Lake Winnipeg, in Canada.

Ann has three children, five grand children, and one great-grandchild. Her home is filled with family, love, and lots of sand every summer.

For more about Ann and her other books visit www.annbrough.com or email her at ann@cmds.ca

www.ingramcontent.com/pod-product-compliance
Lightning Source LLC
Chambersburg PA
CBHW020943260626
47169CB00006B/1799